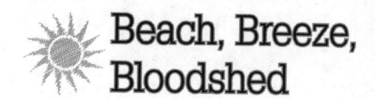

Beach, Breeze, Bloodshed

Also by John Keyse-Walker
Sun, Sand, Murder

Beach, Breeze, Bloodshed

JOHN KEYSE-WALKER

MINOTAUR BOOKS
NEW YORK

This is a work of fiction. All of the characters, organizations, and events portrayed in this novel are either products of the author's imagination or are used fictitiously.

BEACH, BREEZE, BLOODSHED. Copyright © 2017 by John Keyse-Walker. All rights reserved. Printed in the United States of America. For information, address St. Martin's Press, 175 Fifth Avenue, New York, N.Y. 10010.

www.minotaurbooks.com

Designed by Omar Chapa

Library of Congress Cataloging-in-Publication Data

Names: Keyse-Walker, John, author.
Title: Beach, breeze, bloodshed / John Keyse-Walker.
Description: First edition. | New York : Minotaur Books, 2017.
Identifiers: LCCN 2017017667 | ISBN 978-1-250-14847-6 (hardcover) |
    ISBN 978-1-250-14848-3 (ebook)
Subjects: LCSH: Police—British Virgin Islands—Fiction. | Murder—
    Investigation—Fiction. | GSAFD: Mystery fiction.
Classification: LCC PS3611.E977 B43 2017 | DDC 813/.6—dc23
LC record available at https://lccn.loc.gov/2017017667

Our books may be purchased in bulk for promotional, educational, or business use. Please contact your local bookseller or the Macmillan Corporate and Premium Sales Department at 1-800-221-7945, extension 5442, or by email at MacmillanSpecialMarkets@macmillan.com.

First Edition: September 2017

10 9 8 7 6 5 4 3 2 1

To my parents, Lee and Alma Keyse

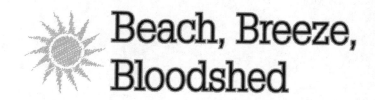

Beach, Breeze, Bloodshed

Chapter One

Violent death is part of a policeman's job—witnessing it, dealing with its aftermath, informing the next of kin, capturing the perpetrators, and sometimes even avoiding having it visited upon oneself. I know because I have done all those things. Only once, it's true, but once was enough, and more than enough, I thought after I had been through it. So I quit, left it behind, thought I had cleansed my life of it the way a *Santerismo madrina* cleanses a home of evil spirits. But then I came back.

I came back after six months away: six months of saying no to the job; six months of my torn flesh healing to become a keloid scar on my chest where the bullet that had awakened me from and almost ended my peaceful, easy, complacent life was removed; six months, less a few weeks, after I stood, a man broken, before the House of Assembly of the Virgin Islands and received the Queen's Police Medal for my distinguished service to home and country.

Now here I was, standing in the bow of my skiff, the *Lily B,* doing what I do best of all the things I do in life, looking through the surface of the water, that impenetrable boundary to the untrained eye, to see the life below. It is a skill I mastered only after years of training, long days of poling and scanning the water ahead, picking through the bouncing rays of sun that veil the surface to spot a shadow, a fin, a flash of movement, beneath the mirrored skin of the sea. It is akin to peering through the daylight sky to discern the stars beyond. It is a skill I learned as a fisherman. I was applying it now as a policeman.

Fishing skill is not a usual requirement in a policeman's job description. It is not a normal requirement even here in the Virgin Islands, where so much of life revolves around the sea. In fact, most Royal Virgin Islands Police Force officers are not anglers, in the professional sense, like me. I daresay most have wet a line on a Sunday afternoon for the purpose of catching a mess of yellowtail snapper for dinner, but I am a fishing guide as well as a police officer, so it was natural and appropriate that my boss, RVIPF deputy commissioner Howard Lane, had assigned the task I was attempting to perform to me.

That task was to catch a perpetrator of violent death at sea off the southwest coast of the island of Virgin Gorda. Deputy Commissioner Lane had made my instructions clear: apprehend and kill, no arrest, indictment, or trial. I was to be judge, jury, and executioner, no niceties of civilization, as it is so often on the brutal sea. Because, you see, the perpetrator I sought was not human. The perpetrator was a shark.

The call had come from headquarters in Road Town about ten in the morning. The mutilated torso of the victim had first been seen at dawn by an early-morning jogger on the beach at The Baths. A jumble of massive volcanic boulders interspersed with powdery white sand, The Baths are dramatic and inviting at the same time. The warm aquamarine waters between the boulders are popular for snorkeling and swimming. Except that no one would venture into them today. The headless, armless trunk of the young woman pulled from the gentle surf had a considerable deterrent effect on swimmers and snorkelers. Great chunks of the torso's thighs had been torn away. Entrails drifted dreamily in the waves. The head, an entire arm and most of the second, and the left half of the chest and ribs had been severed from the body.

The jogger who found the remains had told the constable from the Virgin Gorda police station who first arrived on scene that he had seen a large brown shark circling and returning to rip away flesh again and again as the body floated in on the incoming tide. Neither the jogger, nor the constable, nor anyone else in the to-be-counted-upon knot of the curious who had gathered on the shore had ventured to retrieve the pitiful lump of meat and bones until it had washed in almost onto dry sand. The shark had eaten and eaten and probably would have finished the entire meal had not the tide cleared the table.

The onlookers remained on the sand among the scattered boulders when Anthony Wedderburn and I arrived from Anegada three hours later. They stared seaward toward us as we anchored. Within earshot of shore, we heard no sound from them except for the vendors who circulated among them hawking guava juice and green coconut water. I guess we were the second act of the morning's entertainment and they were waiting for the curtain to go up.

"Let's anchor here, Anthony," I said as the current carried us over a hole, its depth showing as a purple-black color, two cable lengths from land. The anchor caught in the marly bottom, spinning the boat to face the southwest current.

Anthony went to the cooler beneath the stern seat of the *Lily B* and pulled out a thirty-pound block of chum, frozen in a mesh potato bag. The hot sun triggered the almost immediate release of an odor that was a mix of dead fish, sweaty feet, and slaughterhouse.

"Where did you get this . . . awful offal?" Anthony winced, holding the bag at arm's length and turning his head aside, as if that could shield him from the smell now enveloping the *Lily B* and the nearest twenty yards of atmosphere surrounding her.

"I made it myself," I said. "One-third mullet for oiliness, one-third leftover lobster trap bait, and one-third roadkill—a cow hit just outside The Settlement last fall. Whenever I get a client who just wants to catch a big fish and doesn't care about species, I take a bag out of the freezer and chum up a shark. It works like a charm."

"Remind me to never accept a dinner invitation from you, old man. Not if it comes out of the same freezer you keep this in." Anthony grinned, always cheerful at any task. He tied the chum bag to a short length of line, dropped it in the water, and knotted the line to the stern cleat.

Before long, an oily slick, augmented with bits of rotting fish and rancid beef, was being carried in the current on a line parallel to the beach.

While Anthony was setting the chum bag, I prepared the big Penn International reel and rod, attaching fifteen feet of stainless steel cable leader to a ball-bearing swivel, attaching that to the 130-pound-test monofilament line from the reel, and crimping on a 12/0 circle hook. When it was all ready, I pushed the hook through the back of the bait—a whole five-pound bar jack. The bait was then dropped into the water beside the chum bag and the line slowly stripped from the reel as the current took the bait back into the chum slick.

"It shouldn't be long now, Anthony," I said. "Give the bag a couple of shakes to keep the chum flowing, will you?"

Catching sharks is never difficult in the BVI. The hoteliers and resort owners are reluctant to speak of it but the sea here is home to plenty of sharks, large and small. Our waters are abundantly filled with reef fish and other marine life, particularly around Anegada and Virgin Gorda due to the close proximity of the Horseshoe Reef and the Anegada Trench. With many fish come many sharks, the cleaners of the sea, feeding on the old, the injured, and whatever is the piscine equivalent of the halt and the lame, dispatching them with surgical precision. Wade a bonefish flat and you are accompanied by sharks. Snorkel or scuba dive and you will see the gray shapes cutting in and out of the periphery of your vision. Amble a few steps from your resort's beach cabana, with its plush towels and attentive waiters, for a cooling dip in the clear waters, and they will be there, keeping their distance, curious and yet wary, as you splash and play.

While their appearance may be sinister, my experience has been that their intentions are not. I have never known a shark to attack a human being in the BVI. There is just too much easy food, in the form of live and dead fish, rays, turtles, and lobsters, for them to bother tackling something as large and troublesome as a man. And a mistaken attack, the kind that occurs in murkier waters the world over, is not possible here with water visibility usually in excess of one hundred feet.

"I see two in the chum line," Anthony said, a hand shading his eyes against the morning glare. Sure enough, two high fins carved the surface a quarter mile in our wake. Soon more dorsals joined the first two, working forward in the current toward the source of the chum, picking up chunks of fish and cow flesh. At a hundred yards off the *Lily B*'s transom, the bodies of the sharks came into view, orbiting the dead jack that was my bait. I could see that they were all small, their length less than a woman's height, and also that they appeared gray or blue in color. This meant that they were reef sharks or blacktips, species not the object of our hunt. The constable and the other witnesses who had seen the shark eating the torso had described a large brown shark, and that could mean only one species in these waters—a bull shark. While its colors vary widely in the bull shark's round-the-world equatorial habitat, in the Virgin Islands they are known as the Man in the Brown Suit.

What I saw circling the bait drifting in the top of the

water column was not the quarry Anthony and I hunted but there was nothing to be done. Soon the blue and gray ghosts moved to the attack, a half dozen small sharks taking turns, charging in, slashing a piece from the bait, until the surface of the water frothed and churned. Ashore the crowd of on-lookers had grown as the morning moved toward noon, and the attack on the bait drew first a murmur from them, and then a horrified exclamation, which made its way across the water to De Rasta and me.

The clicker on the reel engaged, a signal that the hook had found one of the sharks, and the battle was on. It was not much of a battle. Given the circumstances, today's fishing was not about giving the shark a sporting chance, and I had used my heaviest gear. The hooked five-foot lemon shark was no match for 130-pound-test line and a rod as thick as a manchineel sapling. The fish found itself at boat-side after five minutes of thrashing.

De White Rasta, no fisherman, exulted in the catch. "We have him already! I'll gaff him!"

"No gaff, Anthony," I said. "That's not our shark, any more than the dozen still out there are. Just put on one of those leather gloves and grab the leader wire when I get it close."

Anthony did as instructed and the lemon shark was soon slamming its tail against the gunwale of the *Lily B*. I reached down with a cable cutter and parted the leader just above the hook. The hook itself would rust out of the shark's mouth in a matter of days.

All this unfortunately took place on the port side of the

boat, in full view of the throng on shore. An outraged "ahhhhh" could be heard from the beach when the assembled realized the shark had been released.

It was then that I saw the RVIPF's only police boat, the fifty-five-foot *St. Ursula*, approaching at flank speed from the direction of Tortola. In the bow, field glasses trained directly on the *Lily B*, was Deputy Commissioner Lane, his six-foot-six-inch frame seemingly at attention, as always, the binoculars unwavering despite the gentle roll of the sea. Two minutes later, the *St. Ursula* had closed the gap with the *Lily B* and cut her engines.

The DC cupped his hands to his face and called, "Constable Creque, I assume you have a good reason for releasing that shark and you are prepared to explain it to me in detail." The *St. Ursula's* momentum had carried her close enough that I could see his face, wearing the same exasperated expression it seemed to wear so often around me.

DC Lane had tried to keep his stentorian voice at a level that would not be heard by the spectators on the beach. A grumble of agreement with his statement welled up from the crowd, telling me he had failed.

"That was not the shark involved in the attack," I said. I thought I had spoken in a conversational tone, enough to discreetly communicate across the thirty feet now separating the two vessels. A further rumbling from the beach told me my words had still carried ashore.

"And you know that, Constable, because . . . ?" The DC held nothing back this time, either realizing the water inevitably carried our voices better than the engineered acoustics of the best symphony hall, or not caring.

Providing an explanation to the DC, even if one is confident it is reasonable and correct, is not the most comfortable exercise for a subordinate. As I had in the past been in the position of providing explanations to the DC that were neither reasonable nor correct, I found myself doubly uncomfortable and cast an almost involuntary look around for help. My eyes fell on a large brown shape astern of the *Lily B* by almost the length of a cricket pitch. I pointed.

"Because the shark that made the attack is over there."

Chapter Two

"Get another bait out, Anthony," I said as I looped the cut end of the cable through the eye of another circle hook and crimped the leader closed with a crimping sleeve. De Rasta placed another bait, this time an oily dead bonito of about six pounds, into my hands as soon as the new hook was attached. In less time than it takes to say it, I threaded the hook through the bonito's back and had it in the water, stripping line to let it float toward the brown shape undulating up the chum line.

The rubberneckers on the beach spotted the big shark and began to gesture with excitement, some clambering onto the tan boulders to get a better view of the action they were sure would come. On the *St. Ursula*, the DC trained his binoculars on the shape, while the crew locked on with their eyes.

The great fish wasted no time, inhaling the bait like an

alcoholic downing the morning eye-opener. After letting her run with the reel in free spool for twenty yards, I engaged the drag lever on the plate of the reel. This action seemed to have no effect, the line spooling off the reel at the same rate as when the drag had been disengaged. Fortunately, the fish ran with the current, allowing itself to be played astern of the boat without risk of fouling the line on the anchor rope or the *St. Ursula,* which was idling in neutral to our starboard.

It was not an epic fight, not like something out of *The Old Man and the Sea,* no tarpon leaps or bonefish speed. The bull fought like most sharks, slow and strong, using its mass and muscle like a heavyweight boxer. The sound of the line peeling off against the pressure of the drag finally slowed after an initial run of three hundred yards. The fish shifted to short, head-shaking bursts of twenty or thirty yards, which sent punishing shocks up the line and through the rod butt held in the socket of the fighting harness strapped to my back and legs.

After long minutes, the bursts grew shorter and finally stopped, and the hard work of pumping the fish began, straining to lift the rod tip six inches, then dropping it to reel in the six inches gained, over and over in the hot sun, until the lion's share of the line run off in the shark's initial rush had been regained. When most of the line was back on the reel, the fish ran again, not as far as the first run, but far enough to elicit an exclamation from Anthony and a slow groan from me.

Two more runs and a punishing hour later, eleven feet

of powerful bull shark arced back and forth thirty feet per-
pendicular to the *Lily B*'s transom. In a normal situation, a
few more pumps on the rod, a gloved hand on the leader,
and the fish would be cut loose to live and fight another
day. Today, though, I unclipped the rod from the harness
and handed it to Anthony, who held it steady, thighs braced
against the coaming pads. I went to the console and unlocked
the electronics box, where I had stored my Webley Mark III
and a box of .38/200 shells that morning before leaving
Anegada. I loaded three shells into the chamber and joined
De Rasta at the stern coaming.

"See if you can pump her in a few feet more, Anthony,"
I said as I readied the heavy pistol.

Tired but not beaten, the shark slid side to side as
Anthony cranked the reel, its massive head and dorsal fin
broaching the water like the prow and mast of a schooner.
I fired once and heard the dull report of the shot echo against
the monumental boulders of The Baths. The shot appeared
to have no effect, the fish continuing its side-to-side fight.
I had missed.

I steadied myself against the movement of the boat, trying to gauge the path of the fish and the sway of the boat in
the current, and still maintain the two-handed shooting
stance I had learned last fall at the Regional Police Training Centre in Barbados. Exhaling as taught, I squeezed the
trigger again. This time the water erupted as the shark
writhed wildly. Anthony had the rod in a death grip, leaning back against the shark's thrashing.

There was blood in the water, blood not from the oily

chum bag but from the great fish drawn by its scent. A few more moments of chaos and then the shark went still. De Rasta leaned into the rod, moving the motionless brown body slowly to the *Lily B*'s stern.

Sighting carefully, I fired the last shell from the Webley, which struck home but generated no additional motion from the fish. Once again, violent death begat violent death.

We slipped a loop of rope around the fish's tail and another just beneath her pectoral fins. I estimated her weight at six hundred fifty pounds; there was no way De Rasta and I could load the fish into the skiff. We attached the tail rope to the stern cleat and the other to the forward cleat, weighed anchor, and started for the Virgin Gorda Yacht Harbour, the nearest place with a winch and gin pole able to lift a fish of that size from the water.

The *St. Ursula* motored parallel to us, the DC in his place in the bow, a sour expression on his great black face. Maybe the expression was caused by my poor marksmanship on the first shot. Maybe it was the prospect of having to explain to the premier and the commissioner that Her Majesty's Virgin Islands now had a problem with shark attacks.

Maybe the deputy commissioner just liked his perpetrators with feet instead of fins.

Chapter Three

When I was a child growing up on flat, almost barren Anegada, the verdant eminence of Gorda Peak seen in the distance was for me an unknown and exotic place. While Anegada, the "Drowned Land" named by Christopher Columbus, hugged the low sea, his "Fat Virgin," named after St. Ursula and her eleven thousand virgins, stretched to the airy clouds. Cleaning fish or cracking conch in the heat of an Anegada afternoon, I dreamed the bantam mountain at the center of Virgin Gorda was a shady jungle bisected by freshets of cool water tumbling to the sea, populated by butterflies, parrots, and other exotic creatures who thrived on its dappled slopes.

I was eight years old before I set foot on Virgin Gorda. Not that I wasn't a man of the world at eight. I had already journeyed to Road Town on Tortola and St. Thomas in the USVI by then, trading and shopping with my dada in those places after the open sea voyage to reach them in his bright red and yellow handmade sloop. Those big towns bustled with an excitement and activity that made me want to return again and again.

By contrast, there was no real town on Virgin Gorda. I sailed there with Dada to deliver a cargo of Cruzan rum and Anegada lobster, the rum for the belongers and the lobsters for the tourists at the relatively new Little Dix Bay resort. The Valley, the flatter south end of the island, was then what it is today—a scattered collection of modest houses and small businesses with no real center. The roads were better than those of my home, chiefly because the development of Little Dix had required the construction of infrastructure for the whole island. The Gordians had piped-in water, while we had cisterns. They also had the trickle-down of tourist dollars from the big resort, while we still lived by fishing, catching conch, and farming.

The people of Virgin Gorda seemed polite but reserved to an outsider like me. They would probably have said the same about us Anegadians. But while you could know everyone on my childhood Anegada in a week and make a bundle of kid friends in an afternoon, the Virgin Gorda of the late 1970s, with its two thousand residents, struck me as too large to be friendly. So my first trip there with Dada was my last until I was grown. I still wheedled rides to Road Town or St. John but from then on I took a pass when Dada's trading took him to Virgin Gorda.

As a grown man, I continued to be out of touch with the island nearest my home. I went there infrequently, mostly to

Little Dix, Biras Creek, and the other resorts, to sell lobsters I had trapped or pick up the occasional bonefishing client. But most of the time my off-island excursions were to Tortola, with its shopping and services. Virgin Gorda and its inhabitants remained a cipher to me.

As Anthony Wedderburn and I motored in the glass-green waters along the scalloped bays of Virgin Gorda's southwest coast, word of our catch must have followed a parallel course northward on land. By the time we edged up to the Yacht Harbour dock nearest the fish-weighing station, a crowd of a hundred or more was waiting. The jetty was lined end to end with children, old men, chatting tourists, even a woman on a rusty bicycle with a scarlet macaw perched on her shoulder. The flashy bird squawked and spoke in tongues, adding to the cacophony generated by the rest of the throng. It seemed our arrival was a spectator sport for the people on Virgin Gorda—Carnival, Boxing Day, and a bloody bar fight all rolled into one.

A surly man in a greasy T-shirt, the dockmaster, pushed his way through the crush to the gin pole and winch, which was usually used for lifting marlin caught by the blue-blood clients of the Yacht Harbour. A lone police officer, treetop tall and barn broad, attempted crowd control with outstretched arms and gentle persuasion, neither of which worked. Children darted beneath his arms and gangling teens jockeyed for better viewing positions when he looked in another direction. After the dockmaster got to the winch and started its engine, the bemused policeman gave up, folding his arms and shaking his head as the human flood swirled around him.

The *St. Ursula* pulled up to the dock on the side opposite the gin pole and DC Lane stepped ashore with two police officers in tow. He immediately ordered them to get the crowd back and they waded in, pushing and cajoling, until a perimeter barely large enough to hoist the shark ashore had been formed.

I tossed the end of the rope tied to the shark's tail across to the dockmaster, who performed a practiced sleight of hand over the gin pole's pulley, ending with the rope's attachment to the winch. The winch was engaged and the stocky body was hoisted from the water, sliding heavily over the dock edge and finally up to swing free from the gin pole.

The watching multitude exhaled a collective "ah" as the fish rotated in a slow circle, revealing precise rows of teeth set in a still-open mouth wide enough to accommodate a large eagle ray or a medium yellowfin tuna.

Or the better part of a human torso.

I looped the bowline to a dock post and stepped ashore while Anthony secured the stern of the *Lily B.* At the same time, on the opposite side of the dock, a rotund figure emerged from the belowdecks cabin of the *St. Ursula.* I had not seen Inspector Rollie Stoutt of the Scenes of Crime Unit for over a year. I could only guess that during that time he had increased his consumption of fungi, fried plantain, and goat patties, and decreased his exercise regime. If he had ever had an exercise regime. Rollie rolled his bulk onto the dock with a graceless two-handed climb over the gunwale, which had him poised for an expectant moment midair between dock and boat. His usual generous application of bay rum cologne succeeded in clearing a space in the crowd on the

dock where fitter officers of the RVIPF had failed. Panting
from the exertion, he paused while the *St. Ursula's* helmsman handed an aluminum equipment case and a folded body
bag up to him. Seizing the case and bag, he arrived in front
of the hanging shark at the same instant as the deputy commissioner and me,

I saluted—fingers together, palm out—as I had learned
twenty-one years ago when I had been trained as a special
constable, and received a crisp responsive salute from the
DC. Inspector Stoutt was exempted from the formality as his
hands were occupied with his equipment and the body bag.

"Is this the culprit, Constable Creque?" the DC asked.
The deputy commissioner was all policeman; even a fish
following its instinct to eat received a label that marked it
as guilty of an offense.

"We cannot really know until we cut open its gut," I said.

"Get on with it then, Constable," the DC ordered.

"Wait a moment please," Rollie countermanded. "I need
to have some photos if the fish contains . . . what you expect."

"Very well, snap to it, Inspector." The DC, and the horde
on the dock, were growing impatient. DC Lane paced in the
tight space in front of the carcass; the crowd rumbled in
muted conversation, except for the macaw held by the bike
lady. It repeated "Very well, snap to it, Inspector" in a loud
and precise imitation of the DC's brusque baritone until
everyone, other than DC Lane, dissolved into titters of nervous laughter. The bird's owner, a statuesque woman in her
late thirties with flawless chocolate-brown skin, hissed,
"Hush, Winston," twice, and Winston hushed, although he

was unable to keep from uttering a fresh "snap to it" every couple minutes, much to the crowd's delight.

Rollie Stoutt fiddled and fumbled his way into his equipment case and came out with a new Nikon D7000. It had probably been purchased with a part of the RVIPF's expanded budget appropriation following my recovery a year ago of fifty million dollars stolen from the BVI. I had a momentary flashback to the evening I recovered the stolen cache at Spanish Camp and nearly lost my life in the process. Despite the rising heat of the day, sweat that felt like ice water trickled down under my arms. I closed my eyes for a moment and thought about my children, Kevin and Tamia. When I reopened them to the sight of the mammoth bull shark swinging from the gin pole, I told myself to focus on the task at hand. Cutting open the shark to reveal whatever its distended stomach contained would be a walk in the park compared to my experience of a year ago.

"Dis do the job for you," the dockmaster said, producing a rust-speckled fillet knife from a tool box next to the winch. As Rollie took his photos, I thumbed the knife's blade. It was honed to a keen edge, a sea tool, unglamorous and practical.

The shark had been hoisted so its belly was head-high. I reached up to begin my cut but before the knife touched the sandpaper skin, an Eton-Oxford-accented voice called from the *Lily B*, "A moment, old man, before you begin."

I stopped, blade poised. All the heads of those present swiveled in Anthony's direction.

"Is there some reason, Mr. Wedderburn, why Constable

Creque should not proceed?" the DC growled. DC Lane is not a patient man when work is at hand and this second halt to the proceedings had pushed his patience to the limit. He had particularly little patience for Anthony Wedderburn, a.k.a. De White Rasta, a.k.a. Lord Wedderburn, even though De Rasta had reformed from his ganja-smoking ways over the last year.

"Why, yes, Deputy Commissioner, I believe there is." Anthony smiled his winning smile and tilted his head, once covered with blond dreadlocks and now cut in a more classic Prince Valiant do. "I thought perhaps you might not wish the ladies and gentlemen, and particularly the small children, gathered around us to be exposed to the sight of what may spill from the fish's stomach when it is opened."

Deputy Commissioner Lane considered for a moment and nodded in sage agreement. "Will everyone here who is not present in an official capacity please disperse," he said. "Go about your business. There is nothing to see here." They teach us that line at the training center in Barbados. I wondered if the DC was the one who had made it a part of the curriculum.

The midday sun shone hot above. The usual dockside scents of clean seawater, motor oil, and decaying bait were supplanted by the acrid perspiration of the bystanders, now grown in number to almost two hundred as the word spread, as it always does on islands. A tourist or two mopped their foreheads but nobody moved, either unwilling to miss the macabre spectacle of body parts spewing from the great shark's belly, or seeking reassurance that the young woman's death had been avenged and the pristine waters of Virgin Gorda were again safe. Most probably, a bit of both.

"It is a public dock and we have a right to be here if we wish," said a voice whose owner was unseen at the back of the crowd. A buzz of agreement rippled through the gathering. The DC knew they were right. This was no crime scene and there was no danger. The people on the dock had as much right to be present as he did.

"You may be upset by what you see," the DC tried for a final time. After a moment more to allow those who wished to to leave, and determining that none in the group fit into that category, the DC shook his head in exasperation. "Proceed, Constable."

The scale on the gin pole showed the shark weighed six hundred forty pounds. It hung blunt nose pointed down, and the contents of the shark's gut bulged just above her pectoral fins. I inserted the point of the rusty fillet knife midway between the two fins, pushed in until the blade was buried four inches into the soft flesh, and sawed upward with two hands. For a moment nothing happened and then the punctured stomach wall gave way, releasing a gray slurry, part liquid and part solid, onto the weathered dock boards.

The flood of stomach contents was so forceful that blood, bile, and gastric juices splashed knee-high against the DC, the dockmaster, the other constables, and the first rank of onlookers, accompanied by a vile stench that defied description. Audible revulsion permeated the air. The crowd froze and gazed at the partially digested carnage before it—most of a cubera snapper, a hank of feathers and bones that had once been a pelican, a plastic motor oil container. Sprinkled throughout the mess were a half dozen embryonic shark pups, miniature duplicates of their pregnant mother, dying now without ever feeling the warm sea against their sleek skin.

Only a part of the gut contents had spilled in the first rush; the remainder had jammed in the small opening I had cut, hung up inside the carcass.

I picked up a discarded wooden fish trap slat from the dock to probe the stomach and dislodge the remaining contents. But just as I was about to push the stick inside, a flash of silver in the offal on the dock caught my eye. I pushed the slat down into the pile and pried upward. The object with the silver gleam popped from the glutinous mass.

It was a silver ring on the finger of a human hand.

Chapter Four

The hand had been bleached white by the shark's digestive juices. The ring, wrought in the shape of a curving dolphin, was unaffected by the process of digestion. It shone brightly from the hand's middle finger.

The emergence of the hand had a transforming effect on the throng of gawkers. After a rooted moment of disbelief at what they were seeing, tourists and belongers, men and women, young and old, alike, scrambled to leave the dock and get as far as possible from the pale hand, which, palm up, its delicate fingers slightly curled, seemed to beckon them in horrific invitation. They fled the hand like mullet avoiding a stalking barracuda, scattering in all directions when they finally alighted from the confining avenue of the dock, all the while uttering cries of shock and disgust at the sight, which they could not now unsee.

The dockmaster remained, a statue next to his winch.

The police officers, myself included, stared down at the hand, each thinking our own private thoughts about grisly death in the jaws of the bull shark. The booming voice of DC Lane snapped us all out of our unsettling musings.

"You there, Constable, what is your name?" the DC said, nodding toward the Virgin Gorda officer who had first tried to control the crowd on the dock.

"Tybee George, sir," the big man said, almost embarrassed. "But most people here call me Bullfoot."

"Bullfoot?"

"After de soup. I loves de soup, sir." He smiled broadly, momentarily forgetting both his timidity before the second-ranking officer of the RVIPF and the carnage on the dock at his feet.

"Well, Constable Bullfoo . . . er, George," DC Lane stammered, "go to the end of the dock and put together some type of barrier to keep the people back now that they have retreated. Inspector Stoutt, do you have some barricade tape you can give to Constable Bullf . . . jeez, George?"

Rollie Stoutt's lips carried a subdued but nonetheless visible smile over the DC's difficulty with the name of Constable George as he rummaged for the tape. In short order Bullfoot had a flimsy barrier stretched between two fifty-five-gallon drums he had placed like sentries at the landward end of the dock.

Rollie turned his attention to the hand, placing a yellow pyramid placard with a "1" on it nearby, and shooting photos of it from multiple angles. Then he snapped on a pair of blue nitrile gloves, spread open the body bag, and, lifting the hand by its slender fingers, placed it inside.

"Constable Creque, let's see what else is inside," the DC said, gesturing toward the hanging carcass.

I probed into the shark's stomach cavity with the fish trap slat, hoping to dislodge a large object there without additional cutting. No such luck, so I picked up the fillet knife to open the gut further. Remembering the pungent splash of offal from the first cut, the deputy commissioner and the others gingerly backed away.

I inserted the knife into the end of my previous cut and pushed upward another foot, causing half a dozen cerro mackerel and a human arm, part of a torso, and a head, to rain down at my feet. Finally emptied, the shark's belly hung lank, moving slightly in the breeze that had thankfully begun to stir.

"It looks like we have most of our victim here," the DC said, almost reverently. Rollie Stoutt would have been pallid if he had not been black. I had been able to tolerate my grisly task to this point but now I felt my breakfast of coffee and johnnycake rise in my gorge. I choked it back, all the while remembering losing it not once but twice at my first crime scene involving a dead body.

While Rollie began his routine of numbered evidence placards and photographs, I leaned in to look at the victim's head. Like her hand, the part of the head remaining was a ghastly gray-white. Lank brown shoulder-length hair, any curl lost to seawater and gastric juices, fanned out from the head in a half halo. The young woman's face was mostly gone, nose, right eye, and right ear shredded by the shark's rows of triangular teeth. The bite pattern was distinctive: slightly curved double rows of wedge-shaped punctures tearing the flesh in parallel lines, one line for each tooth, until a hunk of meat was detached and swallowed whole.

The left ear and eye remained untouched. The earlobe held an earring with a dolphin design similar to the ring found on the victim's hand. The eye was closed. I reached down and pulled the lid back, revealing a blue iris surrounding the fixed and dilated pupil. I closed the lid and heard a voice inside my head utter an inarticulate prayer for the young woman dead in shattered pieces on this pleasant morning.

An examination of the torso revealed the same bite patterns as those on the head and neck. I also looked for scars, tattoos, or other marks that might help identify the victim. The head had been severed from the neck in a single bite, leaving a jagged stump at the neckline. I searched along the neckline and gently lifted the torso to check both shoulders as likely places for tattooing. It was then that I noticed an injury ever so slightly different in appearance from the other bites and tears, an elongated slice of about three inches very near to the carotid artery. With all the ragged, torn, and damaged flesh in the area, it was probably just another slash from an errant tooth. It could have been something different, but given the way the rest of the body was battered, I assumed it wasn't.

The sun was transiting the noon meridian by the time Inspector Stoutt had finished with his photographs and the various parts had been placed in the body bag. Bullfoot was sent to the Virgin Gorda Police Station with two assignments. First, pick up the lower portion of the victim's torso, which had been pulled from the sea at The

Baths earlier in the day, and, second, stop at the Supa Valu Market near the station for ice to preserve the body from further damage until it could be delivered to the coroner in Road Town. The big man departed with a spring in his step, whistling a tune by the time he hit the end of the dock.

Half an hour later Constable George returned in the Virgin Gorda station police vehicle, a Land Rover. In its rear was a hundred-fifty-quart cooler containing ice and the lower portion of the victim's body. The remains from the bull shark's belly fit neatly inside the cooler, on top of the rest. Two of the Road Town officers wrestled the cooler aboard the *St. Ursula*, stowing it against the transom as if it were the day's catch of grouper rather than the remains of a human being.

With Bullfoot came his boss, Station Sergeant Isaac Chalwell, the only other officer on duty of the total of four RVIPF officers assigned to the Virgin Gorda station. Sergeant Chalwell was the ranking member of the RVIPF on the island and must have pulled a double shift due to the shark attack. His eyes and, indeed, his entire countenance showed he had been up all night. He saluted the DC smartly despite his obvious fatigue. Like Bullfoot, he was unusually tall and broad. Unlike his subordinate, he had a sharper edge. Maybe it was his command authority coming through. Maybe it was his pencil-thin mustache, a fashion throwback to the thirties and forties that might have finally made its way to Virgin Gorda by the fifties. Who knew why Chalwell wore it now. The mustache perched like a peaked roof over two rows of dazzling white teeth.

"Do we have any idea who the victim might be?" DC Lane asked.

"No, sir," the sergeant said. "I cannot identify her from the parts recovered from the shark. The portion that washed ashore was clothed only in a blue striped bikini bottom. Points to the lady being out for an early morning swim or falling from a passing boat. The condition of the body doesn't indicate she was in the water for very long, certainly no more than a few hours. But we have no reports of anyone missing from a boat or ashore." Sergeant Chalwell spoke with such smooth assurance that you would have thought mangled bodies bobbed ashore in Virgin Gorda at least once a week. "My guess is that we will have a report of a missing person within the next twenty-four hours."

The DC considered for a moment and said, "I agree, Sergeant, but we should still be proactive on this. Call in your other shift of officers and have them start canvassing. If our victim was from The Valley or staying on a boat in the area, I would think that we would have heard from someone that she was missing by now. Maybe you should send a man to the North Sound area. She may have come down from there to spend the day at The Baths." The North Sound is at the far northern end of Virgin Gorda, on the other side of Gorda Peak, and home to a number of resorts.

"I would, Deputy Commissioner, but two of my men are out. One is on vacation, gone for a week to San Juan, and the other is down with a pretty nasty case of the flu. I can send Bullfoot to knock on doors in the North Sound but I need to stay at the station. Most citizen reports and inquiries here are walk-ins, so keeping someone at the desk is important."

"Perhaps you could use some canvassing assistance, Sergeant. I can temporarily assign Constable Creque here to the Virgin Gorda station for a few days," the DC volunteered. It was most unusual for him to offer rather than order. The DC gives out orders like a clown gives out candy at a toddler's birthday party. Only without the joviality.

"That would be most helpful, Deputy Commissioner," Sergeant Chalwell said. This was the most courtly giving and acknowledgment of an order I had ever seen. I surmised that drinks were ordered at the Arts Club in London with far less panache. "And Constable Creque's reputation precedes him."

Teddy Creque, Queen's Police Medal for conspicuous gallantry. Shot while his guard was down. Recovered millions for the BVI. Quit the force and then returned. I wondered which part of my reputation had preceded me to Virgin Gorda.

"Constable Creque has shown particular aptitude for the identification of crime victims under difficult circumstances in the past, Sergeant. I'm certain you will find his assistance helpful," the DC said, eyeing me. I thought I detected the slightest smile at the corners of his mouth for a very, very brief moment as he spoke. A smile from the DC appeared with less frequency than Halley's Comet.

DC Lane continued. "Constable Creque, I think Anegada can survive without you for a few days. I'm assigning you to the Virgin Gorda station, under Sergeant Chalwell's supervision, for the next week, or until the victim of the shark attack is identified, if it takes less time. You can begin by canvassing The Valley to see if anyone is missing, and then wherever else the station sergeant deems appropriate. But first, take your Mr. Wedderburn home to Anegada and while you are there make any necessary family arrangements and pack a bag for a week. It is thirteen hundred hours now. Report to the Virgin Gorda station by sixteen hundred hours. You should be able to get three hours of canvassing in before nightfall." He turned to Sergeant Chalwell. "Keep me posted on all developments, Sergeant."

Five minutes later, Anthony Wedderburn stood alone at the end of the dock. The *St. Ursula,* bearing Rollie Stoutt, the DC, the other officers from Tortola, and its sad cargo of the shattered bones and ripped flesh of an unknown young woman, knifed away across the Sir Francis Drake Channel to the southwest. Sergeant Chalwell and Constable George had gone back to the station. De Rasta climbed aboard the *Lily B* and I was about to do the same. Before boarding, I took a minute to wash the viscera from the dock with a few buckets of seawater drawn from the harbor.

As we pulled away, only the great bull shark remained, cut belly flopped open like a sail, catching the afternoon trade wind and rotating languidly on the rope from the gin pole.

Chapter Five

The hazy profile of my home island grew more defined after a quarter hour at sea. Another quarter hour and it had morphed into a dusty green line of scrub thorn, a smattering of coconut palms, and the low concrete form of the Reef Hotel at Setting Point. Arriving, we tied up to the government dock and, after exchanging greetings with a couple of Anegadians there, piled into the RVIPF Land Rover to make for Anegada's only town and my home, The Settlement.

On the way from the dock, we passed by my dada's one-pump gas station, its tiny shed unoccupied, a sign indicating it was "closed for the day." Woe to anyone who needed a fill-up on the island that day, but you could always catch a ride with a neighbor. Further along the road from the dock was the Reef Hotel bar, an outdoor affair where you bought drinks on the honor system twenty-four hours a day, doing your own pouring and keeping your own tab. I knew that system well.

I had run a pretty heavy tab at the Reef Hotel bar last year. After I was released from Peebles Hospital in Road Town, I still hurt badly. Not just from the gunshot wound, though that was severe enough that the RVIPF declared me temporarily disabled. I hurt from the loss, the foolishness, the indignity, the crushing, mind-destroying, awful, utterly debasing turn I had allowed my marriage to Icilda, and my life, to take.

I went through the motions for the first week or so and everyone was solicitous but slightly embarrassed for me. The physical pain had me at the Reef bar by the end of that first week; the mental pain kept me there. At the end of two months, I could be found daily at midmorning on a rickety corner stool, Special Constable Teddy Creque, QPM, hero of the RVIPF, drunk as a lord. At the end of three months, my children, Kevin and Tamia, were living full-time with Madda and Dada, and Lawrence Vanterpool, proprietor of the Reef, had taken to pulling down the hurricane shutters on the outdoor bar at three a.m. and not reopening them until the more aggressive bareboaters became insistent about their vacation cocktails the following morning at ten.

I remember little about how I filled the hours when the Reef Hotel bar was closed. I know I staggered to the RVIPF Land Rover each night and drove home, a weaving danger to friends and neighbors, safe from arrest because Anegada's only policeman was on disability leave. I know the home I reached at the end of each perilous drive was empty, so empty, a black pit of despair, void of wife and children, as dead and vacant as my soul.

During that time, help sought me out. Dada and Madda were gentle and cajoling, then firm, then severe and insistent, all to no avail. Friends, so many on close-knit Anegada, tried as well, giving up as I rebuffed them time and again. My wounded chest hurt, my wounded soul hurt, and I refused all ministrations.

One morning at the end of five months, half-hungover and still half-drunk from the night before, I drove to the administration building in The Settlement; borrowed a pen and paper from Pamela Pickering, Anegada's administrator; wrote, "I resign from the Royal Virgin Islands Police Force, effective immediately," above my tremulous signature; and asked that Pamela send it to the DC on the next run of the *Bomba Charger,* the fast ferry to Tortola. I handed the keys to the RVIPF Land Rover to her and began the walk to the Reef bar, hoping to make it in time to be the first customer when Lawrence Vanterpool raised the shutters for the day.

Pamela held the letter for days, until she felt in good conscience she could no longer do so. Deputy Commissioner Lane had no such compunction; upon receiving it, the resignation traveled no further than his bottom desk drawer.

A few days after I thought I had resigned found me seated in my customary place at the Reef Hotel bar. It was noon and I was passed out or asleep, I know not which, balanced delicately on my wobbly stool, a skill I had mastered in recent months. A squat glass of my usual, straight Cruzan rum with a squeeze of lime, sat half-consumed before me. Three couples on vacation, all from the same chartered boat, shared the bar with me, drinking sun-just-over-the-yardarm rum smoothies. I could hear them joking about me through the fog of my morning's consumption and I did not care.

"Share a drink with me, old man?" an aristocratic voice said as a hand gently shook my shoulder. I lifted my head from the pillow of the bar and turned to see the smiling visage of Anthony Wedderburn, known on Anegada as De White Rasta and in his native England as Lord Wedderburn, Viscount of Thetford. His amiable smile shone from a face no longer framed with dreadlocks. His eyes, for many years as red and unfocused as mine were that day, danced in the shade of the bar. He was my friend and thus not to be refused.

"Here we are," De Rasta said, pushing a glass of ridiculously pink guava juice at me. I drank.

"Another. To old times and cracking the code," he said, raising an equally pink glass to his lips. I drank.

"Let's walk, Teddy," he said, and had me on my unsteady feet, steering me by the elbow before I could protest. We went out the gate of the Reef Hotel to my old RVIPF Land Rover, parked on the sand road outside. I became vaguely aware that Pamela Pickering was waiting by the vehicle and opened the passenger door as Anthony guided me in. I passed out in the seat and woke on a narrow bed in a sunlit room I did not recognize. I later learned it was Anthony's new home in The Settlement.

"Ah, awake at last, old man," a cheerful Anthony said. "Today is your second sober day! How are you doing?"

The unintelligible mumbling from me, clearly negative despite the lack of coherence, did not faze him. "Well, it's all swings and roundabouts, now, isn't it?" he said, not expecting or receiving an answer.

I could not move, and did not move from that bed for days. I hallucinated, no stranger to such things following my desperate crawl to Flash of Beauty after being shot. I cried, awake and asleep. I wailed, threatened, begged, pleaded, why and about what I can't remember.

Anthony and Pamela doctored me, one of them always by my side. They talked to me incessantly as I shook and sweated in that room, reminding me I had family and friends who loved and cared for me. And as the rum worked its way out of my system, I began to talk to them, to Anthony mostly, but Pamela as well. I talked until the blackness on my soul had departed the same way the rum had left my body. I talked of the mistakes I had made with Icilda, with our marriage, with my life. For days I talked, first haltingly, then without restraint, exposing the darkness that had enfolded me to light. And in the end I realized that my many mistakes were just that—mistakes, not intended, foolish perhaps but not malicious, and to be put behind me.

After two weeks, I got out of bed, ready and determined to go back to living again, back to Kevin and Tamia, Madda and Dada. Back to being human, and not just a bundle of sorrow. Anthony shook my hand as I walked out his front door into the sun. Simply put, I owe De White Rasta and Pamela Pickering my life.

My children proved their resilience again, forgiving and

working as hard as me to bring our little family back together for the second time in two years. Madda and Dada
were there as always, a steadying influence as parents and
grandparents, old eyes who had seen it all.

Of course, I had lost my second job at Anegada's two-
diesel-motor power plant. The power fails often enough
without having a drunk as an operator; when you have one
at the controls, the odds of power failure increase considerably. My third job as a fishing guide was always irregu-
lar, and now that I needed the income the most, the season
for tourists and fishing was at its low point.

That left my job with the RVIPF. For my twenty years
as Anegada's special constable, the job had been a breeze.
Six weeks of training, then nineteen years of patrolling the
sandy roads of crime-free Anegada. All brought to a close
by a forty-year-old crime, the island's first murder since its
days as a pirate haven in the seventeenth century, and a taw-
dry affair, the end of which saw me bleeding on an empty
beach at the hands of . . . well, it is painful to think or say.
So, the job, the real job of policeman, the job performed
when the chips are down, was too tough for me, and I had
resigned—I thought.

The day I had walked out of Anthony Wedderburn's
house a sober and somewhat functional man, Pamela Pickering had placed a call to RVIPF headquarters. Deputy
Commissioner Lane had listened intently as Pamela wound
her way through the story of my recovery from "disability,"
as she put it. After many digressions and deviations, Pamela
got to the point, asking on behalf of herself personally, and,

as Anegada's administrator, on behalf of the two hundred residents of the island, whether I could have my job back. The DC's immediate answer was yes. My resignation had not seen the light of sunny Caribbean day since he had received it and placed it in the dark recesses of his desk drawer.

In a matter of days, I began the training to become a full-fledged constable at the Regional Police Training Centre in Barbados, the first trainee ever to enter the course having already won the Queen's Police Medal. Weeks later, I received my commission as an RVIPF constable, finally a "real" police officer in the eyes of the deputy commissioner, and was assigned as the sole officer on Anegada.

After a dash to my house to pack a bag for a few nights, and a stop at the police station to let Pamela Pickering know that she would be the sole face of government on Anegada until our return, De Rasta and I set a course for my parents' home.

We found my dada, Sidney Creque, dozing in an easy chair on the back porch of the three-room house where he and my madda had raised my nine siblings and me. Like most houses in The Settlement, the diminutive plot of land it sat on was marked by a low rock wall. Dada's beat-up porch chair had a view of the limestone rock yard, a few cacti, a century plant about to bloom, and the cement cistern that caught the infrequent rainfall that was the house's water supply. Dada had been working hard, and looking out at that same dreary scene, for most of his eighty-seven years but it didn't have a negative effect on his sunny disposition.

When Anthony and I scuffed into the yard, he popped awake, fresh as a pygmy orchid after a rain shower.

"To what do I owe this honor, gentlemen?" he said, rising to clap me on the back and shake De Rasta's hand.

"I have a favor to ask of you and Madda," I said. "I have to be away, maybe for several days, and I am hoping you can watch Tamia and Kevin for me."

"Why certainly, boy. This house is used to kids. What's taking you away?"

"Police business," I said.

Dada's demeanor darkened. "It's not something like the last police business you had, is it?"

"No, Dada. I have to go to Virgin Gorda for a day or two to help identify a shark attack victim."

"Shark attack? In Virgin Gorda? Why, boy, I've swum, fished, and sailed these waters for eighty-seven years and I never heard of anyone being attacked by a shark. Unless they were already dead, like the body of a drowning victim."

"I guess this proves there's always a first time, Dada. I caught the shark myself, found parts of the victim in its stomach."

"Don't seem right to me. Man or woman?" he said, curious now.

"A white woman."

"Tourist? No telling what a tourist might have done to provoke an attack."

"I don't know. That's what we have to find out."

"Well, you go and stay safe. Anyway, it's not like people; at least with a shark you know exactly what you're dealing with. Madda and I will watch Kevin and Tamia. Looks like I can skip my nap now, since your madda goes cold in bed when there's grandchildren in the house. Funny, never bothered her when you kids were home." The old man grinned a leathery grin and gave a chicken-wing nudge in the ribs to De Rasta, who responded with a knowing smile and a chuckle.

There are some things a child should never hear from a parent.

Chapter Six

It was midafternoon by the time I eased the *Lily B* into the Yacht Harbour basin at Virgin Gorda. The docks were devoid of all life; even the bull shark's carcass had been taken down and spirited away, now bait for a thousand lobster traps. De Rasta and I walked straight east from the docks on Millionaire Road, bound for the police station at the intersection of Crabbe Hill Road.

The island Christopher Columbus had named Virgin Gorda, "Fat Virgin" in Spanish, did appear fat, or at least prosperous, when compared to Anegada. The road we walked on was paved, the houses neat and large compared to the two- and three-room dwellings in The Settlement. There were banks, stores, and businesses, even a post office. The dollars brought in by the resorts on the island, many multiples of the amount earned on Anegada, showed in the form of fresh paint on houses, new construction under way in several places, scooters, and late-model cars. The signs on shops weren't hand-lettered. Yes, there were goats, but fewer than on Anegada, and they were tethered. Only the chickens ran free.

The people we met on the road nodded and said "good afternoon" in greeting but made no further attempt to engage us in conversation. They were polite but seemed hurried and busy, on their way to something important, unlike Anegadians, who always had time for conversation.

"The torrid pace of life here reminds me a bit of London," Anthony joked.

We stepped onto Crabbe Hill Road and were immediately at the front gate of the police station. We knew because there was one of those freshly painted signs proclaiming it as such, unlike the police station in Anegada, which had no sign and seemed to be striving for shabby anonymity.

The low building was cool upon entry, the natural tempering effect of the concrete block walls aided by actual air-conditioning, a luxury one could only hope for in the cramped Anegada station. A waist-high wood railing, with a swinging gate like the bar in a courtroom, separated a public area with four wooden chairs from the sergeant's desk. A dim interrogation room, with a wooden table, a single chair on one side and two on the opposite, with an attachment point for shackles in front of the single chair, was visible on the left. Behind the sergeant's desk were two cells, both unoccupied, with a toilet, basin, and bunk platform, all stainless steel, in each. On the wall to the right of the desk was a corkboard covered with yellowing wanted posters and announcements and two paper flags, the Union Jack and the BVI flag, a blue ensign with the Union Jack in the canton, defaced with a green coat of arms featuring St. Ursula and the golden lamps of her eleven thousand virgin followers. The wall tableau was completed by a central portrait of HRH Queen Elizabeth II, her expression either severe or bored, depending upon the inclination of your mind.

Sergeant Chalwell rose from his seat at the desk when we entered. I saluted and he returned it, a casual wave to the brow without the snap of the salutation he had delivered earlier to DC Lane. The gesture said he was in charge here and we had better understand it.

"You can put your bags in the cells," he said, tossing his head in their direction. "I'm afraid those are the best accommodations I can provide on short notice and in season like this. I'll have Mrs. Scatliff, the housekeeper, get you blankets and pillows. She'll provide you with your meals while you're here; she does that when we have prisoners. It's not bad food but don't count on seeing too much meat. She gets paid a per-meal stipend, so expect johnnycake, rice, pumpkin, and a little fish. But she ain't poisoned anyone yet." Sergeant Chalwell's deadpan attempt at humor was not reassuring. I silently wished I had eaten more for breakfast.

The sergeant turned to business. "I have Bullfoot out with the police vehicle canvassing the North Sound and all points north of Little Dix Bay and Olde Yard Village. Constable, why don't you work south, down Crabbe Hill toward the Episcopal church, and some of the back roads in that area. I can't give you a vehicle or a radio—Bullfoot has both—but folks with a telephone will usually let you call if you ask. Call in with any leads and if we get a report here at the station or if Bullfoot turns up anything in the North Sound, I'll have him swing by to pick you up.

"Mr. Wedderburn," Chalwell said, turning in De Rasta's direction, "as you are an assistant to Anegada's administrator, I have no authority over you and cannot order you to take part in canvassing the neighborhoods. But you are welcome to accompany Constable Creque on his rounds and I assume you intend to do so or you would not have returned with him."

"Quite so, Sergeant. We try not to let Teddy go out alone too often—he has a habit of getting himself shot and needing rescue and such—so I'll be keeping an eye on him." Anthony grinned.

Chalwell did not. "Very well, Constable, you better get started. You only have about three hours of daylight left."

Anthony and I worked south on Crabbe Hill Road, knocking on doors. The process was faster than it would have been on Anegada, even though the distances separating houses on Virgin Gorda were greater than they were among the puny cluster of homes in The Settlement. The reason we moved quickly was the people. They always answered their doors, responded to our questions about whether anyone in the household was missing or unaccounted for, and then said "good afternoon" and closed the door in our faces. In Anegada, questions of this nature would guarantee fifteen minutes of conversation at each household, the owner's entertainment for the day but also a useful tool to spread the word through the community. Not happening on this island; the Gordians were as aloof as a pampered Siamese cat.

"Must be your cologne, old man," Anthony said after the last door of our first twenty houses clicked purposefully shut in my face.

"I'm not wearing any cologne," I said.

"Maybe that is our problem."

But it wasn't us. It was them. With the tourist economy on Virgin Gorda, the belongers there saw more strangers in a week than an Anegadian saw in a year, and they had learned the way of the world with strangers. Be firm, be polite, understand they are not important to your life, and if they show up at your door, they are intruding on your privacy. The more people who surround you, the more important your privacy is, and the more rapidly you move to reestablish it when you feel it has been invaded.

We reached a series of short unpaved side lanes just south of the Episcopal church. The houses there, while still widely spaced, were older and smaller. After another "No one missing here" and another door shut in my face, we came to a tin-roofed bungalow painted buttercup yellow, with a lavender door. A rusting bicycle leaned against the front porch. The place had an ancient catchment system for water, the stone dome of the cistern almost as large as the house itself. The yard was lush with papaya, lime, soursop, and mango trees and suspended from almost every branch of those trees were wind chimes, wind chimes with delicate glass bells, with mellow metal tubes, with shells that clicked and clacked like the bones of a fast-played domino game. The late-day breeze through the trees set in motion a river of sound, not cacophonous, a soothing berceuse of tones and tinkling.

My knock at the door received an immediate response, though not the one I expected. A deep male voice inside called urgently, "Raatid! It Babylon! Hide de kali! Hide de kali!"

Chapter Seven

De White Rasta took two steps back, hissed, and waved me away from the door. His eyes were wide.

"Hide de kali!" from inside the house again. If the voice was any indication, its owner was not someone I wanted to tangle with.

" 'Babylon' is police and 'kali' is ganja," Anthony whispered, the irony of a white English aristocrat translating Rastafarian patois for someone born and raised in the Caribbean lost on him.

"It Babylon. Hide de kali," the voice behind the door implored. It sounded closer.

I had a split second to make a decision. It is RVIPF policy to make no entry into a suspected drug house without an armed officer present. While our country makes it illegal to own or possess a handgun, and that law has been very effective for decades, today's drug dealers had shown little regard for the law. On Tortola, in Road Town, and in the tough Huntum's Ghut and Long Look neighborhoods, several guns had been found during raids in the last year.

I was pulling Anthony down the steps when the door burst open and a laughing woman, with a scarlet macaw perched on her arm, stepped out.

"Hide de kali!" said the bird in a Barry White bass-baritone.

De Rasta and I stopped in midretreat.

"I'm sorry, officers, but the prior owners of Sir Winston Churchill here were less than law abiding," said the lady with the avian arm candy. "He picked up some of their vocabulary and sayings and kept them when they went to jail. Anytime someone comes to the door, he says the police are here. Apparently the Royal Virgin Islands Police Force visited his old owners fairly often."

"It de fuzz," Sir Winston Churchill said, frilling his neck feathers.

"Winston, that is so rude," said the bird lady. "Tell the officers you are sorry."

"Sorry, fuzz. Sorry, fuzz," the bird repeated.

The adrenaline from the anticipated encounter with an armed drug gang fueled a bout of hysterical laughter from De Rasta and me. The bird lady was incredulous for a second and then broke up, too, understanding that we had expected something other than a regal-looking bird and his keeper to emerge from the door.

And what a keeper Sir Winston Churchill had. She was the same woman, and Sir Winston the same bird, who had been at the Yacht Harbour dock earlier when we brought in the shark. The press of business and the crowd had not allowed me to fully take in and appreciate the bird lady's comeliness at that time, but those distractions were absent now and I used the opportunity to focus completely on what I had missed earlier.

The woman before me was tall and lithe. When she stepped further toward us, she moved with balletic grace. Her laughter settled into a smile that showed just the right amount of her white teeth and crinkled the skin at the corners of her eyes in a way that was both attractive and sensuous. Those eyes were blue, the deep, deep blue of the Anegada Passage.

I realized in that moment that I was looking at this woman whose name I did not know in a way I had not looked at a woman since Cat Wells. That thought brought with it a rush of memories, of loss and fun, of lust and regret, of what should have been, what might have been, and what had been.

"I'm Jeanne Trengrouse," she said. "And, officers, don't worry, there is no ganja in my house, nor any other drugs. I live a natural life here, grow my own food, take fish from the sea, and don't pollute my body with drugs, or my soul with greed, sloth, pride, or envy."

I noticed she had omitted wrath. And gluttony. And lust, at one time my favorite and most frequently committed of the seven deadly sins. I thought to remind her that she had missed three sins but it occurred to me she might have left these three from her list on purpose. I refrained from their mention. No use incurring her wrath. It was, after all, not on her forbidden list. I decided then that if we were to explore the omissions from her forbidden list at some point, wrath would not be my first choice. Nor would gluttony.

Anthony, noticing my lack of focus, jumped in. "Begging your pardon, but I am no police officer and need not be addressed as such, ma'am. Anthony Wedderburn, assistant to the administrator of Anegada and civilian assistant to the RVIPF on that sister island, at your service." De Rasta delivered his lines with a dramatic flourish. "The silent gentleman to my right is the real police officer here, Constable Teddy Creque, QPM."

The bird lady reached out to De Rasta and shook his hand. Turning to me, she did the same, saying, "Constable Creque, the one from Anegada?"

I nodded, still tongue-tied. The blue eyes held mine for a time long enough to seem like an encouragement, an encouragement of a nature I had not received in quite some time. It made me relaxed and oddly pleased.

"That's correct, Ms. Trengrouse. Mr. Wedderburn and I are both from Anegada," I said.

"So you are the hero? Oh, of course, QPM. Queen's Police Medal," she said. Some women, the type my friend Detective Sergeant Donovan of the Boston PD calls "badge bunnies," might have said this to be coy or coquettish. The bird lady said it with admiration, like I was some kind of . . . well, hero.

"They did give me the medal," I said. How do you acknowledge it when someone calls you a hero without seeming immodest?

"What you did was brave, very brave," she said, eyes once again locked on mine.

"Thank you," I said, embarrassed and unable to think of anything else to say. A brief but portentous silence fell between us.

De Rasta, oblivious to what was going on, filled the conversational gap. "I had a small but important role in those events, too."

Neither Ms. Trengrouse nor I paid him the slightest attention.

Anthony followed through with an exaggerated throat-clearing, to no avail.

"He's a hero, he's a hero!" Sir Winston squawked in the same voice as the one he had used to warn of the approach of the police a minute earlier.

The trance, spell, rapture, or whatever it was that the lovely Jeanne Trengrouse and I were experiencing was broken. She called over her shoulder into the house, "Jemmy Jim, come take Sir Winston back to his perch."

A young boy, no more than seven or eight years old, appeared shyly at the door. Like the bird lady, he had the same velvety chocolate-hued skin, and when he turned his face momentarily to mine, the same gentle blue eyes.

"Hello, young man," I said. He turned his eyes downward, then, and, accepting the transfer of Sir Winston to his arm, retreated into the house.

"Please excuse my son, Constable, he is very shy," Ms. Trengrouse said. "Now, how can I help you gentlemen?"

I repeated the same query that had generated so many

negative head shakes and closing doors for De Rasta and me in the last few hours.

"I don't know of anyone who is missing," she said. "Jemmy and I live alone, unless you count Sir Winston as a human, which sometimes I think he is. Does this have to do with that horrible shark attack?"

"Yes. We are trying to determine the identity of the victim, and, as you saw today at the dock, her remains are in a very . . . damaged condition. We are hoping to identify the body by ascertaining if anyone is not accounted for on the island."

"I'm sorry, Constable. I guess I'm no help to you." She paused. "Unless . . ."

"What is it, Ms. Trengrouse?"

"It may be nothing."

"Any information may point us in a direction to help identify the victim."

"Well, my Jemmy sometimes wanders at night. He's . . . different from other children his age. Anyway, he does most of his wandering just before dawn. I can't tell you how many mornings I've heard the back door slam closed just as the sky lightens and the pearly-eyed thrasher begins to sing. Jemmy usually goes out to the beach at The Baths and watches the first light play over the water. He was there this morning, Constable, and he says he saw a boat."

Chapter Eight

      The main living area of Jeanne Trengrouse's home consisted of a single open combination sitting room and kitchen, in the old Virgin Islands style. The room's teak flooring, battered but spotlessly clean, had probably been salvaged by the builder from a shipwreck. A wicker sofa and chair furnished the quadrant of the room devoted to sitting. A simple wooden table with four mismatched chairs provided a dining area. The kitchen corner held an ancient propane stove and a companion refrigerator. The remainder of the room was dominated by a massive wooden perch for Sir Winston Churchill, who lorded over his kingdom in scarlet splendor, emitting a series of beeps that precisely mimicked the sound made by a disconnecting cell phone. Jalousie windows on all sides allowed for the passage of the late-day breeze, carrying the sound of wind chimes from the yard on its back.

A single door at the main room's left side opened onto a hallway where I could see the doors of two bedrooms.

Jemmy was nowhere to be seen.

"You must understand about Jemmy," Jeanne Trengrouse said. "He is a very special child. He does not speak much, never has, but when he speaks it is important. And it is always the truth, the unvarnished truth, as free from embellishment and opinion as any human being I have ever known. And he likes order, Constable, no disruption in his surroundings or in his life. I try to give him that and he gives me more than I could have ever hoped for in return. I hope you understand that, Constable, and that you will respect that in your dealings with him."

This last was delivered with a surprising fierceness, and I nodded in agreement. I expect if I had done otherwise, De Rasta and I would have been asked to leave and thus completed our circuit of The Valley one slammed door at a time.

"Certainly, Ms. Trengrouse. I will treat him as I would expect my own son to be treated," I said. The response caused the fierceness to evaporate from her face, replaced by a warm smile.

"This way, Constable," she said, pushing open a plank door. It led to a bedroom, no more than ten feet by ten feet, with a single bed and a chifforobe made of Caribbean heart pine. The wiry Jemmy sat in the middle of the floor, rapidly adding Lego blocks to an astoundingly complex structure that filled all the remaining floor space. The edifice had a familiar look and then I realized it was because I had seen a picture of it somewhere before, probably in one of Kevin's schoolbooks when I was helping him with his homework.

Then I saw, in the space at the back corner of the bed, a book open to a photograph of the actual building. The Lego construction replicated the photo in precise detail, every tower, spire, and transept, except for an incomplete portion of a wall along the seaside. That wall was being constructed by the boy at a pace so rapid his hands fairly flew, adding block upon block so that the wall seemed to grow of its own accord, as in a time-lapse film.

Jemmy did not refer back to the book as he built, nor did he deviate from his work to see who had entered the room.

"That is Mont St. Michel, and a striking likeness it is!" Anthony exclaimed.

"Yes, Mr. Wedderburn," said Ms. Trengrouse in a matter-of-fact tone. "Yesterday Jemmy did the entire grounds of Buckingham Palace and the day before the Sagrada Familia in Barcelona."

"That is incredible," I said.

She smiled. "I told you, Jemmy is a special child." Turning to Jemmy, she said, "Jemmy, this is Constable Creque and Mr. Wedderburn. They want to ask you about what you saw this morning at The Baths."

The boy did not even seem to have heard his mother. The blocks continued to fly onto the seawall of Mont St. Michel, the small hands working at a blinding pace.

"Sometimes it takes a while," she said, an explanation but not an apology. "Jemmy, look at me for a moment." The blocks continued to fly, the structure almost complete. "What

did you tell me you saw at The Baths this morning, poppet?"
Not so much as a twitch of response.

I knelt down to the boy's level and asked, "Jemmy, what
did you see?"

The hands stopped for a moment and I thought I was
going to get an answer. But then I saw that the boy had
stopped because he had finished the building, which now
filled the room except for the area where Jeanne, Anthony,
and I stood.

"The building you have built is truly marvelous," I said,
meaning it but also hoping the compliment might breach the
barrier the child had erected around himself.

The rapid little fingers began their work anew, this time
in reverse, dismantling the Lego Mont St. Michel a block at
a time, nearly as quickly as the eye could see. With the blocks
Jemmy removed, he began another structure, not a building
this time, but a compact central core, lapped and expand-
ing outward on its own perimeter, the colored blocks in the
same pattern of blue, red, black, yellow, and white, repeated
over and over again until the French monastery was gone
and in its place was a solid cube of Legos, waist high, and of
the same width and length. The process took no more than
ten minutes and when the last block was removed from
Mont St. Michel it completed the cube in a precise pattern
of colors.

We three adults had watched this occur without a word.
When Jemmy finished, he said, "Time for bed," to no one in
particular, kicked off his flip-flops, and climbed into bed.
Placing himself in the center of the bed, he crossed his arms

on his chest like a Mexican bandit wearing two bandoliers and closed his eyes. It was clear there would be no further communication from Jemmy this evening.

Jeanne Trengrouse motioned for us to leave the room and we followed her back to the main room.

"I am sorry, Constable, but when Jemmy goes to bed, he will speak to no one until morning, not even me," she said, apology in her eyes.

"I understand, Ms. Trengrouse," I said. "He is a remarkable boy."

"He did say he had seen a boat, Constable, and he would not have mentioned it unless something important had occurred. He is used to seeing boats at The Baths. Perhaps you can stop back tomorrow if you haven't identified the victim. Jemmy may be more forthcoming by then." Her eyes met mine. Standing near to her, I thought I detected the light scent of lavender. I found myself pleased at the prospect of visiting Jeanne Trengrouse again. No. "Pleased" is too mild a word. I was thrilled, and in a most unprofessional way. The most thrilling part was that Jeanne Trengrouse's smile and the way she moved her body close to mine conveyed that she felt the same way.

"With your permission, then, I will stop over sometime tomorrow morning," I said.

"Certainly. Until tomorrow, Constable," she said, her voice an octave lower. Whether it was intentional or not, she succeeded with those words in stirring something inside me I thought had been long put to rest.

"Until tomorrow, Constable," said Sir Winston Churchill

in the same sultry voice, as De Rasta and I walked out into the dusk.

"It appears that bird has taken a liking to you, old man," De Rasta said, a glimmer in his eye.

And I don't think he was talking about the macaw.

Chapter Nine

Anthony and I arrived back at the station on Crabbe Hill Road at the same time Bullfoot returned from scouting the North Sound. We all gathered around Sergeant Chalwell's desk to report.

"Dere nothing in de North Sound," Bullfoot said. "All white belongers, non-belongers, and tourists are accounted for. I covered everything north of Gorda Peak, and all de west side south of de peak down to Pull and Be Damn Point." He had covered much more territory than Anthony and me. Of course, he wasn't walking.

I described our equally unsuccessful partial canvass of The Valley, Sergeant Chalwell nodding in understanding as I relived the myriad doors closed in our faces for his benefit. "The only hint of a lead is from a Ms. Jeanne Trengrouse, who says her son was at The Baths early in the morning and saw something on a boat."

"Jeanne Trengrouse, the crazy lady with the crazy son and the parrot? The parrot is the only one of them not sick in the head. What kind of story did she tell you?" the sergeant scoffed.

"Just that the boy had seen a boat and remarked on it to her. When I tried to get more information from him, he wouldn't speak to me. Or anyone else."

"Watch her and watch that boy. He made a complaint of indecent assault against one of our more prominent citizens a couple years ago. When I investigated I found it to be unsubstantiated. The mother pushed and fussed till crown counsel charged the man anyway. He was acquitted when the boy was called to testify and wouldn't speak a word in court." Chalwell shook his head in disgust. "A good man's name dragged through the dirt for no reason."

"I still think it would be worth a follow-up visit tomorrow morning to see if he might have information that would help," I said.

"Let me be clear, Constable Creque. Do not waste your time with that woman or the boy. They are nothing but trouble. Complete your canvass of The Valley tomorrow. Bullfoot will help now that he is finished with the North Sound. Am I understood?"

"Yes, Sergeant," I said. Why do I always clash with superiors? All it would take is a few minutes, I wanted to say. We'll be passing by the Trengrouse house on our way to finish the rest of the canvass, I wanted to say. But I had learned my lesson last year and I kept my mouth shut.

"Good. I'm going home now. It's been a long day.

Mrs. Scatliff should be by with your meal shortly. Bullfoot has the station shift tonight. I'll see you in the morning." And with that Chalwell was gone into the night.

The mood in the station lightened considerably with Sergeant Chalwell's departure. Bullfoot took off his check-banded uniform hat, flopped into the desk chair, and propped his surprisingly-small-for-a-big-man brogues on the desk. He hummed a vacant tune, a hymn, I think, as he settled into his spot for the night.

Mrs. Scatliff, a round, quiet woman, appeared shortly with thin pillows, blankets, and three tiffins of food. My mouth watered at the smell of the meal and I realized I had gone without food since the morning.

When Mrs. Scatliff left, the three of us turned the station desk into a dinner table, pulling in two battered chairs from the waiting area. The tiffins contained johnnycake and a thick fish stew, as predicted. The first bite of the stew, redolent with thyme and island sage, confirmed that Mrs. Scatliff knew her way around a kitchen, even if the ingredients were simple and homely.

Digging in, Bullfoot became expansive. "Ah, de sergeant eatin' good tonight. She saves de big bits for him."

"Who? Mrs. Scatliff?" I asked.

"Yeah, she a widow lady, husband died a few years back, fallin' off a roof he was repairin' at Biras Creek." Bullfoot waved generally northward in the direction of the resort. "She and Sergeant Chalwell, well, it's a long time dey been married, dey just never been churched." He laughed uproariously at his own joke and pounced on another piece of johnnycake.

Since Bullfoot was being talkative, I thought I'd try him out on Jeanne Trengrouse. "The sergeant really doesn't seem to like Ms. Trengrouse."

Bullfoot's mood sobered. "She go her own way all de time, even if it makes trouble. Sergeant don't like trouble an' he don't like folks who go dey own way."

"It can't really hurt to talk to her and her son again, can it? If they have information that might help?"

"One thing I know," Bullfoot said. "The sergeant like things done his way, an' if he say to do or not to do a certain thing, you better do or not do what he say."

Bullfoot's downcast eyes told me he was speaking from experience and it was not the type of experience I wanted to undergo. The conversation turned to lighter topics—fishing, the Loro Piana regatta—and Anthony and I retired to our jail cells early, while Bullfoot dozed his shift away at the desk.

We were awakened by the song of a mockingbird outside the cell windows, followed by Mrs. Scatliff banging her way into the police station with three more tiffins of food and a thermos of coffee. The tiffins contained a breakfast of flying fish fillet topped with a poached egg and a drizzle of homemade curry-pepper sauce, a broiled tomato, and the ubiquitous johnnycake, cooked in bacon drippings and still smoking hot. If I were ever incarcerated, I would want it to be in one of the two cells at the Virgin Gorda Police Station, just so I could pass my sentence eating Mrs. Scatliff's home cooking.

Fortified by Widow Scatliff's fare, Bullfoot, De Rasta, and I were champing to work the remainder of The Valley when Sergeant Chalwell rolled in at eight, the start of the morning shift. After a brief conference, it was decided that Bullfoot would drop Anthony and me along Church Hill Road where we had left off the day before. He would continue to Tower Road, starting at its southernmost point and working north to the Yacht Harbour.

Minutes later, De Rasta and I watched the RVIPF Land Rover, Bullfoot at the wheel, round an arc in the road after dropping us off. The noise of the SUV receded quickly and the light morning air stirred just enough to remind me of our proximity to the chime-filled yard of Jeanne Trengrouse. I made a beeline for it, Anthony on my heels.

"Do you really think this is a good idea, old man, after what the stern-faced Sergeant Chalwell said to you yesterday?" Anthony warned.

"I do," I said, applying my knuckles to the front door of the yellow bungalow.

"My thoughts exactly, Teddy," said De Rasta with a broad smile.

A deep masculine voice on the inside of the door yelled, "Raatid! It Babylon!"

"We're at the right house," said De Rasta.

Chapter Ten

The door opened wide and I decided that, if it were possible, Jeanne Trengrouse looked even more fetching in the morning light than she had the prior evening. The climbing sun caused her blue eyes to spark with good cheer and welcome. A night's sleep had refreshed and filled the gentle laugh lines at the corners of her eyes and mouth, softening them not quite enough to eliminate them altogether. Ripe curves, neither too great nor too small, enhanced her white linen chemise dress.

"Good morning, Constable Creque and Mr. Wedderburn. You are both looking chipper today," she said. The words were directed to both of us but she never removed her eyes from mine. We stood in the doorway, gazing at each other like two first-crush adolescents.

"Ahem . . ." Anthony said after the doorway standoff continued for a time beyond his comfort level. When the gazing persisted, he said, "Good morning, Ms. Trengrouse. As you can see, we are here to take up where we left off yesterday." Then, *sotto voce*, he added, "In more ways than one."

"Of course. Come in," she said, stepping back to allow us in.

"It de fuzz," Sir Winston Churchill said from his perch, taking a break from his breakfast of soursop and nuts.

"Jemmy is in his room." Jeanne lead the way to the bedroom, I followed, and De Rasta brought up the rear. I was glad neither of them could see my eyes; let's just say Jeanne Trengrouse swayed in all the right places as she walked.

"Jemmy, Constable Creque and Mr. Wedderburn are back to speak with you again."

The boy was on the floor surrounded by Legos, putting the finishing touches on an ornate structure with massive wings. I glanced to the bed and found the same book from yesterday, open to a photograph of the Palace of Versailles. The Lego structure matched the original to a T.

"Hello, Jemmy," I said. "It looks like you are almost done. While you are working, can we talk about what you saw yesterday morning?"

No response. The hands flew along, adding Legos at an even pace.

"Your madda says you went out to The Baths at dawn yesterday; do you remember?"

Not a flicker of acknowledgment.

"Did you see something while you were there? Something to do with the lady who was killed by the shark?" Versailles was nearing completion. I was nearing giving up.

"Jemmy, what you saw may help that lady . . . help us to get that lady back to her family." For the briefest of moments, the hands hesitated before resuming the flow of Legos to their appropriate places on the walls, columns, and enfilades.

"What did you see, Jemmy? Help us get that poor lady back to her madda," I said.

"Constable, I don't want you to upset—" Jeanne Trengrouse began.

"Boat," the boy said. Versailles was complete, standing full-blown in all its glory on the teak floorboards in that bungalow half a world away from the original. It only lasted a moment before Jemmy reversed the process, quickly removing blocks to be placed in a new structure he began in the scant space not already occupied. I recognized the beginning of the cube I had watched being constructed last evening.

"Who was on the boat?"

The Legos flew from the wing of the palace to the base of the cube in the same sequence of blue, red, black, yellow, and white as yesterday. Silence hung heavy in the room. I thought we were done, and then . . .

"The lady, two men, bad men."

"What happened, Jemmy?"

The blocks moved in a blur. The child's concentration on the cube seemed complete but then he said, "The lady screamed. One of the men pushed her over."

"Who were the men?"

"A white man and a black man. Bad men."

"Do you know them?"

"Couldn't see."

"What about the boat? Was it a boat you had seen before?"

"Bad-men boat."

"What color was the boat?"

The cube of Legos was quickly taking shape while the walls, roof, and windows of Versailles melted like sands out of an hourglass. Jimmy said nothing in response to my last question, redoubling his efforts on the blocks.

"Did the boat have a motor? A sail?" I tried again, feeling a sense of panic rise within me. What if I could not get this information from the child? Had a crime been committed? It was as if I were not in the room, as if none of us were in the room with this boy. Jeanne tried but Jemmy was no more responsive to his mother than he was to me. Minutes passed with only the music of the wind chimes and the click of the Legos snapping into place. Finally, the cube with its perfectly sequenced pattern of colors stood completed on the floor. I tried the question again. In response, Jemmy arose, walked to the book on his bed, turned the page to reveal the Kremlin, and began dismantling the cube and creating walls and onion-domed towers. In a few more minutes, the home of the tsars was recognizable.

Jeanne Trengrouse led us from the room. "You have to understand, Constable, that sometimes weeks pass without Jemmy speaking at all. In fact, that was the most I have ever heard him say to a stranger." She said it like a compliment and maybe it was one.

"Did what Jemmy said jog your memory at all?" I asked. "Did he give you information on the boat or the two men?"

"He only told me he saw a boat and a bad thing happened. That was what he said, 'a bad thing.' "

"What he said is valuable information. I need to report it now. Do you have a phone I can use?" I surveyed the room as I spoke, guessing that the interior of the bungalow had never seen Alexander Graham Bell's invention, under this owner or any of the previous ones.

"A telephone is an unnecessary intrusion into the joy of life, Constable. I never learned anything through a telephone that wouldn't as easily have reached me through word of mouth or a letter. I don't have one."

"Well then, Ms. Trengrouse, thank you for your time and assistance. If you think of anything further or Jemmy provides additional information, please contact the police station. And if it is all right with you, I may follow up with you and Jemmy every few days until this matter is resolved." I must confess, while this practice might sound like good police work, I said it because I wanted an opportunity to see Jeanne Trengrouse again.

"We will help in any way we can, Constable," she said, lowering her eyes behind long lashes and then raising them to meet mine. When I was fifteen and first taking serious notice of girls, my madda told me shiny-eyed women are trouble to a man. With Cat Wells, I had learned how right she was. Yet, here I was, only a year after all the trouble that shiny-eyed Cat had created, losing myself in Jeanne Trengrouse's luminous eyes. A man in his forties should have learned most of life's lessons. Sometimes I thought I had not even signed up for the class. I knew I would return to this woman's cozy home off Church Hill Road, whether I had reason to or not. I knew I couldn't stay away.

I knew when I returned she would not turn me away.

Chapter Eleven

Anthony and I caught up with Constable George on Tower Road, outside a nameless bodega painted with magenta steps and bright turquoise siding. He was in animated conversation with two weathered codgers who sat rocked back in plastic lawn chairs beside the outdoor chest cooler that served as the bodega's primary display case. He broke off the conversation with a combination low five and hand pump as we approached. I decided that had to be the Virgin Gorda secret handshake, and that I must learn it. De Rasta and I had not received such a warm send-off from anyone on the island in our two days there.

"Dem my uncles Wilfred and Cheebie," Bullfoot said by way of explanation as he strolled up to us. The old boys waved. Any friend of Bullfoot was obviously considered a friend of theirs. "You have any luck, Constable Creque?"

"I don't know if you would call it luck, Constable George."

I stayed with Bullfoot's formal title, even though we were equals in rank. I noticed that he always used my title when speaking to me. I suspect because he was impressed that I had been awarded the QPM. If he only knew the entire story. "It appears we have a crime on our hands. A boat was seen off The Baths at dawn yesterday, with two men, one black and one white, and a woman aboard. The witness heard the woman scream and saw one of the men push her over the side. I think the woman is our shark attack victim."

Bullfoot stepped to the RVIPF Land Rover he had parked beside the bodega in the shade of a gumbo limbo tree. Every time I looked at this vehicle, I was irked. The police vehicle I drove on Anegada was a ten-year-old hand-me-down no longer fit for motor patrol on Tortola. The Virgin Gorda station had been equipped with this year's model. It was air-conditioned. It was not scratched and dinged from a thousand scrapes against scrub thorns, cacti, and cows. It even had a professional police-band radio, not a CB like I used on Anegada. As Bullfoot picked up the mic to call the station, he asked, "Who de witness?"

"The Trengrouse boy, Jemmy."

Bullfoot's hand dropped, carrying the mic from his lips. He frowned. "Sergeant Chalwell say dat boy is a liar and a troublemaker. You sure you want to do dis?"

More than a little surprised that Bullfoot would even consider not reporting the information, I opened my hand to receive the microphone. Bullfoot placed it there, saying, "I hope you know what you doin'."

"What is our call sign?" I asked.

"Unit one," said Bullfoot. Of course.

Thirty seconds later, I had Sergeant Chalwell and explained the information Anthony and I had learned, carefully omitting the source.

It didn't take Chalwell long. "You didn't get that from that crazy Trengrouse kid, did you, Constable?" Chalwell's gravelly voice barked.

"Yes, Sergeant, but—"

"No buts, Constable. I thought I told you that boy and his mother are not trustworthy. You know they have made false reports in the past and yet you bring me another. Is that where you spent the morning, instead of canvassing like you were supposed to?" The sergeant had obviously studied at the Deputy Commissioner Howard T. Lane School of Subordinate Scolding, even if he might not have graduated with honors.

"Sergeant Chalwell, I think it is worth—" I got out before the radio roared, "Constable Creque, this is an order." Uncle Wilfred's and Uncle Cheebie's heads turned in the direction of the angry voice thundering from the radio. "You will not waste any further RVIPF time speaking to that psychotic child or his troublemaking mother. Get out there and canvass as you were ordered. Is that clear?"

"Yes, Sergeant."

"Is Constable George there?"

"Yes, Sergeant."

"Put him on."

I handed the mic to Bullfoot, who took it shaking his head, a wry smile on his lips, and said, "Here, Sergeant."

"Constable George, did you hear what I just said to Constable Creque?"

"Yes, sir." You don't "sir" a sergeant, I knew from my training at the Barbados Regional Police Centre, but Bullfoot's experience obviously told him that rule didn't apply where Sergeant Chalwell was concerned.

"You make certain Constable Creque obeys that order, and you report to me immediately if he does not."

"Yes, sir." Bullfoot looked as if he were a five-year-old about to feel the wrong side of his dada's belt. The radio clicked out at the police station and Bullfoot clipped the mic back into its holder.

"Well, that was pleasant," said De Rasta. "I guess if we get any more information from that household it will have to come from the beak of Sir Winston Churchill."

Anthony and I were on the ninth house of our late-morning canvass before the sting of Sergeant Chalwell's rebuke began to wear off, replaced by a string of negative answers to our questions about persons missing at each house, and the punctuating slamming of doors in our faces.

House nine held no promise of being different. A sour-looking old man sat on the porch, whittling away at a piece of tamarind wood with a penknife. As we walked down the long path to the house, I saw that the rocking chair on which the old fellow sat was intricately carved, as were the porch rails and the posts supporting the rusted tin roof. The shapes of the carving had an abstract flow to them. If they had been glass, I would have thought the old chap was a disciple of

Chihuly, if Chihuly had devoted himself to fashioning supports for tin roofs.

"Good morning, sir," I said in my best official but cheerful voice. "I am Constable Creque and this is my associate Anthony Wedderburn. We wonder if we might take a moment of your time to ask if anyone in your household is missing or unaccounted for." Best to get right to the point, as the fellow on the porch did not strike me as a patient man, even if he was not in a position to immediately slam a door in our faces.

"What's that you say?" the old man boomed out. "Speak up, son!"

I repeated the request, slowly, and, I thought, loudly enough for my own dada back on Anegada to hear.

"Why does everybody mumble?" the old man said. I am sure he thought he was speaking under his breath; I am also sure most of the population of The Valley could hear what he said. Then, louder, if such a thing was possible, he said, "Woman, come here. The police have finally come to take you to your just reward for all the years of misery you have inflicted on me."

"Man, will you stop your infernal deef yelling at me and the entire world," said an equally elderly woman, wiping her hands on a dish towel as she stepped from the house onto the porch. She was thin as orphanage porridge and light skinned, with a splash of freckles across her nose. Only a ragged wisp of white hair at the very top of her head prevented her from being as bald as a Buddhist monk. She appeared surprised to see us, perhaps concerned that the old man had somehow managed to have her taken into custody, and then the surprise morphed into a visage of sweetness and light.

"Why, gentlemen, what a pleasant surprise to have a visit from the Royal Virgin Islands Police Force this morning," she purred. "What can I do for you? I hope Luther, the worthless scoundrel, was not rude to you."

At last, someone on Virgin Gorda concerned about being rude to me. "Oh, no, Mrs. . . . ," I said.

"Mrs. Quince, Dessie Quince. And this creature"—she gestured toward the old man—"is my husband, Luther." She fluttered her eyelashes at me in the exaggerated manner of a silent film starlet. Who knows, maybe she had never seen a talkie.

"What do these boys want?" Luther interrupted. Calling it an interruption doesn't do it justice; I thought I heard Luther's voice echo back off Gorda Peak.

I explained the reason for our visit to Mrs. Quince. She translated it to Mr. Quince by screaming at him in a shrill voice that I am certain woke the dead in their brick tombs in the shaded yard beside the Methodist church. Not Virgin Gorda's Methodist church; the one on Anegada.

"Me and the witch are the only ones live here. And, as you can see, she intends to stay, despite my best efforts to send her on her way," Luther replied. It must have been a laugh a minute with these two when they weren't constrained by the presence of company.

"What about Michele, out back in the bachelor house?" Dessie screeched at the old man.

"Ain't seen her for a couple days. Why?"

Chapter Twelve

The bachelor house, Luther told us, had gotten its name from Dessie's bachelor cousin who lived there "until Dessie's cooking carried him to the great beyond." While Dessie took us back to the house, Luther stayed on the porch, carving and muttering at a hundred decibels about his concern that he would be next.

To say the bachelor house was small would be an understatement. The bougainvillea-covered wooden cottage was the smallest residence I have ever seen, which in the sister islands of the Virgin Islands is saying a lot, as tiny houses, at least for ordinary belongers, are the rule. As we approached, Dessie explained that Michele was Michele Konnerth, a physician who conducted cancer research at Duke University and had come to Virgin Gorda as a part of her work.

"What is she doing research on in Virgin Gorda?" I asked.

"Some kind of fish to cure cancer, I guess," Dessie said.

"We really don't see much of her. She spends most of her days on the water and at night she is either typing up her field notes or making the rounds of the bars. She usually is up and out before we get up in the morning and she comes home after we go to bed at night. But she is never any trouble and her private life is her own business." Compared to most landlords, Dessie had an unusually charitable attitude about the activities of her tenant.

We knocked on the door and received no answer. I peered in the vine-shaded front window. There was no one inside.

"Do you have a key?" I asked.

"No need. She leaves it open."

I pushed open the front door and called, "Police," into the room. I don't know why. It was clear the single room of the house was empty. I guess I did it because that is what police do, at least on TV.

The room had a spartan neatness about it. A single bed, made to military standards, took up a third of the space. The kitchen area consisted of an open cupboard, a tiled counter with a cold-water sink and a hot plate, and a mini-refrigerator. The fridge held some bottled water, a bottle of Carib beer, and a jar of olives. Apparently Ms. Konnerth had not graduated from the Cordon Bleu before attending medical school.

The remaining space in the room was taken up by a metal table and a folding chair. The table held an accordion file of bills and receipts, and a journal with "Field Notes" inscribed on its olive-drab canvas cover. I certainly had no authority to perform an invasive search but as long as I was this far in, I flipped open the journal to its last entry. Looping, precise handwriting filled half a page below a sketch of two lumpy objects depicted side by side. The date on the notes was January 18, over three months ago. Turning back further revealed more notes and lumpy drawings, some beneath labels in Latin. All of the notes were about the habits of *Holothuria mexicana*, which I recognized from my time poling the flats as the donkey dung sea cucumber. No wonder Michele Konnerth had to hit the bars in the evening for entertainment.

Under the bed I found a footlocker filled with female island apparel—shorts, tank tops, bathing suits, and a floral-print wrap dress, probably her going-out-to-the-bars dress. At the very bottom, under all the clothing, was a photo, a glossy eight-by-ten of a man and a woman in the stern of a boat. The man, dark haired and what in another era would have been called rakishly handsome, flashed a pearlescent smile at the camera. The woman looked not at the camera but at the man, obviously smitten. She had blue eyes and shoulder-length brown hair, both of which seemed familiar. The source of my familiarity was the examination of the stomach contents of the bull shark De Rasta and I had caught yesterday morning. This was confirmed by the woman in the photo's clothing—a blue-striped bikini—and her ring, barely visible but clear enough to see that its design was a curving dolphin. Michele Konnerth was our victim.

While I was convinced the victim's identity had been established, I looked further for a purse or wallet, hoping to find a passport or other photo identification. This didn't take much time, as the only place I hadn't looked was the bathroom. The size of a phone booth, it had unmistakably been added after the advent of modern plumbing to replace the outhouse that had served at the time of the house's original construction. The bathroom was crammed with a toilet and shower, but no purse.

Dessie and Anthony had lingered in the doorway, watching while I searched. I brought the photograph to Dessie and asked if the woman was Michele.

"Sure is. And that man"—she pointed—"is Robin Kingsmill. He's the manager of the Yacht Harbour. The fassyhole." Tell us what you really think, Dessie.

"Do you have any emergency contact information for Michele, Mrs. Quince?"

"No, Constable." Dessie smiled sweetly at me and batted her lashes again. I wondered when Luther had last been accorded that treatment and decided it was probably decades ago.

"Well, it appears that Michele is the victim of the shark attack that took place yesterday at The Baths. Is there anyone who might know who her next of kin is?"

Dessie thought for a moment. "I don't mean to speak ill of the dead, Constable, but Michele . . . she was very serious and dedicated in her work but she was less than scrupulous in her private life. She had a lot of men 'friends,' if you know what I mean, and a lot of women 'friends.' Sometimes more than one friend at a time. She never brought any of them here, but she confided in me on a couple of occasions. She went back and forth between men and women. She said she was confused, and she wished she could know just who she really was, but she never could settle in, one way or the other. Poor child, it just wore on her and she never seemed to get close to any of 'em, just one-night stands. I guess the closest she was to anyone was that fassyhole Kingsmill, or maybe that bartender lady. The three of them hung around together for a while. The bartender is a photographer. I'll bet she took the picture you found."

"Do you know the bartender's name?"

"I did but I can't remember it now. It's hell to get old, 'specially with a crotchety old deef man as your only company." She gestured toward the main house, where I assumed Luther remained on the porch, carving and "mumbling." I could still hear him. She continued. "But you can find her. She works at the Mine Shaft Cafe out on Coppermine Road."

"That is helpful, Mrs. Quince," I said, rewarded with a gap-toothed smile for my comment. "I will need to take the photograph with me but all of Ms. Konnerth's other possessions will have to stay here for the time being. Will you lock the door here when we leave and not enter or allow anyone else to enter the bachelor house without approval from the police?"

"Yes, Constable, of course."

"Very well, then. Mr. Wedderburn and I will be leaving now. Thank you for your cooperation."

Dessie walked us back to the main house and lingered on the porch beside Luther as we started along the road in the direction where Bullfoot was conducting his canvass. We were a few hundred feet away when we heard Luther bellow, "Woman, is that girl Michele in trouble with the law?"

Dessie's ear-piercing reply minced no words. "No, man, you old goat. She been et by de shark."

Chapter Thirteen

My feet were hurting as we walked along Tower Road's macadam. The heat radiating from its blacktop coating, the unforgiving hard surface, and the pinch of my uniform boots made me long for Anegada's soft white sand paths and the non-regulation sandals I wore on patrol there.

Actually, there was not much I found comfortable about Virgin Gorda and my instincts told me it was about to become less so. If I had to guess, I would have said that Sergeant Chalwell would view the identification of Michele Konnerth as the conclusion of the investigation of her death. But Jemmy Trengrouse's terse description of what he had seen, the victim's sexual promiscuity and confusion, and her missing purse, identification, and most recent field journal told me otherwise and I knew I would end up confronting the sergeant over it. Hardly a comfortable situation, but one I had been through before.

We found Constable George leaning on a garden fence, talking to a couple of teenage boys clad head-to-foot in Chicago Bulls gear. The smiling and joking from the boys ended as we approached, even as Bullfoot turned his wide grin in our direction. It took only a moment to fill him in on our findings and he immediately attempted to call the station on the radio.

There was no answer from Sergeant Chalwell but that was not unusual in the world of out-island policing. If someone had come to the station with a matter needing attention, it was likely that Sergeant Chalwell had done what I would do on Anegada—close the station and go to attend to it. We all jumped into the RVIPF Land Rover and were at the station three minutes later. Sergeant Chalwell was nowhere to be seen, but a shriveled old woman watering her pumpkin patch across the road said the sergeant had headed north on Crabbe Hill Road toward Olde Yard Village.

"Constable, you and Mr. Wedderburn stay here and I'll go get de sergeant," Bullfoot said. "The station ought to be manned, and, if I am right, it just Benjamin Hewson, drunk an' yellin' an' strippin' naked in de middle of de road. He did it twice last month."

"Do you think you'll need help?" I asked.

"Naw. Benjamin always puts his clothes back on and goes inside his house when de sergeant tells him it's a police order," Bullfoot laughed. "But de sergeant probably don't want to walk all de way back in de heat. I'll go give him a ride." De Rasta and I exited, and Bullfoot turned the Land Rover up the road.

"Glad we don't have such raucous conduct to deal with on Anegada," Anthony said, smirking. I had once, but only once, caught him doing the same thing on the main road in The Settlement, back in the days before he had reformed. Now that he had put his penchant for ganja aside, De White Rasta was arguably Anegada's most respectable citizen.

"Well, old man, it looks as if our work here is done, if you follow Sergeant Chalwell's edict," Anthony said, entering the station. "I will pack my bag so that we may leave promptly on the good sergeant's return."

Anthony was right. If I followed the order from Chalwell to disregard Jemmy Trengrouse's report, our work on Virgin Gorda was done. Downcast, I trailed De Rasta through the door of the station. The first thing I saw when my eyes adjusted to the dim interior was Sergeant Chalwell's desk. The first thing I saw on the desk was the station's landline telephone.

"Don't start packing yet," I said, lifting the receiver from its cradle.

"I should have known," Anthony said, an amused look on his face.

I rang the direct line of Deputy Commissioner Lane and was greeted by the cool voice of Consuela Lettsome, his loyal longtime secretary. "Deputy Commissioner Lane is in a meeting with the commissioner, the governor, and the premier, Constable Creque. He probably will not be available until after lunch," she said in response to my request to speak to her boss.

After lunch would probably find me back on Anegada,

all but kicked out of Virgin Gorda by a Sergeant Chalwell eager to close the book on this tourist-off-putting shark attack. I knew there was no way Consuela would interrupt the high-level meeting to ask the DC to take a call from a lowly constable, QPM or not. That left one alternative, and not a very promising one.

"Miss Lettsome, will you please put me through to Inspector Stoutt?"

"Certainly, Constable," she said, pleased to allow DC Lane to emerge from his meeting with one less call to return.

"Scenes of Crime Unit, Inspector Stoutt," Rollie said a moment later, clearly thinking the source of the call was DC Lane. I knew because he failed to answer with the slightly annoyed exhalation that usually precedes his greeting when the call is not routed through the DC's office.

"Hello, Inspector, this is Constable Teddy Creque." Now the sigh drifted through the line, crossing the Sir Francis Drake Channel in a cable on the sea bottom.

"Hello, Constable. Any news from Virgin Gorda?" As Rollie asked the question, I had an image of his wrinkling his nose in disgust, remembering the contents of the bull shark's gut splashing against his fastidiously pressed trouser legs.

"Yes, Inspector. We have the name of our victim, Michele Konnerth, a doctor from the States, here to do medical research. We have located her residence and spoken to her landlords."

"Good. We can use her passport information to inform her next of kin."

"I'm sorry to report her purse and passport are missing. And her landlords have no emergency contact information."

"That shouldn't be a problem. You know with a little effort we can obtain the information we need to have her remains"—his voice quavered at the word—"sent home. I'll inform the DC. I'm sure you and Mr. Wedderburn are ready to get back to Anegada."

Now or never. "Inspector, I don't think we should return home yet."

The sigh. Rollie smelled trouble, and worse yet, the unwelcome possibility of extra work, in the wind.

"Why?"

I launched into Dessie Quince's description of the victim's sexual exploits and Jemmy Trengrouse's sighting on the morning of the attack, and finished with a reminder of the missing purse, passport, and field journal.

"You should report these things to Sergeant Chalwell. He knows you are assigned to Virgin Gorda for as long as he needs you on the investigation."

"Well, Inspector," I said, trying to balance the timbre of my voice somewhere between recognizing my duties under the chain of command and the desire to convey the impression that Sergeant Chalwell would simply close the case if given the opportunity, "Sergeant Chalwell doesn't think much of the child's story."

"Oh?" A hint, the most minimal hint, of rare curiosity. From Rollie Stoutt, who viewed curiosity as a severe failing in a police officer. I treated it as an opportunity wide enough to navigate a barge through.

"According to Sergeant Chalwell," I said, "the boy once reported an inappropriate touching by a prominent Virgin Gorda citizen. The sergeant did not believe the boy, but the child's mother persisted, going over his head, and charges were brought. The trial resulted in an acquittal. Now Sergeant Chalwell refuses to believe anything the boy says."

"I remember the case," Rollie said. "Three years ago. The boy was only four or five years old. Intelligent, very intelligent, but . . . odd. I did some forensic work on the child's clothing but found nothing. I was there when the kid testified, or should I say, was put on the stand. He wouldn't say a word, but his body language told everyone in the courtroom that he was terrified of the defendant. Of course, the jury couldn't convict on that, but I believe that something, something very wrong, happened to the boy at the hands of the defendant."

"I believe him now," I said. "I think we may have a murder, not a shark attack. Or maybe a murder where the murder weapon was a shark." It was bizarre to even say it aloud.

"That's pretty far-fetched, Constable. Then again, you didn't get the Queen's Police Medal for being wrong. What is it that you want?"

I hadn't thought that far and hesitated for a moment before replying, "I want to stay here on Virgin Gorda for a few days and investigate. Talk to the victim's boyfriend, talk to the boy again, just run down those leads and see where they take me."

"Better ask the deputy commissioner if you want to do that."

"He's in a meeting. With half the government. They are probably telling him how they want him to spin the news about the shark attack. He won't be out until the afternoon and I suspect I'll be sent packing from Virgin Gorda by then."

"I tell you what, Constable. You stay put, on my authority. I'll fill the DC in on our conversation as soon as he gets out of his meeting. The coroner is holding a special sitting of the coroner's inquest on the woman's death in three days. Maybe the DC will let you stay on Virgin Gorda until then. I'll tell him about Sergeant Chalwell and about my impression of the boy."

Could Rollie Stoutt be going out of his way to help? Wonders never cease. "Thank you, Inspector. I'll await word here at the station."

"You're welcome, Constable. I hope for your sake you can turn up something more than just that boy's story, or the DC won't be happy."

"No one knows better than me, Inspector," I said. The line clicked dead.

De White Rasta lounged against the wall, having heard only one side of the conversation yet reading the outcome. "I take it that we are to remain as cellmates, Teddy?"

"I'm staying here for the time being but you do not need to remain if you don't want to. We can have a boat take you back to Anegada."

"And miss the opportunity to see you flaunt the command structure of the RVIPF and 'take arms against a sea of troubles'? Not on your life. I missed most of it the last time and I'll not miss it again." He grinned.

As we settled in to await the DC's call, if we were lucky, or Sergeant Chalwell's return, if we were not, I wondered if Hamlet's soliloquy had ever been quoted within the dingy walls of the Virgin Gorda Police Station before today or if De White Rasta had just broken new ground.

Chapter Fourteen

There was not much time for contemplation of Shakespeare's words and their meaning in my professional life before Sergeant Chalwell and Constable George returned. The pair came in accompanied by a man with wide friendly eyes, a deeply tanned face, unruly hair, and a merry laugh. Both Chalwell and Bullfoot were laughing, too, as they entered the station.

"That was the most dignified and artful striptease I have seen since I caught a performance at La Vie en Rose in London in 'eighty-two," the tanned man said.

"Mr. Hewson changed today's show in the street from a rant to a striptease. He was wiggling out of his boxers by the time I arrived," Sergeant Chalwell sputtered by way of explanation. Bullfoot's silly simper spread from ear to ear.

"Have a seat in the reception area, Yuri, while I get the paperwork ready," Chalwell said to the man.

But the irrepressible fellow instead stepped over to Anthony and me, hand extended. "Yuri Gribanov, former KGB," he said warmly, in a perfect British accent that couldn't quite be placed as to its region. "I always like to lead with that, get things out in the open."

"Constable Teddy Creque, Mr. Gribanov. My associate, Mr. Anthony Wedderburn." I shook his hand, a bit bewildered. What was a former KGB agent doing in Virgin Gorda? Besides working on a killer tan?

Mr. Gribanov read the look on my face. "What's an old spy doing here? A long and twisted tale shortened, I worked for the *rodina mat*—the 'mother homeland' is the best translation—from the time I was old enough to enlist until things broke up in 'ninety-one. By then I had been stationed at the embassy in London for five years and had acquired a taste for all things British. Rather than return to the chaos in Russia, and the uncertain fate regime change always brings to those in my line of work, I traded what little I knew of value to MI6. My bargaining chips bought me UK citizenship and a house in London. It turned out that no one at the security service cared that I had left their employ. I set up a modest import-export business, did well for myself, and after a decade, decided I needed some sun. I fled the dreary London winters for the BVI like any self-respecting Brit and opened a dive shop here, Captain Tankhauler's. The KGB had done a good job training me to dive. I've been here ever since."

"Much as he enjoyed the striptease, Yuri will be the complaining party against Mr. Hewson," Sergeant Chalwell said.

"We can't have the tranquility and the moral rectitude of the neighborhood disrupted. At least not before a decent hour in the early evening," Gribanov said with a wink.

"Have a seat here, Yuri, and write what you saw on this form," Chalwell said, surrendering his chair to Mr. Gribanov. As Gribanov picked up the pen with a flourish, Sergeant Chalwell turned to me. "Bullfoot tells me you have identified the shark attack victim as a Michele Konnerth, a tenant of the old Quince couple."

"Yes, Sergeant. Though we were not able to locate her passport or other identification, I recognized her bathing suit and some jewelry she wore in a photograph that Mrs. Quince said was of her with a male friend, Robin Kingsmill."

"I know Robin well," Chalwell said. He extended his hand. "I'll take the photograph and speak with him later today to confirm the identification. Why don't you sit down and write out your report and then you and Mr. Wedderburn can be on your way home to Anegada."

I could tell we were about to clash but I had to try. "With all due respect, Sergeant—" I began, only to be interrupted by the mellow ring of the landline phone. I stopped speaking, leaving Sergeant Chalwell nothing to do but answer.

"Royal Virgin Islands Police Force Virgin Gorda Station, Sergeant Chalwell," he said, his face already folding into a frown, whether from the interruption or because he anticipated what I was about to say, I could not tell.

He listened for a moment, his expression changing. If a face could come to attention, Sergeant Chalwell's did just that. He nodded and spoke the occasional "Yes, sir" for the next four minutes but otherwise the caller dominated the conversation. A final "Yes, sir!" and he held the black receiver out to me. "Deputy Commissioner Lane wishes to speak to you."

"This is Constable Creque, Deputy Commissioner," I said with trepidation. Just because Rollie Stoutt had said he would go to bat for me did not mean he had hit a six.

"Constable, Inspector Stoutt has told me you believe our shark attack victim may have died from something other than misadventure," said the DC, to the point as usual. "He has explained the basis for your belief and it is not very convincing to me. After I informed Inspector Stoutt of this, he reminded me of the last occasion when I doubted a theory advanced by you, your insubordinate actions following my expression of doubt, and the culmination of those actions proving your theory correct. The inspector makes something of a valid point and so, against my better judgment, I am going to keep you on Virgin Gorda for a few more days."

I do not think I made a sound but the DC read my mood through the phone line nonetheless, the kind of clairvoyance that makes a good superior officer into a great one, and strikes justified trepidation into the hearts of his subordinates.

"Do not think for a moment that this gives you carte blanche to run around Virgin Gorda like you did on Anegada last year." The DC's sternest Voice of Doom boomed through the line. "You will be subject to the regular line of command, with Sergeant Chalwell as your immediate superior. However, you will be exempt from all patrol and regular duties until further notice. I am assigning you to special duty—the investigation of the circumstances of the death of Michele Konnerth. The coroner has scheduled an inquest for this Friday. Unless my thirty-five years of experience count for nothing, absent further facts—and I mean facts, Constable—the coroner will hold that Ms. Konnerth died of accident or misadventure, her specific cause of death being attack by a bull shark. If the coroner's inquest results in that determination, I will not be able to justify keeping you on Virgin Gorda any longer. So you have three days, Constable. Understood?"

"Yes, sir," I said. "And, sir?"

"Yes, Constable Creque," the DC said, drawing out the c-o-n-s-t-a-b-l-e and deepening his voice more ominously, if that was possible.

"It would be helpful to me to have Mr. Wedderburn remain here to assist."

There was a prolonged period of silence before the DC answered in a resigned tone. "All right, Constable, Mr. Wedderburn can remain there to help you. Just see that you both don't end up in Peebles Hospital like the last time." The DC hung up.

Sergeant Chalwell cut his eyes toward me but said nothing. Mr. Gribanov, who had stopped filling out his statement to take in this little drama, smiled a knowing smile and said to Chalwell, "Not to worry, Isaac, I've seen this in the old KGB. One minute you are the *corps kommissar* and the next you are on your way to the *gulag*. Bide your time in the *gulag* and the next regime will reinstate you, perhaps with elevated rank as compensation for your loyalty to the *rodina*."

Gribanov turned to me and said warmly, "So, Constable, you have the power but not the rank. This is the truest power of all. I salute you." And he actually gave me a bluff salute.

Gribanov's gibes did nothing for Sergeant Chalwell's mood. He muttered to Bullfoot, "I'm going to lunch," and was out the door just as Mrs. Scatliff arrived with our noon meal of johnnycake, stewed okra and tomatoes, and a steaming pail of Bullfoot's namesake soup. The arrival of the soup derailed any inclination Constable George had to follow his commander to an off-premises lunch. In moments he was slurping the savory soup with Anthony and me.

Ten minutes later, Anthony leaned back from his bowl, sated, and said, "As they once asked the dog with his teeth embedded in the tire of the lorry, now that you have it, what are you going to do?"

What, indeed?

Chapter Fifteen

It did not seem prudent to await Sergeant Chalwell's return from his lunch break. It also did not seem prudent to appropriate the Virgin Gorda Police Station Land Rover, so De White Rasta and I set out on foot for the Virgin Gorda Yacht Harbour and a conversation with Robin Kingsmill.

The facilities of the Yacht Harbour, like all facilities for tourism in the BVI, are in top-notch condition. While we belongers may have rusting tin roofs, walls in need of paint, and fences crying out for repair, you will be hard-pressed to find a hotel, restaurant, dive boat, or souvenir shop on even the most remote sister islands that doesn't look like it was repainted, refurbished, and redecorated yesterday. Quality tourist accommodation demands it.

The pocket-sized Yacht Harbour, most tourists' first glimpse of Virgin Gorda, is no exception. Sailboats in for the day, week, or month marshal in neat rows along its three dock arms, each boat with its own finger pier. Set foot on land and you are greeted by a velvety manicured lawn, lush bougainvillea tumbling along the fence beside the walkway, and a Caribbean-cute wood-frame building with a discreet sign directing you to where the iced Heineken awaits to slake your sailor's thirst. The manager's office is a cubbyhole buried to the left of the bar, which the barman directed us to after we asked to see Mr. Kingsmill.

The still rakishly handsome Robin Kingsmill greeted us with a scowl, depriving us of the pleasure of a gander at his lustrous dentition. He remained seated when we entered his office.

"I don't like cops in my place. Puts off the visitors, makes them think there's trouble," Kingsmill said by way of greeting. "And you"—he nodded at Anthony—"what are you, some kind of plainclothesman?"

"Just a humble civil servant, sir, along to carry the constable's bags," Anthony said, bowing deeply.

The bow drew a "phfffft" from Kingsmill, and he turned his attention back to me. "So what is this about?"

"Constable Teddy Creque, sir, and RVIPF civil assistant Anthony Wedderburn," I said, determined to make a courteous introduction in accordance with RVIPF protocol and good manners, which Robin Kingsmill sorely lacked, if you were not a paying patron of the Yacht Harbour. "We are here investigating the death of Michele Konnerth."

Most people find news of the untimely death of a lover, friend, or even acquaintance as the stuff of at least mild upset. Kingsmill's reaction couldn't have been more indifferent.

Without a whit of sadness, he said, "How sad, but what con-cern is it of mine?"

I pulled out the photo of him with Michele Konnerth and placed it on the desk before him.

"Did you have a relationship with her?"

"I did, if you can call hooking up when either of us felt like it a relationship. But if you use that definition, she had a relationship with anyone who had a zipper on their trousers. And I don't mean men only. I played along for a while until I found out what a completely crazy bitch she was, and then I broke off whatever 'relationship' we had, in a manner of speaking. I just stopped calling and she moved quickly on to the next hood or tunty, as you boys say. You see, not only did she like it both ways, man or woman, she liked it both at the same time. That amused me for a while but the drama got old. So if you want to hear about her relationships, you might want to work your way down the bar at each water-ing hole on the island."

"When did you last see her?"

"Three, maybe four, days ago. She was having trouble with her boat motor and she came in for a repair. Couldn't stand the sight of her, so I turned her over to Johnny Harley, the dockmaster, to get the work done."

I remembered Johnny Harley from yesterday, operating the winch to hoist the shark that had eaten Michele Kon-nerth and getting his ankles splashed when her torso spilled onto the dock. I would speak with him next.

"Where did she keep her boat?"

"Right here. She rented it from us on a long-term rental

when she first came down, for her work, she said. Twenty-one-foot Boston Whaler."

"Is it here now?"

Kingsmill rose from his seat and poked his head out the office door for a moment. "It's not in its slip."

"Do you know when it was there last?"

"Can't remember the last time I saw it. You'd have to ask Johnny. He might know. Are we about done? Because I have a report I'm working on for the directors and I need to get it done this afternoon."

"Just a few more questions." I'd seen the cop shows on my DirecTV dish. And the lawyer shows. They always say that, right before they get the perpetrator or the witness to crack. Hearing myself say it sent a thrill of anticipation down my spine. This was where Robin Kingsmill, unsavory Lothario, would crack.

"Do you know anyone who would want to harm Ms. Konnerth?"

Kingsmill scoffed. "You mean other than the dozens of men and women whose minds and bodies she's fucked with?"

"Someone in that category or otherwise," I said.

"No, not really. The little whore wouldn't be worth the effort."

I could see we were going nowhere. Might as well get to the point. "Where were you the night before last, Mr. Kingsmill?"

"Here, at the bar, until we closed at three in the morning and steered the drunks back to their boats. Then home to bed. By myself."

"Can anyone confirm that?"

"Johnny was here until closing, and half a dozen bar patrons. Two or three of them probably weren't too drunk to remember. Why, do you think I did something to her? Fed her to that shark? Bugger off, copper, I've got work to do." He pointed to the door.

"Thank you, Mr. Kingsmill. If we have any follow-up questions, we'll be back," I said.

Kingsmill grunted and returned his attention to the paperwork on his desk. "Bugger off," he mumbled.

Chapter Sixteen

"Mr. Kingsmill does not seem to harbor warm, fuzzy feelings toward his former lover," De White Rasta said, blinking in the noonday sun as we stepped from the shaded interior of the bar. It was only then that I noticed it was another glorious Virgin Islands afternoon, cottony clouds on the horizon, the diamond glint of sunshine spread on the cerulean waters of the Yacht Harbour, the musical ring of rigging against the spars. Police work has the unfortunate effect of making one ignore beauty, so intent is the search for the ugliness in life. I find it the most disappointing aspect of the job, apart from people shooting at you.

"He certainly does not. I wonder if it actually was him who ended the relationship. Let's see if we can find Mr. Harley and hear what he has to say about the two lovebirds."

The Yacht Harbour and its grounds are small, almost quaint, and it didn't take long to locate Johnny Harley, sweating over the exposed guts of a dismantled outboard motor on a dinghy tied to the seawall. Real fear showed on his face at the sight of my RVIPF uniform. I suspected this was not Johnny's first encounter with the police, and the earlier ones had not gone well for him.

"I ain't done nuthin," were the first words from his mouth, followed by "I ain't talkin'."

"Fine, Mr. Harley," I said. "I will talk and you listen. We just spoke to your boss, Mr. Kingsmill, about where he was night before last, and he says he was drinking at the bar here, with you. Is that right?"

"What dis about?"

"Right now this is about whether you answer my questions here or if we need to do something more formal involving handcuffs and a trip to the police station."

"Okay, okay, take it easy, mon. I jus' got salt wit Babylon couple times an' I a lilly bit 'prehensive, sight?"

"There is nothing to be apprehensive about if you tell the truth," I said.

"I tell you de truth. Mr. Kingsmill not drinkin' *wit* me at de bar, but he at de bar drinkin' an' I dere too."

"Who was he drinking with?"

Johnny thought for a moment and said, "Peoples from de boats, tourists. He all yaga yaga wit dem. I not know de peoples."

"How late did he stay?"

"I stay, he stay, mos de peoples stay till de bar close at three. Den I go home an' he go home."

"Where is home, Mr. Harley?"

"De blue house on Little Road, 'tween de ferry dock an' de gas station."

"What about Mr. Kingsmill?"

"Him place on Lee Road goin' south, jus' pass de bank. Big white house."

"So the last time you saw him that night was . . . ?"

"After de bar close, we walk out to de road, him go south an' I go north."

"When did you see him next?"

"De nex' mornin', jus' before you brought dat big shark kill de lady in."

"Did you know the lady who was killed?"

"Nah. Who was she?"

"Michele Konnerth," I said.

"Dat doctor lady? I know her." Johnny looked squeamish. "I not recognize her from de . . . parts."

"Was she Mr. Kingsmill's girlfriend?"

"Dey was aroun' together for a while but den broke up." Johnny averted his eyes.

"Was there a problem with the breakup? Did they fight?" I asked. Johnny's eyes explored the edges of the concrete seawall. "Look at me."

He brought his eyes up to mine. "No, dey not fight. Not her an' Mr. Kingsmill, anyway."

"Did somebody fight?"

"Mr. Kingsmill an' Henna, de bartender at de Mine Shaf', fought over Miss Michele." Johnny fidgeted with his hands.

"Go on," I said.

"Miss Michele, she nice enough, but she have . . . a reputation. She sleep wit a man, sleep wit a woman, she not care. She sleep wit both, all three together, I hear." Johnny stopped. "You goin' tell any o' dis to Mr. Kingsmill?"

"I'll use discretion wherever possible," I said. That seemed to satisfy Johnny, or maybe he just had to get it out.

"I think Mr. Kingsmill, Miss Michele, and Miss Henna have a ting goin' together, a three-way ting. For a while, dey was always together, de three o' dem. Dey go off to islands, together, go to Mr. Kingsmill's place. Dey all drink in de bar here, get drunk, an' den go off together. I see, dey make de eyes at one another, all three, I seen many times."

"So why did Mr. Kingsmill and Henna fight?" I asked.

"Henna end de threesome, took Miss Michele away from Mr. Kingsmill."

"How do you know that?"

"Mr. Kingsmill, he talk when he drunk."

"Did he ever talk about harming Michele?"

"No." Johnny's face closed down.

"Okay, Mr. Harley. When was the last time you saw Michele Konnerth?"

"Few days ago she come in wit motor troubles on her boat. She ask Mr. Kingsmill about fixin' it an' he told her to find me. I fixed it."

"What was the problem with the boat?"

"Bad spark. I pulled 'em, put in new, an' it worked okay. Maybe she got bad gas, fouled de plugs."

"What day was that specifically?" I asked.

"Let's see . . ." Johnny scratched his chin. "Four days now."

"Where is her boat?"

Johnny scanned the harbor. "Not here. I know when I fix de motor she took it right out. I don't think it's been back since."

"And this is a boat rented from the Yacht Harbour?" I asked.

"That right. She rent it when she first come here, said she needed it for her work. A yellow twenty-one-foot Boston Whaler. It a good little boat."

"Did she ever keep it anywhere other than here?"

"Not so's I know," Johnny said.

We left Johnny Harley with an admonition that just as he expected us to keep his comments private from his boss, we expected him to do the same. He agreed, bowing and scraping like a Savile Row tailor to a ten-suit-a-year customer.

"Nice job, Teddy," Anthony said as we stepped clear of the Yacht Harbor grounds. "I am certainly glad I never encountered the hard-bitten version of Constable Creque during my time spent on the wrong side of the law. Threatening a trip to the station in handcuffs. My, my."

"As I recall," I said, "I once told you I would put you in a holding cell and it was not that long ago."

"Ah, Constable, those days are remote in sentiment, if not in time." De Rasta's mischievous eyes sparked in recollection. "To change an incommodious subject, to where do you propose we stroll next?"

"I feel the need for a cool one, Anthony. What do you say we stop in for a drink at the Mine Shaft Cafe?"

"Capital idea, Teddy, except for the fact that you are on the wagon. As am I, come to think of it."

"Club soda all around, Anthony. I'm buying," I said.

Chapter Seventeen

It was a lengthy hoof to the Mine Shaft Cafe, or would have been if Bullfoot had not come along on patrol in the RVIPF Land Rover. He pulled alongside us as we sweated our way south on Lee Road.

"You gentlemen need a ride?" he asked, all toothy grin, air-conditioning roaring in the cab. We piled in, thankful for the respite from the afternoon swelter.

"Are you sure you want to give us a ride?" I said, now safely in the passenger seat and not about to leave. "You might get in trouble."

"Wit de sergeant? Naw, what he not know, him not hurt. Where you headed?"

"The Mine Shaft Cafe."

"Where little Henna work? She don't have anything to do with de lady's death, does she?"

"Not that we know or suspect, Constable George. But

I think she may shed some light on a relationship that does."

Bullfoot raised a brow but said nothing more about our destination or its propriety. Soon he and De Rasta were in animated conversation about the upcoming England vs. West Indies test match, which evolved into who was the best batsman of all time. Anthony, showing his old-school roots, stood by Sir Jack Hobbs. Bullfoot championed Viv Richards, the Master Blaster from Antigua. Chided by both to break the tie, I managed to remain neutral as we wound our way from sea level upward.

The Mine Shaft Cafe perched atop the most prominent of the low hills south of The Valley, with panoramic views of the open Atlantic to the east and the Sir Francis Drake Channel and Tortola to the west. Had not the knob of Gorda Peak intervened, I am sure I could have seen Anegada from there. Bullfoot dropped De Rasta and me in the dusty parking lot, waving merrily as he headed back to The Valley.

The Mine Shaft Cafe was as much a mine shaft as a lobster is a bicycle. It had windows all around, to take advantage of the trade winds and the stunning view. Light filled the place, from the outdoor seating of the ubiquitous white plastic chairs, the bane of every island restaurant, to the semicircular stone and wood bar, where petite Henna Beckles presided.

"Good afternoon, officers," she said, mistaking De Rasta for a white plainclothesman. Did he look more like a policeman out of uniform than I did in one? "What can I get you to drink while you tell me to what I owe the pleasure of your company?"

"Two club sodas, please, ma'am," I said.

"Oh, official business," she said, mock serious. With bird-like quickness, she sent a cascade of ice cubes into two tall glasses and, popping open two stubby bottles of Schweppes, placed glasses and bottles before us on the varnished bar top. "Must be something special, 'cause you boys ain't local. I didn't even know the RVIPF had any white officers, other than the commissioner." Henna's black eyes flitted from me to Anthony and back, sizing us up.

"Mr. Wedderburn is an administrative assistant, not an officer. I am Constable Teddy Creque. We are here about Michele Konnerth." I watched for her reaction.

"Michele's not in trouble, is she?" Henna's attitude shifted from imperturbable bartender cool to genuine concern. "She's okay, isn't she?"

"I'm very sorry to inform you that she is dead." It was the first time in my twenty-plus years with the RVIPF that I had delivered that unfortunate news to someone who cared. The expression on Henna Beckles's face made it one of the most difficult things I had done as a police officer. Maybe it became easier if you did it more often. I suspected it did not.

Henna crumpled onto a stool behind the bar. Tears gathered in wet wells along her lower eyelids. "How?" she managed to ask.

"You may have heard about the incident with a shark at The Baths yesterday morning," I began. I knew that was enough. Every bartender in Virgin Gorda had to have heard, and contributed to, a dozen versions of what had transpired at The Baths during the extended cocktail hour the previous evening.

The tears overflowed and ran in rivulets down her cheeks. "That's . . . horrible, so horrible," she said, barely audible.

"We are looking into the events preceding the shark attack, Ms. Beckles," I said. "We have reason to think Ms. Konnerth's death may not have been an accident or misadventure."

Henna Beckles reached somewhere, very deep, in the next moment; lifted her chin; and asked, "You mean you think that someone may have done something to Michele? That someone got the shark to attack her on purpose?"

"We do not know if that is what happened. We are looking into the circumstances of her death. When was the last time you saw her?"

"Three days ago, in the afternoon." She paused. "Oh God, I feel so awful. We fought, the last time I saw her . . . oh, God."

"What did you fight about?"

"We were . . . she was my girlfriend, Constable. I know those kinds of relationships are frowned on here. They were in Barbados, where I grew up, too. But One Love, mon." She continued. "You asked what we fought about; it was what we always fought about. She wanted others. Usually one other, that one so bad for her, that man."

"Who?"

"Kingsmill, Robin Kingsmill. He didn't really care for her; he used her. For a while, I wanted her so badly, I let him use me. But then I persuaded her that he was bad for her and she left him. Instead of the three of us, it was the two of us together. She was never happier. He was mad—insane-mad and angry-mad at the same time. He loved his little threesome. I heard he used to brag about it with some of the boys." She stopped. The rush of words seemed to have exhausted her.

I showed her the photo that had been found in Michele Konnerth's footlocker. "Do you recognize this?"

"I should. I took it. That's Michele and Kingsmill. Out near Fallen Jerusalem Island, where she did most of her fieldwork. It was when we three were together. The thought of it disgusts me now."

"You said Mr. Kingsmill was angry-mad?" I said, my inflection making it a question.

"When she came to be with me, a week ago, he was enraged, barged in here one morning before we opened. He broke a few glasses and threatened to carve up my face. He had a knife, a mean-looking job with a square black blade, and he waved it around until I pulled a kitchen knife from under the bar and let him know it wouldn't be a one-sided fight. He backed off, the coward, screaming that we, Michele and me, hadn't heard the last of it."

"Did you report this to the police?"

"No. I was opening by myself, so it would have been my word against his, and the police on Virgin Gorda take a different attitude toward the manager of the Yacht Harbour than they do to a non-belonger bartender. Besides, I can handle myself." Her face crumpled. "I just didn't realize he would take it out on Michele."

"Did Michele ever say he had confronted her after she broke off the relationship with him?"

"No. And she would have told me. It was me he was mad at, because I had taken her away from him. Oh, he liked it with both of us, called us his 'little salt and pepper,' but that was just because he thought he was more of a man if he had two of us at one time, the perv. No, I was only icing on the cake. It was Michele who he wanted."

There was enough evidence here to arrest Robin Kingsmill for common assault, though no battery had occurred. From there I could proceed with a search of his office and residence, to see if any further evidence would surface. It would be a fishing expedition, but then I remembered my last fishing trip. Poor Michele Konnerth deserved better, regardless of what people might have thought of her sexual proclivities. Still, there was the obvious question to ask. "Where were you two nights ago, Ms. Beckles?"

"Here. There was a group of Texans from the US who had rented a villa in Princess Quarters. It was their last night on the island and they came in for a final blowout. Good tippers but they stayed until they couldn't stand. I'm glad I didn't have a seat beside them on the next day's flight to San Juan. Rhodni, the busboy over there"—she pointed— "and I closed about four thirty a.m."

Anthony and I bid Henna Beckles good-bye, leaving her with her grief and a half-dozen tourists shaking empty glasses in her direction. We confirmed her alibi with Rhodni the busboy on our way out.

It was time to make an arrest. As we set out, I realized I would be making the first arrest in all my years with the RVIPF.

Chapter Eighteen

Traveling on foot meant that we could not simply speed over to the Yacht Harbour and arrest Robin Kingsmill. We could not speed anywhere. Anthony and I walked down the gravel road Bullfoot had taken to bring us to the Mine Shaft Cafe. The walk was not unpleasant, as we were at high elevation and the trade winds were steady from off the Atlantic. Moving downhill, we kept a brisk pace, hoping Bullfoot would come round on patrol and pick us up before we had to cover the entire distance to the station.

Two miles later and no Bullfoot in sight, going on foot seemed like less of a good idea. Even De White Rasta, seasoned from years living in the elements and walking everywhere he needed to travel, fell into glum silence. Only a ride from my cousin Ellis Creque, an Anegadian transplanted to Virgin Gorda by his marriage to a Gorda girl, saved De Rasta and me from having to slog the whole way.

Sergeant Chalwell was seated, feet up, at the station desk when we entered. I reported our conversations with Kingsmill, Johnny Harley, and Henna Beckles and he listened without a word until I was done.

"Sounds like a clear case of common assault," Chalwell finally said. "Hard to prove without corroboration but enough for an arrest. I'll radio Bullfoot and you go with him and bring Kingsmill in. Maybe we'll get a confession."

I had expected a hard time from the sergeant but he was businesslike and civil while we waited for Bullfoot and the Land Rover, chatting about diving for conch and lobster. It turned out that the sergeant spent most of his spare time in the water, either after food or trying to locate what he called "marine artifacts." When you live in a place where treasure is more than a myth, everyone, sooner or later, is a treasure hunter.

A jovial Bullfoot took me straight to the dock of the Yacht Harbour. Anthony, as a civilian, was prohibited from going along on the arrest. We stopped at the *Lily B* first, so I could retrieve my Webley from the dry locker where it had been stored the last two days. RVIPF procedure required at least one armed officer to be present when arresting a suspect who had used a weapon in the crime charged. I opened the gun's break-top cylinder and ejected the shells, discarding the three discharged when I had fired to kill the bull shark. I replaced the discarded shells with three new .38/200 rounds and shoved the heavy gun in my pocket. The smell of gunpowder from the spent shells summoned a memory of the time the old revolver had been used to shoot me. I put it quickly out of mind as Bullfoot backed the Land Rover to the Yacht Harbour bar and the manager's office behind it.

I could hear Robin Kingsmill talking as we approached, and another voice, Johnny Harley's, responding.

We stepped in the door. Kingsmill was seated at his desk. Johnny Harley stood just inside the door, and retreated to a far wall as we entered.

"I thought I told you to bugger off, policeman," Kingsmill said.

"Robin Kingsmill, we are here to arrest you for common assault on Ms. Henna Beckles," I said. "Please stand and step out from behind the desk."

Instead, Kingsmill lunged for a desk drawer and pulled out a large knife with an odd blunted blade. He slashed wildly at Bullfoot, who was approaching him with a set of handcuffs. Bullfoot dodged, successfully, losing his balance and falling down backward in the process. Kingsmill turned his attention to me next, as I fumbled the Webley free from my uniform pants pocket.

Kingsmill raised the knife and moved toward me. I pointed the gun, not really aiming, and pulled the trigger. Concussive sound filled the small room, causing everyone to freeze in place. Kingsmill ran a hand over his chest and stomach, seeming to take stock, while looking at me with fear written in his every feature. He opened his other hand and the knife fell to the floor. I am sure it made a noise as it struck the tiles, but I detected none, my ears still ringing from the shot.

I had missed, missed from four feet away, to Robin Kingsmill's good fortune.

The spell of the Webley's discharge broken, Bullfoot scrambled to his feet and snapped the handcuffs on Kingsmill. I held the gun toward Kingsmill while this occurred, not so much keeping it on him as in his general direction, worried that I might accidentally shoot him. Johnny Harley demonstrated his prior experience with situations such as this; he lay splayed on the office floor, facedown, fingers interlaced behind his head. Bullfoot put his second pair of cuffs on Johnny, I suppose for good measure.

"I'll go quietly, no problems," Robin Kingsmill said, his face pale. Maybe he was thinking about what might have happened if I had been a better shot.

Constable George and I marched Hawley and Kingsmill through the bar and locked them in the rear seat of the Land Rover. Drawn by the sound of gunfire, a curious knot of boaters and barflies gathered on the lawn outside the bar to watch. Shows how behind the times we are in the BVI; here, we run toward gunshots to see what the excitement is about.

While Bullfoot kept an eye on the prisoners, I returned to the office to secure the knife. I borrowed a fairly clean plastic bag from the frightened barman on the way in, pulled it over my hand, and thus shielded, picked up the knife. It was a wicked-looking instrument, meant to terrify as well as wound. On close inspection, there was a rust-colored smear the size of a bananaquit's eye on the ricasso, near the blade guard. Thinking it might be dried blood, I rolled the inside-out bag over my hand to envelop the knife. Remembering the singular unusual wound on Michele Konnerth's shark-ravaged torso, I wondered if this was the knife that had made it.

Chapter Nineteen

Constable George seemed unfazed by the difficulty of the arrest, calmly and slowly navigating the Land Rover to the police station. During that same short trip, the adrenaline wore off, and I was visibly shaking by the time we escorted the prisoners inside. Anthony and I packed our belongings and moved them from the two cells, and placed Johnny Hawley and Robin Kingsmill in separate cells.

Bullfoot provided Sergeant Chalwell with a verbal report and the sergeant suggested that we arrange to transport both prisoners to Road Town. I put in a call to Inspector Stoutt for that purpose and to discuss whether we could even hold Johnny Hawley.

The long delay in answering and the unusually emphatic sigh before he spoke told me Rollie Stoutt was not having a particularly wonderful day. "Scenes of Crime, Inspector Stoutt," he said at last.

I explained, as briefly and succinctly as I could, the circumstances giving rise to Messrs. Kingsmill and Hawley being invited guests of Her Majesty at the Virgin Gorda Police Station, and my suggestion that they be transported to Road Town. I also asked whether he thought Johnny Hawley could be held. At the mention of the name, Rollie gave me a "Hold on." After five minutes of *Mantovani's Greatest Hits for Elevators and Customer Service Numbers* drifting through the line, Rollie was back. "I thought the name was familiar. There's a *capias* outstanding for him, for failure to pay a fine following a conviction for forgery. He passed a forged check at a liquor store. The good news is that you can hold him.

"The bad news," Rollie continued, "is that you can't send him or Mr. Kingsmill here. The holding cells in West End, Long Swamp, Cane Garden Bay, and here at the main station are full. Jeezum, it's a god-awful mess. A bunch off one of the cruise ships got into a brawl with one of the local vendors, haggling over prices. Things got out of hand, and we had to call the entire watch down to the cruise ship docks. We got the fight broken up and then everyone got more belligerent and wanted to press charges against everyone else. Transport vans just kept unloading tourists in handcuffs. I never saw so many beer guts, comfortable walking shoes, and I'm-with-stupid T-shirts in my life. We'll be lucky if it doesn't turn into some kind of international incident. But that's not your problem. Your problem right now is that there's just no room at the inn, and there probably won't be for the next day or two until charges are withdrawn or we work them all through magistrate's court. You'll need to hold your prisoners on Virgin Gorda for now."

"I understand," I said, thankful that cruise ships cannot navigate the reefs and shallow waters surrounding Anegada, and that I would never have to deal with such nonsense. "But I do need assistance from Scenes of Crime."

"What kind of assistance?" Rollie, wary of anything that might involve work or responsibility, asked.

"I have a knife, taken from Mr. Kingsmill, which has a spot of what I think may be blood on it."

"Blood? I thought you arrested him for common assault, not battery."

"I did," I said. "I think the blood may belong to the victim of the shark attack at The Baths."

Rollie became all business. "Do you have it bagged?"

"Yes. And I have it in my possession, so there is no chain-of-custody issue."

"Who touched it? Did you touch it?" Inspector Stoutt was doubtless having unhappy memories of my difficulties handling evidence in our last case together. And I can't say I blame him.

"Robin Kingsmill had it in his possession and used it in an attempt to escape when we arrested him. I only handled it through the plastic evidence bag."

"Jeezum, he pulled a knife on you? What did you do?"

"I shot at him."

"You discharged your service revolver during an arrest? There's going to be a stack of paperwork as high as Mount Sage to fill out on that. You weren't carrying that old Webley, were you? The one with 'HM West Indies Police Force 1932' stamped on the receiver?"

"That's it." I have a soft spot in my heart for that gun. Once upon a time, it didn't kill me.

"You're lucky it didn't blow up in your face," Rollie said.

"Did you wound him?"

"I missed. But he gave up after I fired. And I think I hit his office credenza dead center."

"Good thing you missed. Hitting him would have been even more paperwork. Anyway, bring the knife over, and I can conduct a Luminol test as a preliminary to see if there is blood on the knife. If the test shows positive, I'll have to send it to the lab in San Juan to see if there is a DNA match with the victim. I can do the Luminol ASAP but the DNA will take several days for the results to come back. I'm glad you found this now, so I can have a DNA sample taken from the victim before her body is released. By the way, we should have the autopsy report tomorrow or the day after. I can fax it to the Virgin Gorda station when it comes in."

"That would be great. I will have Anthony Wedderburn transport the knife over to you immediately," I said, raising a brow to Anthony. He nodded affirmatively.

"Just remember to have him receipt for the evidence when you put it in his possession."

"I will. And thanks, Inspector, for all your help on this case," I said, and I meant it. Without Rollie's taking my suspicions up to DC Lane, Robin Kingsmill just might have gotten away with murder. Not that the case was airtight yet, but I felt like I had the right man. Now it was a matter of making the case stick.

"My pleasure, Constable. I'll call as soon as I do the Luminol test on your knife. Good-bye." Rollie sounded almost cheerful, like he was actually beginning to take to police work.

"So I'm off to Road Town. Are you certain you trust me with the *Lily B*?" Anthony said as soon as I placed the receiver in its cradle.

"Of course. You've operated her more than a few times and you can't get lost going to Road Harbour. Tie up at the RVIPF Marine Base where the *St. Ursula* is docked. One of the boys there can give you a ride to headquarters, or you can walk. And, Anthony, now that we have made an arrest, there is no need for you to stay, especially since we have lost our accommodations to Hawley and Kingsmill. When you finish up in Road Town, go back to Anegada. I'll give you a call when I need a ride back. And I'm sure the RVIPF can provide a place for me to lay down my head for the next night or two until I tie this up in a neat ribbon." Such confidence.

"You can bunk at my place," Bullfoot interjected. "It not much but de fish fresh and de rum good."

"Thank you, Constable George," I said.

"All right, old man, I'll take my leave. Say, give me a paper bag to cover the knife. If I walk to headquarters, I don't want to cause a panic when I come in the door. The boys with the check-banded hats in Road Town are not as well acquainted with me as you gents on Anegada and Virgin Gorda."

Bullfoot found a paper bag, the evidence bag and knife were placed inside, and he and Anthony left for the *Lily B.*

Sergeant Chalwell and I remained with the prisoners. Chalwell said, "That was an impressive bit of work you did. I see now why they awarded you the QPM."

"Thanks." I did not want to tell him that the reasons I had received the Queen's Police Medal were because I was stubborn, because I was lucky, and because I didn't die when I should have. I changed the subject. "I think we need to spend some time speaking to the prisoners."

Robin Kingsmill piped up from his cell. "You'll have no talk from me. Not till I speak with my barrister."

"I not saying nuthin," Johnny Hawley chimed in, riding his neighbor's tough-guy coattails.

"Well, Sergeant, there are other things to attend to, so perhaps I'll let our guests cool off a bit and see to other matters."

"Suit yourself, Constable. I'll keep an eye on these two," Sergeant Chalwell said.

One minute later I was out in the lambent Virgin Gorda afternoon, walking the macadam of Crabbe Hill Road again. I had a possible murder weapon, a suspect in custody, and a witness to what I was sure was a crime. But confirmation and details make a case, so I turned my steps toward the bungalow with the wind-chime-filled yard, and the reluctant boy, his lovely mother, and their sassy macaw inside.

Chapter Twenty

Lust, desire, libido, craving, infatuation, passion, yearning, even love—we have these words and a hundred others like them for the need of a man for a woman or a woman for a man, a need both base and exalted, the subject of art, poetry, midnight assignations, and juvenile fantasy. From the time our bodies awaken to the need until we are put in the grave, hardly a day, or maybe even an hour, goes by that our thoughts do not stray in that direction, truth be told. I must admit, after my recent bad experience with lust, desire, love—well, let's just say "it"—after my recent experience with "it," I thought I had succeeded in putting "it" out of my mind. The fact that "it" had gotten me shot provided a strong impetus toward this particular amnesia. The rum I so diligently applied during my physical recovery certainly helped. And the healing of the gunshot wound and the relinquishing of the rum hadn't hindered my ability to keep "it" out of my mind. Until now.

The lengthy walk in the slanting sun along the road to Jeanne Trengrouse's house gave me plenty of time for impure thoughts, and I proceeded to use the time for just that. Azure eyes, tawny skin, and long slim legs seemed to dance before me, just out of reach and spurring my progress nicely. By the time I stood at her front door, listening to the wind chimes bong and tinkle, I was in a state of desire I had not experienced since my ill-fated liaison with Cat Wells.

It didn't hurt that Jeanne Trengrouse answered the door wearing, well, wearing not much at all. The shortest of cut-off shorts and a tangerine blouse, tied to expose her midriff and missing a button at a strategic point above the knot. She had been washing dinner dishes in the early evening warmth and her face and arms were aglow with little beads of perspiration. A tendril of damp hair clung to the edge of her forehead. She smelled faintly of dish soap, not like any dish soap I had ever used, but clean, fresh, and light. She was drying her hands with a dish towel, an expression of "Who can this be?" on her face, when she opened the door. That expression's transformation to a welcoming smile only added fuel to the fire I had been stoking with my imagination on the long trek up Church Hill.

From his perch in the corner, Sir Winston Churchill squawked, "Babylon back, he back. Hide it! Hide it!"

Jeanne Trengrouse laughed. "Constable Creque, what a pleasant surprise. Come in. I see your colleague Mr. Wedderburn is not accompanying you this evening."

"That's right. He has gone to Tortola on business." Since I had actually sent him to Tortola, saying this gave me a twinge of conscience. Had I sent De Rasta away so I could be alone with Jeanne Trengrouse? No, this was strictly official. "I am sorry to intrude so late in the day but there are developments in my investigation which make it necessary to speak with your son again."

"Of course, Constable. He is in his room, as usual," she said, leading the way. My eyes strayed to the swaying back of her cutoff shorts. Come on, Teddy, keep your mind on the job. Be professional.

Jemmy was on the floor of his room with his Legos, about a third of the way to completion of his current project, a precise version of the Taj Mahal, albeit in the multicolored pattern he followed for all his constructions. He did not look up when we entered, continuing to lay blocks rapidly.

"Jemmy, you remember Constable Creque, don't you?" Jeanne Trengrouse said. The boy gave not a flicker of response. "He is here to speak with you again."

"Hello, Jemmy. Do you remember when we talked about the lady and the two men you saw in the boat at The Baths?" The blocks progressed at a steady pace, the boy never lifting his eyes. Had Shah Jahan employed the child to erect the original Mahal, the twenty-two-year time for its construction would have been halved.

"Jemmy, I need to know the color of the boat. Do you remember the color of the boat the lady was thrown from?"

The boy's only response was to shift the focus of his work from the dome of the tomb to the crenellated exterior wall.

Jeanne Trengrouse interjected, "Constable Creque needs your help, Jemmy. Please answer his question."

"What color, Jemmy? That is all I need to know."

No response.

"I'm sorry, Constable. Jemmy has not spoken at all today, and usually if he goes into the afternoon without speaking he doesn't talk at all that day."

"Please, Jemmy," I said. "The lady who was pushed into the water was killed. We need your help. She needs your help."

The child said nothing but his hands quickened, the blocks snapping down to form the wall faster and faster, blue, red, black, yellow, and white, repeating constantly, the wall rising as if it were a live, growing entity.

"Jemmy, please." My voice rose, a mix of frustration and urgency.

The small hands stopped, poised above the partial wall for three long beats, and then began again. But now the blocks they placed were different, not in a repeating pattern, or in multiple colors. Instead, the blocks alternated blue and yellow.

I guess I had my answer. The boat Michele Konnerth had been thrown from was blue and yellow.

"Blue and yellow. Thank you, Jemmy," I said.

The child did not acknowledge my thanks but the next blocks were laid in the now-familiar multicolored pattern beginning with blue and ending with white. After two more rows, Jemmy abruptly stopped and, without looking to me or his mother, climbed into bed, crossed his arms on his chest as he had done the last time I had been present at his bedtime, and closed his eyes.

Jeanne Trengrouse and I retreated to the living room area.

"I think I have the information I need, Ms. Trengrouse. Thank you—" I began, and then she was in my arms, her lips on mine, her pliant body pressed full against me, all soft warmth and clean scent. I was taken aback for a moment, but only a moment, and then her tender embrace became more carnal, her tongue flicking and probing, hands caressing, clothing falling away, until we were both on the floor, naked, she atop me, her face buried in my shoulder, our bodies working together in the rhythm as old as life itself. She suddenly shuddered, biting hard on my shoulder to suppress her cry. After an instant of stillness, she rolled to her left, surrendering the initiative, and I took it up, the cleansing euphoria carrying away the last year of my life, the hurt, the shame, the pain that had traveled with me during that time, gone. I was alive again.

Half an hour found us in a spent embrace, delicious exhaustion now substituted for passion. We remained that way as darkness descended, our bodies entangled in quiet communion, our bliss too complete to allow the intrusion of speech, or movement, or even thought. The moon rose, its silvery light advancing across the floor as it ascended, until it found Jeanne's blue eyes and they found mine. Our eyes held each other, our bodies held each other, for one long last minute, and then we parted, giving ourselves over to the practicalities of picking up clothing, dressing, and putting on the lights.

I thought she might be embarrassed then, or displeased with herself for giving in to the "it"—lust, love, desire—but she smiled, and poured us two glasses of water, and we drank, standing side by side, thighs and shoulders touching, smiling and saying nothing. Then she broke away to where Sir Winston Churchill, silent voyeur to our passion, stood on his perch, and covered his cage for the night.

That was the last thing she needed to do before she took me to her bed.

Chapter Twenty-one

The faintest light of dawn had just begun to show when I heard the door to Jeanne Trengrouse's house creak open and then close.

"It's Jemmy on one of his morning walks," she whispered, curled against my chest.

"I'd better go now, so I won't be here when he returns," I said, sitting up.

She reached to pull me back against her. "Stay. Stay for breakfast. Stay longer."

I opened my mouth to speak but she had the good sense to squelch the reply with a languid morning kiss. Good thing, because I wasn't sure what I would have said. Part of me, the caveman part, said, *Run, run fast.* Part of me, the widower who had known a once-happy marriage, yearned to stay, not for breakfast, not for the day, but forever. I sensed Jeanne Trengrouse had a place in her heart and home for me, and the temptation to accept that place was overpowering. I was almost ready to do that when the kiss ended and she immediately spoke.

"I'm sorry, Teddy. I shouldn't have said that. Not the breakfast invitation, the 'stay longer' part. All that does is put awkward pressure on you and you do not deserve that." She gave a leering grin. "Not after your fine performance last night. Good Lord, you must be starved. I know I am."

I started to speak, started to say that the invitation to stay longer was not only not off-putting but very, very welcome. Instead, she touched a finger to my lips.

"Not a word, Teddy, not a word. It's too early in the morning for me to get shot down and too early in the morning for you to be accepting invitations that extend beyond breakfast." With that she was up, wrapping herself in a short silk robe decorated with Chinese characters, and bounding, laughing the laugh of the carefree, out the door toward the kitchen quarter of the cottage.

I lay back as the morning sunlight flooded the room, listening to the first notes of the wind chimes, and thought about how good this all was. How good it was to have the affection of a decent woman. How good it was not to sneak around. How good it was to be on the cusp of a love that was not a duty or an obligation.

The mellow perfume of black coffee snapped me out of my reverie. By the time I reached the kitchen, the floral scent of fresh-cut mango, the richness of baking johnnycake, and the buttery bouquet of sautéed snapper joined with the coffee's aroma to ignite in me a raging appetite. Even the sight of Jeanne Trengrouse's sleek tawny legs below the hem of her robe proved only momentarily diverting. I enveloped her in my arms, and was given a quick kiss and an invitation to be seated. I followed that instruction with alacrity and was rewarded with a mug of coffee; a plate of mango, buttered johnnycake, and fish; and Jeanne's smiling face seated across from me, each of us holding the other's left hand while we scarfed down food and coffee with our right.

We had not gotten beyond smiles and terms of endearment when the front door popped open, Sir Winston announced, "Jemmy's home!" and the young man entered. I expected an uneasy moment at the least, and prepared myself for something worse, but Jemmy took my presence in stride. In fact, he did not seem to recognize my presence, determinedly helping himself to fruit and johnnycake. Jeanne simply said, "Constable Creque will be joining us for breakfast today, Jemmy," and suddenly it all seemed normal—as normal as being with an unspeaking eight-year-old who doesn't acknowledge your presence can seem. Jeanne did not release my hand and I did not release hers, and soon there were more smiles, and small talk, and a feeling of home. I thought of Tamia and Kevin, and wondered how they would take all this, until I reminded myself that they had spent the last year with a wounded, sometimes drunken father and had more than proven their resilience. I thought perhaps they might enjoy having a mother again, a crazy thought, premature and probably unfounded. But then I looked across the table at Jeanne and read her beautiful face as thinking the same.

The breakfast drifted through a half hour of relaxed beatitude. Jemmy, steadily dispatching a wedge of johnny-cake, did not speak to either of us but it didn't feel rude; it was just him. When he was done, he left the table and went to his room.

"Don't let Jemmy's silence bother you, Teddy," Jeanne said. "He never speaks at breakfast. Ever. It's just part of his routine. Most days I clean up the dishes, do some small chores, and then go to his room, where I find out if we are going to have a lot of conversation that day. And 'a lot' usually means a few sentences responding to what I ask or, on the best days, a question or two from him."

"Are you sure it was a good thing for him to see me here?" I asked.

"I thought about that," Jeanne said. "I woke up just before Jemmy went out this morning and thought, What will Jemmy think if he sees Teddy here this morning? You know, he's never awakened to a man in the house. He's never had breakfast with a man at the table. Jemmy's father was a wonderful man. I loved him with all my heart. We found out he had cancer just three days after I learned I was pregnant with Jemmy. He died a month before Jemmy was born."

"I'm so sorry," I said.

"Thank you. It was the hardest thing I've ever been through. Sometimes I think I might have died, too, if it hadn't been for Jemmy. He is my blessing."

"A child can keep you going, through the darkest of days," I said.

"And Jemmy did, he kept me going, he and I in our own

little world here," Jeanne said. "Our own little world. That's what I realized this morning. I've kept the two of us in our own little world, kept Jemmy from the big world out there. To protect him, I thought. But our little world isn't real. In the real world, there are men. And laughter, chaos, fear, tragedy, happiness. Life means not being sheltered from any of it. In life, sometimes there *is* a man at the breakfast table. I decided Jemmy needed to understand that, and process it in his own way. And I thought that if there was going to be a man at the breakfast table, it was good that the man was kind, respectful, and gentle. Not to mention, well, manly." Jeanne smiled. "So that's why, partly why, you weren't chased out the door this morning. Jemmy's hard to read, but I think he handled it well. I think that he accepted it as something that's normal, as much as he sees anything as normal."

"I'm glad you didn't chase me out the door, for the reason you said and for my own selfish reasons," I said.

"I'm sorry. I shouldn't have said 'chased out the door,'" Jeanne said. "It's just that I'm not used to this. I don't do this, Teddy. I don't have men staying overnight. My love life is rather . . . tame."

"Tame?"

"'Nonexistent' might be a better word."

"Tame is not a bad thing," I said. "And I must admit there have been times when nonexistent would not have been a bad thing in my life."

"You were married. For a long time." There was a question somewhere in Jeanne's statement.

"I was married. I thought I was in love for a long time. Then things between us became . . . routine. I know now that I wasn't giving her what she needed but I didn't understand it then. And I cheated on her with another woman, a woman who was using me while I used her. It was ugly, so ugly, and it was mostly my fault. And you know it ended badly."

"Yes," Jeanne said. "I read the stories in the papers. It must have been horrible."

"It was," I said. "But no more horrible than you losing the man you loved. The things that happened to each of us were horrible in their own way."

Jeanne looked at me evenly. "Last night wasn't horrible."

I laughed. "Talk about faint praise. No, last night wasn't horrible, it was wonderful. And life hasn't felt this wonderful in the morning for a long, long time."

"You too, eh?" She took my hand in hers. "Teddy Creque, I feel wonderful, and happy, and excited, and content, and a little bit frightened that I am feeling all those things so quickly."

"One thing the last few years of my life have taught me is that we feel what we feel, and there is no too quickly, nor too slowly, nor too strongly, as long as there is honesty in the feelings."

"It's so easy to talk with you, Teddy," she said. "All right, I've been honest with you and with myself, even down to the frightened part. Where do we go from here?"

"I guess we don't do anything that feels uncomfortable. Is that too simple?"

"Not for me."

"We let each other know if it gets uncomfortable."

"Deal," Jeanne said. "Pinkie swear."

"What?"

"Whenever Jemmy and I agree on something important, we pinkie swear."

"Well, this is important." We hooked small fingers, and sealed the swear with a kiss.

I stood. "I'm sorry, Jeanne. I have to go to work."

Jeanne Trengrouse rose and walked me to the front door for a lingering kiss and a long embrace.

"You can come back tonight," she said.

"I will." And I knew I would be back, not just on this night but on every night I remained on Virgin Gorda. At that second, I selfishly wished that the investigation of Michele Konnerth's death was not so far advanced so I might draw a few more days, and nights, on the island. I knew it was not to be. Robin Kingsmill had caused Michele Konnerth's death. He was in custody. My witness, young Jeremiah James Trengrouse, would place the victim in a boat with two men, one white and one black. Kingsmill had a motive and a possible willing accomplice in Johnny Harley. If it was Michele Konnerth's blood that stained Kingsmill's knife, the case was probably over. On the last murder I had investigated, nothing fit. Now, when I would not have minded if things took more time, the evidence and the case were falling neatly into place. Just my luck. I bid Jeanne Trengrouse good-bye and turned my steps toward the police station.

The world of Virgin Gorda was brighter than it had been the day before. The sun was sunnier, the air was lighter, the breeze more refreshing, the flowers in the yards more resplendent with color. A Gordian hand or two even waved in friendly greeting as I picked my way along Crabbe Hill Road.

"I was about to declare another search," Constable Tybee George greeted me, good-naturedly, as I came in the station door. A knowing look pasted on his broad face told me he was cognizant of where I had spent the night, no doubt thanks to his network of cousins and uncles. Nothing is really secret on an island; I had learned that lesson the hard way.

"I found a place to stay." I tried to be ambiguous. "I probably won't need to bunk with you tonight either, Constable, but thanks for your earlier offer."

"Found better accommodations, huh?" Bullfoot smirked. "Okay by me, but you're always welcome in de Bullfoot 'ouse."

"Anything new here?" I hoped to shift from our oblique discussion of my love life.

"Sure is. Virgin Islands Search and Rescue has a report of a boat washed ashore on de beach at Fallen Jerusalem Island. No one aboard and it fits de description of de Yacht Harbour boat rented to Michele Konnerth. Sergeant Chalwell and Mr. Gribanov went out about five minutes ago to pull it off de beach and tow it in, if it's seaworthy."

"What's Gribanov got to do with it?" It seemed unusual to involve a civilian.

"He's a VISAR volunteer. De sergeant call on him pretty often if we need his boat—a twenty-five-foot Parker. It a real workhorse an' it looks sharp, too. It got a sea-green custom gel coat."

"When do you think they'll be back?"

"De sergeant say dey would radio when dey begin de tow-in. Once dey start it shouldn't be more den a couple hours for dem to get back to de Yacht Harbour."

There was nothing to do but wait for them to bring the boat in. I glanced over Bullfoot's shoulder into the two cells. Johnny Harley sat sullen on his cot. Robin Kingsmill was stretched out on his, an arm thrown back over his eyes. I could not tell if he was sleeping. "Anything new from our guests?"

Before Bullfoot could answer, Johnny piped up. "I ain't talkin' to no one."

Bullfoot rolled his eyes. "All last night, 'I ain't talkin' to no one, I ain't talkin' to no one.' Why's he have to say it so often if he ain't talking?"

"What about Mr. Kingsmill?" I asked.

"When my barrister finishes with you, you'll wish you had been a better shot yesterday, copper," Robin Kingsmill said, never lifting his arm from his eyes.

I was about to remark that both prisoners seemed happy with their lodgings when the phone rang. Bullfoot answered, listened for a moment, and thrust the receiver in my direction.

"It's Inspector Stoutt," the voice on the other end said when I answered. "I have a couple of items for you on your investigation. First, on the knife you sent over, the Luminol test shows the spot you found might be blood. The test is only presumptive, so I have to send it to the lab in San Juan for confirmation and DNA testing if confirmed. I'm sending a swab sample of DNA from Ms. Konnerth for testing at the same time. We should know in a week or so if that's her blood on the knife."

"That's great news, Inspector," I said. "You said a couple of items?"

"Yes, the other is the coroner's report. He shows the cause of death as being massive trauma and exsanguination. He was able to locate a few shark's teeth actually remaining in the body, so he attributes the trauma and exsanguination to shark attack. No surprise there. But here's the interesting part. He also located an antemortem incised wound at the neck of the victim, about three centimeters in length, with enough depth to create a half-centimeter laceration in the anterior wall of the common carotid artery. The edges of the wound were not as jagged as the other wounds made by the shark's teeth; the coroner calls the wound 'consistent with a cutting or slashing motion by an edged weapon.' "

"And it would have bled . . ." I began.

"A lot," Rollie finished. "I'm no shark expert but I would think a wound of that nature would put enough blood in the water to prove very attractive to a shark or sharks."

"And with the currents in the area of The Baths, it would not be long before sharks would be drawn to the source of the blood from up to a mile away," I said.

"The coroner's report says that the incised wound alone might not have been fatal if direct pressure was applied and prompt treatment obtained. It does not establish the wound as a direct cause of death. The coroner is labeling the cause as 'undetermined,' rather than 'accident' or 'misadventure.'"

I glanced back at the two cells. The two prisoners, unable to hear both ends of the conversation, remained unmoving. What a horrible death for Michele Konnerth, injured and bleeding, cast into the dark waters to wait for the first, inevitable bump as the shark tested, and then the flesh-ripping violent end. At least one, and maybe both, of the men in the cells had perpetrated this outrage. I was certain of it.

"If we tie up the forensic loose ends," Rollie went on, "it looks as though we should have enough to convict."

"Yes." I visualized the night waters, imagined the rasping nudge of the shark's snout against an arm, and the shudder of horror sure to follow.

"Oh, another thing, Constable. Late yesterday I spoke to the victim's parents, Tom and Judy Konnerth, about arranging for release and transportation of the remains. Nice people, very polite, but as you can imagine they are just devastated. They had a request. They asked to speak directly with the officer investigating their daughter's death. I figured they just wanted direct news on your efforts but they said they had information they urgently needed to discuss with you. I gave them your name and the station number there on Virgin Gorda. I wouldn't be surprised if you heard from them today."

"I'll speak to them," I said, wondering what could be so urgent. But grief, I knew from recent experience, does strange things to people. Whatever information they considered urgent was indeed urgent to them, even if useless to the RVIPF. They would receive my condolences on their loss, my sympathetic ear, and my respect for their grief, regardless of the manner in which they dealt with it.

Chapter Twenty-two

    I only had time to thank Rollie Stoutt, hang up, and get a second cup of coffee before the call from the parents of Michele Konnerth came in. There was static on the call, a poor connection that also echoed every thirty seconds or so, the words careening back and forth on the line somewhere between Virgin Gorda and its origination point, the flat farming country just south of Blue Earth, Minnesota.

    Both Mr. and Mrs. Konnerth were on the line, on two extensions in their home, I imagine. Judy Konnerth let her husband do most of the speaking, sniffling softly in the background throughout the call. Tom Konnerth took the lead in the conversation, his voice a bland twang that exuded calm, whether speaking of the effects of a dry spring on this year's crop or the gruesome death of his only daughter in a manner he could never have imagined when he held her as a newborn thirty years before.

"My condolences on the loss of your daughter," I said after the couple introduced themselves. "We are doing everything within our power to determine the circumstances of her death. I will be glad to keep you posted on any developments in the case if you wish."

"Of course, Constable, we would appreciate your doing that. Michele was the joy of our lives. We were getting on in age, had given up on having children, when she came along. Our little miracle, we called her. She was a bright child, always happy, and became a wonderful adult, a daughter any parent would be proud of."

Judy Konnerth sniffled agreement in the background. I resolved to spare the Konnerths from the details of their daughter's checkered private life, if possible.

"People here on Virgin Gorda who knew your daughter spoke highly of her," I said, a white almost-lie to spare the feelings of these grieving parents.

"That is comforting to know, Constable," Tom Konnerth said, and then fell silent, clearly uneasy speaking about his emotions, especially to a police officer in a foreign country.

The silence was so long I thought he was preparing to end the call. "If you will be so kind as to give me the best number to contact you—" I began.

"Getting information on the status of your investigation is not the only reason we contacted you, Constable," Tom Konnerth interrupted. "We also have some information which might assist you."

"What information is that, Mr. Konnerth?"

"Michele wrote to us regularly, once a week, Constable.

We really aren't telephone people," he said, his awkwardness confirming his statement. "She kept us up on her life, and her work, that way, and she was steady doing it. I mean, you could always count on that one letter a week. In the last few letters, there was something different, something not quite right about the way she wrote, like something was bothering her but she didn't want to say it. It was difficult for me to put my finger on it, but then the last one . . ."

Judy Konnerth, sounding suddenly strong, jumped in. "In the last one Michele said she suspected that someone on Virgin Gorda was smuggling, Constable Creque, smuggling right from the area where she was doing her research at a place called Fallen Jerusalem. Do you know the place?"

"Yes, ma'am. Fallen Jerusalem Island, less than a mile off the south coast of Virgin Gorda. It's uninhabited and mostly rocks." I decided not to mention Michele's rental boat being found there, since it had yet to be confirmed. "What did she say was being smuggled?" I naturally thought drugs, the bane of the Caribbean and the ruination of many an island Eden.

"She didn't say what it was and she never said who was doing it," Tom Konnerth said. "She said she suspected but she couldn't be certain. She said she was documenting it, along with her fieldwork, and she planned to go to the authorities when she had enough evidence. That was two weeks ago, and now she's gone." He stopped for a stoic breath. "She was careful, Constable. Thorough and careful, particularly when she was working in the field. She was meticulous about safety when she scuba dived. We talked about it many times, though I am not a diver. She always dove in bright daylight hours, never at dawn or dusk when there might be danger of sharks, and never in turbid water. She wrote on more than one occasion that she had exited the water when a large shark was seen in the area. In short, Constable, Judy and I don't believe Michele would have been diving or swimming where she was at the time of day she was found. We think someone or something brought her there, and placed her in harm's way, possibly against her will. Michele was not an alarmist and neither are her mother and I. Michele stumbled onto something and it resulted in her being killed. And it wasn't a shark that killed her, Constable, any more than a gun or a knife kills. Someone, not something, killed our little girl."

There was a silence then, on both ends of the line, followed by weeping, not just from Judy Konnerth but from Tom as well. What do you say to a parent in this situation? Is there anything that is truly comforting, anything that can assure them of your concern, anything that is not cliché and trite? What can be said to convince grieving parents that an unknown stranger at the end of a phone line in another country will truly investigate the death of their only child, exhausting all avenues and leaving no stone unturned? Could I tell them of the grief I had known and how it must pale when compared with the loss they had suffered?

No. I said the only words I could. "I will do my very best for your daughter, Mr. and Mrs. Konnerth. If Michele was killed, her killer will be brought to justice."

Those words were dust in my mouth. I did not even

mention having Robin Kingsmill in custody. Nothing pointed to any involvement by him in smuggling and I now had to question whether this was more than a murder by a jealous lover.

"Thank you, Constable. Your assurance that you will do that is very comforting. Please keep us informed." Tom Konnerth gave me the phone number in a near-whisper and, somewhere south of Blue Earth, Minnesota, two telephone receivers were replaced in their cradles, leaving the aging couple with only each other to share their sorrow.

And leaving me to wonder if I had the wrong man in the dingy cell a few feet from where I stood.

Chapter Twenty-three

I decided to make the ten-minute walk to the Yacht Harbour to be there if and when Sergeant Chalwell and Yuri Gribanov towed the abandoned boat in from Fallen Jerusalem. Maybe the boat would contain evidence that would further incriminate Robin Kingsmill, close the case, and put Tom and Judy Konnerth's concerns to rest. Hope springs eternal in the investigator's breast.

The Yacht Harbour was the picture of calm when I arrived, with just a handful of chartered bareboats at the docks, season tail-enders who had yet to rouse themselves to begin the trip to the next sun-drenched island, reluctant to continue on a journey that had as its inevitable end a spring-muddy suburb in Pennsylvania or a confining condo in Chicago. A steady twelve-knot wind from the southeast nudged cottony clouds across the water, creating a changing tableau of shadow and sun. A lone boy dangled his legs over the dock's edge, hand-lining foot-long grunts chummed in with scraps of their cousins left from a fishing guide's clean-up earlier in the day.

"How is the fishing?" I posed the eternal question between anglers.

"Dey bitin'," the boy said, displaying a gap-toothed smile. He lifted the lid on a stained Styrofoam box at his side to display a dozen grunts going stiff inside, a small brick of ice in the middle losing its battle against the morning warmth. "Madda makin' grunts and fungi tonight."

"You see a policeman and a white man leave in a boat?" I asked.

"You mean Sergeant Chalwell an' de Russian dude owns de dive shop?"

No flies on this kid. "Yes."

"Dey lef' mebbe an hour ago in de dive boat."

"Thanks."

"Dey gone ta look for more parts o' dat lady got sharked?"

"Something like that. You know her?"

"Yeah. She give me dulce de coco every day." The cloyingly sweet coconut candy had been a favorite of mine when I was his age. Dada used to bring it for me from a Puerto Rican trader in St. Thomas.

"You know where she went when she took her boat out?"

"She say out to Fallen Jerusalem, to look at de fish. Don't know why. She can see fish right here."

"Did she ever have anyone go with her?"

"Not's I see."

"Did you ever see her on anyone else's boat?"

"Sometimes she go with Mista Kingsmill an' Miss Henna, de lady from Mine Shaft, but lately no one."

"What's your name, son?"

"Garfield. What's yours?" The boy lifted his chin, his expression saying he could give as good as he got.

"Teddy."

"I pleased to meet you, Constiple Teddy."

"Same here. Good luck with the fishing."

It would be a while before Chalwell and Gribanov returned. I decided to wait in the shade of the bar. I took a seat at one end, and after giving me a bottle of sparkling water, the barkeeper retreated to the sink in the opposite corner, washing glasses with his back to me. Shooting at his boss yesterday probably did not do much to endear me to him, or maybe he had the polite but aloof attitude that marked most Gordians.

An hour of waiting allowed me the luxury of introspective thought. I took advantage of the time to first consider why I maintained the niggling doubt that Robin Kingsmill was Michele Konnerth's murderer.

He deserved to be guilty. He was an arrogant libertine. He threatened women. He had assaulted me and another police officer. He was uncooperative. The latter was hardly as serious as his other actions and characteristics, but it grated on me, not fingers-on-a-chalkboard, but rather a vague irritation that the man might be able to help himself and refused to do so. True, he had a motive. Evidence, in the form of a threat and a weapon, was present. And if the blood on Kingsmill's knife proved to belong to Michele Konnerth, the case would be almost open and shut. But somehow I doubted the blood would be hers, and the conversation with her parents only added to the doubt. Perhaps her missing field notes, or other items from her boat, would put my doubts to rest. Perhaps the blood on Kingsmill's knife would be hers. I decided the best course would be to allow the evidence to come to me, in the form of the boat being towed in at that moment, and the testing results on the knife certain to arrive in the next few days.

With that conclusion, my thoughts turned to Jeanne Trengrouse. Had what occurred between us last night meant anything? Was it the beginning of something good and right and true, or had I succumbed, as I had all too recently before, to desire, or lust, or whatever it was called when a man and a woman are just that and nothing more? Jeanne Trengrouse was beautiful. She was strong. She was different. All those attributes were attractive. All those attributes had attracted me to the wrong women in the past. Was I headed in the wrong direction again?

The boy Garfield ambled off the dock, fishing line wound around a Coke can in one hand, Styrofoam cooler full of grunts in the other. He whistled, an aimless out-of-tune happy whistle, and smiled to himself. Maybe he was thinking of home, his mother, and eating the fish he had caught. The simple pleasures of a simple place, the pleasures, the very existence, I had enjoyed for the first four decades of my life on Anegada. Pleasures lost to me now, the past year a string of complications and rude awakenings I had barely survived. Were the pleasures of a simple life, the life my

Anegada home provided, now lost to me forever, or could they be regained? Was it Jeanne Trengrouse who would return me to them, her laughing blue eyes feeding the hunger in my soul for that simple happy life? Or was I moving into further complication, difficulties with only hard solutions?

I watched with envy as Garfield turned from the dock and walked toward Lee Road and the way home. When I turned back toward the water, two boats had appeared to the southwest. As they neared, the figures of Mr. Gribanov and Sergeant Chalwell could be seen in the green lead boat, as well as a towline running to the yellow trailing craft. The second vessel appeared empty.

In actuality, it was carrying a cargo of complications.

Chapter Twenty-four

The two boats entered the Virgin Gorda Yacht Harbour at no-wake speed, and, once inside the break wall, Gribanov reversed course while Sergeant Chalwell dropped the tow-line. Gribanov then expertly nudged the empty yellow boat into the pilings of the dock with his own, at half the speed at which a toddler walks.

I donned blue nitrile crime scene gloves and secured the empty craft with bow and stern lines. Sergeant Chalwell and Mr. Gribanov were wearing identical gloves in the dive boat, their hands no doubt sweating profusely inside, as were mine. With the towed boat secured, Gribanov rounded the dock with his boat and tied up on the opposite side. Soon the three of us stood looking down into the derelict Whaler.

"I thought sure this would be wrecked by the time we got to it," Sergeant Chalwell said. "Fallen Jerusalem is nothing but a pile of boulders. But somehow this ended up bow-in on the only twenty feet of sand beach on the island. We were able to float her off after waiting for a half hour for the tide to rise. Not a scrape on her."

"Did you need to get in the boat to tie the towline?" I asked. I was, you see, now a stickler for crime scene integrity after botching it on my first case on Anegada. No sinner is more righteous than the reformed sinner.

"No," Gribanov said. "We looped a line around the outboard cowling to ease her off the beach and then tied the towline to the bow cleat while standing in the water. We wore gloves while doing it." He seemed pleased that they were able to accomplish this without entry into the Whaler.

"It's been out in the open but we should still get Scenes of Crime over here for a look," Sergeant Chalwell said. "I'll go back to the station and make the call. You keep an eye on it, Constable."

I settled down on the dock, dangling my feet over the edge. As the sergeant walked away, Gribanov plopped down beside me.

"Are we sure this is the boat Ms. Konnerth was using?" I asked.

"The Yacht Harbour only has two rental boats. The other one has been tied up in its slip"—Gribanov gestured to another yellow Boston Whaler three dock fingers over—"for the last week. This one went missing the same day Ms. Konnerth was attacked by the shark."

"How do you know that?"

"Remember, Constable, I am former KGB. We make it our business to know." Gribanov smiled slyly. "No, I jest.

Johnny the dockmaster mentioned it was missing on the same morning you brought the shark in. I had a group dive that day but they canceled after seeing what you brought to the dock." He chuckled. "I somehow could not persuade them that any threat had been removed or, at the least, had its hunger satisfied."

We fell silent then, not the uneasy silence of some awkward social situations; ours seemed the relaxed silence between old friends with no need to speak, our understanding of each other complete and comfortable. I could see how Yuri Gribanov had been a good spy. His amiable nature encouraged ease, trust, and disclosure.

After a few minutes, Gribanov said, "I understand from Sergeant Chalwell that you are a hero." He raised a hand when I began to protest. "Enjoy it, Constable, while you can. Me, I was a Hero of the Soviet Union, the highest honor from a country which now does not exist. I guess that means I am no longer a hero. Now, I am just a man." He said this in a matter-of-fact manner, not sad or wistful. "But you, you are still a hero, here in the BVI. A hero in paradise. An enviable position, my friend. Savor it." He rose and left.

I thought about what he had said as I waited. I never felt like a hero, though many had treated me as one, a treatment I believed unwarranted. After all, I had failed. Failed at marriage. Failed to find a murderer until the murderer found me. Failed to stop a thief. Almost failed to keep on living. And yet I was called a hero precisely because of all those failures. Maybe Yuri Gribanov was right. Deserved or not, it could all be gone in the wink of an eye, as it was for him. Maybe I should just go on, stop thinking about what had happened, and enjoy life. My thoughts turned to the surprising and happy occurrences of last night with Jeanne Trengrouse, and I savored and enjoyed them, basking there on the dock in the noon sun, until I heard a familiar sound, the engine of the *Lily B*, up on plane and approaching the Yacht Harbour mouth.

"The *St. Ursula* is tied up on drug interdiction patrol with the US Coast Guard, so Inspector Stoutt called me to get a ride from Road Town," De White Rasta said, explaining his and the *Lily B*'s presence. Rollie Stoutt, just bounced and rocked in the shallow-draft boat through a dozen miles of swell in the Sir Francis Drake Channel, appeared prepared to kneel and kiss the dock when he disembarked. Instead, he knelt and none-too-delicately deposited his breakfast roti into the pristine waters of the Yacht Harbour. Wiping his mouth with the back of his hand, he rose and asked, "Where's the boat?" Rollie seemed to be getting more resilient with age.

Five minutes later, he was dusting the boat's wheel and console for prints. After another twenty minutes, he shook his head.

"None," he said.

"No fingerprints other than the victim's?" De Rasta asked.

"No. None. No fingerprints, palm prints, nose prints, any prints. At all. The wheel, throttle, and console are wiped clean. I'll bet when I dust the gunwales, rails, and coaming there won't be any prints there either." Another hour spent spreading gray dusting powder on likely spots on the cockpit's white gel-coat interior and white powder on all its chrome and glass surfaces confirmed Rollie's speculation— not a print, even a partial, anywhere.

"Whoever wiped this down was thorough," Rollie said, shaking his head. Then he brightened and dropped to his hands and knees, his eyes mere inches above the foredeck anchor locker.

"Yes!" he said, as if he were about to lay down four aces in a hand of Texas Hold'em. He scrambled to his feet in a stunning imitation of a balletic hippo, grabbed his print powder, and was back at the anchor locker before you could say Jack Robinson. Seconds later the outer edge of a shoe-sole print emerged as he spread powder. It was a ripple pattern, and only about a quarter of the sole surface showed when Rollie stopped feathering with his brush.

Then Rollie was up again, pirouetting to his equipment case, shooting with his Nikon from multiple angles before he stopped for a breather. If I had encountered him on the street at that point, I would have been convinced that he had just run at least five miles. After a minute, he puffed out, "Man's shoe, probably UK size eight or US size eight and a half." The look of triumph on his face could not have been greater if he had just run and *won* a five-mile race.

"Are you sure, Rollie? About the size, I mean?" I remembered that both Robin Kingsmill and Johnny Harley shared one characteristic—they both had unusually large feet. Johnny must have worn at least a UK size thirteen and Kingsmill only a half size or, at most, a size smaller. The print did not belong to either of them.

Rollie produced a measuring tape from his pants pocket, placed it beside the gray-black print, and said, "No larger than UK eight."

"Any chance it could be a woman's shoe?" I said, trying to remember the footwear I had seen in Michele Konnerth's personal effects—flip-flops, dive booties, and strappy sandals suitable for dancing and resting on the brass rail of a bar. No ripple-soled closed shoes wide enough for a man's foot.

Rollie thought briefly. "Not like any woman's shoe I have seen, although I guess a woman could wear a man-type shoe." This was as close to an unequivocal answer as you would ever get from Inspector Stoutt. "My guess is that whoever wiped down this boat left the print as they were exiting."

After more photographs, Rollie declared his efforts to find prints on the boat's exterior surfaces complete. I stepped down off the dock into the Whaler to join him for the opening of the console locker, hoping Michele Konnerth's missing field notebook was inside.

"Chart of Virgin Gorda and surrounding waters, tube of sunscreen, box of three condoms, a granola bar, a pint of Cruzan rum—half-empty," Rollie listed as he pulled items from the toaster-sized locker. He went to work with his print powder and, after several minutes, declared, "Damn, whoever wiped things down even did the stuff in the locker."

I pored over the chart, hoping to find markings or something else that would make the afternoon going over the Whaler more worthwhile. No such luck. By the time the sun was low in the sky, we were done. Whatever the sturdy little boat had seen would not be further disclosed to us.

Anthony and Inspector Stoutt departed for Road Town, the *Lily B* cutting a graceful arc southwest after clearing the Yacht Harbour break wall. I turned my steps inland. It had been a long afternoon in the broiling sun. An icy drink would be in order. I decided to get it at the Mine Shaft Cafe.

Chapter Twenty-five

If Michele Konnerth had spoken to anyone about her suspicions of smuggling taking place at Fallen Jerusalem, it likely would have been her lover Henna Beckles. Maybe Henna even knew an acquaintance of the murdered woman who wore ripple-soled shoes. It was worth a try, mainly because I had nowhere else to turn.

I arrived at the Mine Shaft minutes before sunset. The Gordians of The Valley seemed to be becoming more friendly; one of them gave me a ride most of the way. The atmosphere at the café was raucous, fueled by rum and the tourists who had been consuming it since the beginning of the early island happy hour. I took a seat at the end of the bar and caught Henna Beckles's eye after a couple minutes.

"Hello, Constable, what'll it be?" Henna looked worn, with the haunted eyes of a refugee, even though she tried to put on a good face for the festive crowd of drinkers.

"Sparkling water with lime, Ms. Beckles. How are you holding up?"

"As well as can be expected," she answered. She placed a squat old-fashioned glass on the bar, tumbled in ice cubes, squeezed in the juice from a yellow island lime, and poured in the soda water.

I sipped and watched as she hustled up and down the bar, sad for her. My guess was that Tom and Judy Konnerth knew nothing about Henna Beckles and their daughter's engaging in a lifestyle that would not dare be mentioned in Blue Earth, Minnesota. So Henna Beckles would not attend the funeral, would not receive condolences, and would not have the ceremony and the closure of being the chief mourner for the woman she loved.

The setting sun hit the horizon and the bar emptied, the crowd of inebriated sailors and holidaymakers pushing onto the outside deck to await the Green Flash. The next day or the next week they would all return to Detroit or Des Moines and claim they had seen that famous feature of the Caribbean sunset. In fact, there was no Green Flash. They were all drunk, pure and simple drunk, and would see what they wanted to see, just as later they would see that stunningly attractive member of the opposite sex staring at them across the room, only to awaken to homely reality tomorrow morning. The temporary quiet at the bar brought Henna Beckles back to me.

"I heard you locked up Robin, but not before you almost shot the snake," she said.

"Word travels fast on this island," I said. Actually, word

travels fast on all islands. On Anegada, if you stub your toe, the whole island knows before you say "ouch."

"It's the barfly telegraph. Billy, the barman at the Yacht Harbour, told everyone at the bar that day, and the barflies made the rounds and finally ended up here and told me. Too bad you're not a better shot." Her eyes shone with tears. "He killed her, you know."

"I spoke to her parents," I said. "They seem like good people."

"Michele talked about them a lot. She loved them. Always told me about growing up out on the farm, her mother baking pies, her daddy playing catch with her 'cause he always wanted a son. She never told them about us. She said they were simple folks, they wouldn't understand. I guess it doesn't matter now."

"They told me Michele wrote to them about smuggling, that she suspected some type of smuggling was going on but she wasn't sure. Did she ever mention anything to you about that?"

"No. Smuggling here on Virgin Gorda?"

"Actually, no. Out at Fallen Jerusalem where she was doing her fieldwork."

Henna frowned. "The place is certainly deserted, which I suppose would be good for smuggling. But smuggling what?"

"Drugs, perhaps?" I said. We have learned in the Caribbean that people who smuggle drugs are the kind of people who kill.

"It's possible, I suppose, but I don't see Michele involved in something like that. I mean, she would not even associate with someone who just smoked a little ganja once in a while, let alone someone who was smuggling it or something harder. She enjoyed her Pusser's or Mount Gay, and I kept a bottle of Don Armando *añejo* under the bar just for her. Booze, yeah, she loved the stuff. But drugs—never."

Henna continued. "And I have to tell you, as much a bastard as Robin Kingsmill is, he doesn't seem like a smuggler to me. He wants two things—women and booze—and he has a perfect setup to get both in his job at the Yacht Harbour. He loves that job—it's not hard work running the place—and hanging at the bar every evening playing host and trolling for tipsy women looking for a little action on holiday. He wouldn't risk that by running drugs."

"What about anyone else Michele associated with?"

"No one comes to mind." Henna's brow knitted. "You don't think she stumbled onto something out at Fallen Jerusalem? But she would have mentioned it to me, I'm sure. And I don't know what there would be to stumble on. Have you been out there?"

"No." Fallen Jerusalem is only fifteen miles from Anegada but even less of a draw to Anegadians than Virgin Gorda.

"It's pretty empty. The national park there is all bird sanctuary. No good beaches, in fact only one place to even get ashore, at North Lee Bay. The rest is rocks and boulders, like The Baths. The snorkeling and diving are great because of the rocks. When Michele, Robin, and I were . . . together"— a veil of disgust clouded Henna's face—"Michele took us out there to snorkel a couple of times. There was no one around and next thing I know Robin had us all naked on the beach. The perv."

Drunk-loud voices approaching from the outdoor deck signaled the end of just another sunset in paradise. Thirty seconds later Henna Beckles presided over a bar again crowded with tourists waving empty glasses and calling for refills.

I lingered for a short time, pondering what could be done to confirm or deny the information on smuggling provided by Michele Konnerth's family. I decided the issue could wait until the next day. I turned my course toward the bungalow on Church Hill. The mental image of Jeanne Trengrouse wearing nothing but a smile called to me. I tossed five dollars on the bar, gave a wave to Henna Beckles, and headed for the door.

Something made me turn just as I was about to exit into the rapidly falling night. From the doorway I saw Henna step out from behind the bar, a tray in her hand as she moved to pick up glasses and empty bottles from a vacant table. She wore the standard Caribbean bartender's uniform of shorts and T-shirt.

And on her feet was a pair of bright blue ripple-soled clogs.

Chapter Twenty-six

     With no good excuse to return to the bar and not wanting to tip Henna Beckles off if she did have some involvement in her lover's death, I turned and stepped from the gaudy lights of the Mine Shaft into the lush black of the tropical evening.

     The moon had not yet risen, and as I put distance between myself and the burnished glow of the café, a wash of stars—the Milky Way—gradually appeared above. I should have been in the best of moods, strolling through the evening warmth to visit a beautiful woman with whom I might have been falling in love. But the sight of the ripple-soled shoes on Henna Beckles had pushed all beauty and anticipation from my thoughts, replacing them with worry and concern. Were the clogs just coincidence or was Henna the person who had wiped down her lover's Boston Whaler, and, if so, why? Was Beckles a smuggler who had killed rather than be exposed? Had she played me by pointing to Robin

Kingsmill as a suspect, only to have her ploy succeed beyond her wildest expectations when he resisted arrest? Did I have the wrong person in custody? Did I have two suspects, two motives, and two items of physical evidence, the shoe print and the knife with blood residue, each pointing to a different suspect? Was Henna Beckles such a superb actor that she could produce sham tears and false grief at the drop of a hat? Where were those high-quality cop instincts I told myself I had acquired in the process of nearly losing my life on my last case?

Those questions, and even harsher thoughts about my abilities as a policeman, swirled around in my head until the funk was broken by the sound of wind chimes and the smell of baking bread carried on the night breeze. I stepped onto the porch of the Trengrouse cottage, to be greeted by Sir Winston Churchill's cry "It Babylon!" and, an instant later, a warm embrace and a passionate kiss from the bird's mistress. After a moment—a very long moment—Jeanne Trengrouse tilted her head back far enough for me to gaze into her lovely blue eyes. That look told both of us what was in store later in the evening.

But civilized people don't greet each other at the door, peel off their clothes, and make wanton love just inside the threshold. At least not two nights in a row. At least not with an eight-year-old child playing quietly in the adjoining room. At least that was how I read it when Jeanne dialed down the heat and cut her eyes in that direction.

"Ohhhhh, Teddyyyyyy!" Sir Winston suddenly blurted out in an almost perfect imitation of a phrase Jeanne had uttered several times during the previous evening. Fortunately, there was just enough cackle in the bird's version to distinguish it from the real thing. Jeanne laughed, a happy musical laugh, the laugh of a woman in love, which soon had me doing the same.

"I missed you, Teddy Creque," she murmured. "All day long, just Jemmy, Sir Winston, and me, waiting for you to return."

She led me into the house. It was a very domestic scene inside, a pot of pumpkin soup bubbling on the stove, the table set with candles, hibiscus flowers floating in a glass bowl, and three place settings. Three? Of course, Jemmy would join us. I asked after him.

"Come see this," Jeanne said, drawing me toward Jemmy's room. As we stepped in the doorway, Jemmy was busy creating an amazing replica of an odd triangular building pictured in his architecture book. I glanced at the text and discovered it was the Flatiron Building. But unlike the other occasions where his concentration on building was undiverted by my presence, he stopped, his hands motionless, and then he pointed to a corner of the room where stood another of his creations. Unlike his other building projects, this one had not been dismantled as soon as it was completed. And it was not a building but a boat, a remarkably accurate model of a boat with a spacious covered wheelhouse or cabin fore and an open workspace aft. It was the type of boat that is the workhorse of island life, used for net fishing, hauling goods, and diving. The upper portion was all white Lego blocks, while the hull was an alternating yellow block/blue block combination, a color scheme I had never seen on any boat in the BVI.

"Boat," the boy said. It was the first time he had ever spoken in my presence without prompting.

"Is that the boat you saw with the two men and the lady?" I asked.

"Bad-men boat." Jimmy barely whispered the words and immediately turned his attention back to the Flatiron Building. I'd seen enough of his body language to know that our little conference was over, as far as Jemmy was concerned.

Jeanne and I backed from the room. "Do you have any idea what the significance of the color pattern on the boat hull is?" I asked.

"No." She frowned. "He's never done anything like that before. Whenever he does a large project that requires most of his blocks, he always uses all the colors he has, repeating the same blue, red, black, yellow, and white pattern. If he does something small, he uses all one color. He has never done just two colors before."

"I get the feeling Jemmy doesn't do much without a reason, even if it's only known to him," I said. "I wish he could give me enough information to identify the boat."

Truth be told, though, he had started me on the road to identifying the boat. If I ignored the odd hull color sequence and concentrated on the shape of the boat, I could probably narrow the field of likely candidates down to a dozen boats on Virgin Gorda. One thing was certain—the shape of Jemmy's handiwork in no way matched the low, broad-beamed profile of the Whaler Michele Konnerth had rented from the Yacht Harbour. Whoever had cut her till she bled and tossed her to the sharks had done it from another boat, if you believed Jemmy.

The pleasurable pressure of silken lips, followed immediately by an exploring tongue, stirred me from my musings. "A penny for your thoughts, Constable." Jeanne tilted her head back and smiled.

"Hardly a bargain, even at that price," I said. I pulled her close against me. She smelled of lavender. My hands explored, found soft flesh. Hers did the same, but the flesh she found grew firm. Buttons and belt buckles were hurriedly undone, heartbeats quickened.

"Ohhhhh, Teddyyyyy," a breathy voice said, coming not from the gorgeous woman in my arms but from across the room. Sir Winston repeated the phase, if anything with more passion, and Jeanne and I fell against each other, laughing uproariously. The mood was broken, not in a bad way, as an easy domestic cheerfulness came over both of us.

Jeanne steered me to the wicker chair in the sitting area, gently pushed me down, pecked my cheek, and returned to the kitchen corner of the room. There she hummed a nameless tune, clattered pots and pans, and cast the occasional fetching glance my way, until she materialized dinner on the wooden table set for three. Sir Winston bonged six times in a perfect rendition of Big Ben just as the food was placed on the table, and a look at my watch showed him correct to the second. On cue, Jemmy appeared and seated himself, and began eating with focused silence while his mother and I made small talk, ate her excellent cooking, and stared into each other's eyes.

The tropic night was far advanced by the end of our leisurely dinner. With his usual "Time for bed," Jemmy adjourned the meal and headed for his room. Jeanne left to tuck him in, returning shortly with an impish expression on her face. She made straight for where Sir Winston stood on his elaborate perch and drew a black cloth down over the bird's cage. In seconds she was back to me.

"Ohhhhh, Teddyyyyyyy!" This time it wasn't the bird.

Chapter Twenty-seven

When I emerged from the house on Church Hill the next morning, the sun shone brighter, the air smelled sweeter, and the chittering of a friendly bananaquit blended mellifluously with the clack and bong of the wind chimes. On the sleepy roads of Virgin Gorda, the few people I passed nodded and smiled. My steps were quick and light on the downhill walk to the police station. I was experiencing something I had not experienced for a long while, perhaps for years.

I was happy.

It was such an alien emotion that I did not recognize it at first. Don't get me wrong; there were moments, hours, and even days of happiness regularly in my life, even during the dark difficulty of the last year. This was different. It felt sustained and substantial. I knew it would continue beyond a minute, a day, a week. It was good and right. It was the kind of happiness men search years to obtain. And some fail, as I had failed, until now. It was, I decided, the finest morning of my life.

My mood was such that it seemed impossible for anything to bring me down. I decided to put it to the test by making a call to someone who had in the past never failed to sour my mood, ruin my day, and generally shake my faith in the goodness of humanity. I decided to call Agent Rosenblum of the US Drug Enforcement Administration.

The last time I had spoken to Agent Rosenblum was the day he had come to Anegada to, as he put it, "clean up your crappy little island." The last words he had spoken to me accused me of being a dirty cop. No, Agent Rosenblum was not on my short list of warm close personal friends. He wasn't even on my list of friendly enemies. He *was* on my list of sarcastic assholes. But in the end, when the RVIPF had needed help and I lay on a deserted beach with a bullet in my chest, Agent Rosenblum and his squad of mongrels from the Joint Interagency Task Force South had pitched in and made the crucial arrest. We'd had no contact on that day, or since, so I didn't know what kind of reception awaited my call. What I did know was that if anyone in the world of law enforcement knew whether there was smuggling going on near Virgin Gorda, it would be Agent Rosenblum.

Constable Tybee George was all smiles when I entered the station. Sergeant Chalwell was out on patrol, he said. Bullfoot had the good taste not to comment on my previous night's sleeping arrangements and amiably produced the JITFS number when I asked for it, with a cup of steaming coffee on the side.

"Joint Interagency Task Force South," said the radio-perfect female voice at the end of the line in Key West.

"Hello, this is Constable Teddy Creque of the Royal Virgin Islands Police Force calling for Agent Rosenblum." As I said this, I realized I didn't even know Agent Rosenblum's first name. It was probably Agent, I thought, hoping the receptionist would not ask.

"We have no one here by that name, sir," came the crisp reply.

I was briefly taken aback until I remembered the nature of Agent Rosenblum's work with JITFS. "If there was someone there by that name, I would leave a message for him to call me at," I said, and I gave the Virgin Gorda Police Station number.

"I would take the message, sir, if there was someone here by that name, but there is not. Can I connect you with someone else?" said the voice with measured politeness.

"No. Thank you. Good day," I said.

"Good-bye, sir," the polite female voice said as the line clicked off.

I had just enough time for two sips of coffee before the telephone rang.

"RVIPF Virgin Gorda, Constable Creque speaking."

"Constable Teddy Creque, a name I haven't heard since me and my boys saved your skinny ass on that backwater shithole . . . what was its name?" Agent Rosenblum said. So much for meaningless pleasantries.

"Anegada."

"Yeah, Anegada. I heard they gave you a big shiny medal for taking one for the team."

"Yes."

"You all right, all recovered?"

"Yes." I was becoming wary now.

"Back on the job?"

"For a few months now."

"Hey, that's great. Honest cops are hard to come by in the Caribbean. Wouldn't want you out of the game," said the man who had accused me of dishonesty the last time we spoke. I suspected this was as close to an apology as I could expect from Agent Rosenblum. "So what can I do for you, Constable?"

"I'm on Virgin Gorda, investigating the murder of a young woman named Michele Konnerth."

"The name doesn't ring a bell, if that's what you're asking. Drug involvement?"

"I don't think so. She was a medical doctor doing research fieldwork in the area and there is some indication that she may have stumbled onto a smuggling operation and was killed as a result."

"What kind of smuggling?" Rosenblum asked.

"I don't know. I was hoping you might be able to tell me if you knew of any smuggling that might be taking place near here."

"Drugs I can tell you about. The taco jockey cartels aren't moving anything through the Eastern Caribbean these days. The coffee beaners—"

"Coffee beaners?"

"Yeah, Constable, the coffee beaners, you know, the Colombians." I could sense Agent Rosenbaum rolling his cold melanoid eyes at my ignorance of the latest slurs for

everyone living south of New York City. "The coffee beaners have moved west of you, too. We've been putting some
real heat on the EC for the last couple of years and the cartels have basically decided to get out of the kitchen."

"So as far as you know, there is no smuggling going on
in the area?"

"As for drugs, none. The JITFS has the EC shut down.
The coke and ganja routes have all moved west. But I hear
there's other smuggling going on, stuff JITFS isn't tasked to
interdict. Antiquities from South and Central America; bio-
logicals like reptiles, fish, and plants; and, of course, people."

"Do you know who I might talk to about those items,
Agent Rosenblum?"

"Yeah, I can give you the name of the ICE public affairs
officer, who will tell you the same shit you could learn by
yourself in a half hour surfing the web. Is that what you
want?"

Agent Rosenblum's tone of voice told me that was not
what I wanted. When I hesitated, he continued. "I thought
not. Listen, Constable, I know a guy at ICE, one of their under-
cover guys, who I can call. He'll give me the skinny, where
he wouldn't even give you his real name. I guess I owe you
that, seeing as how that little episode you stirred up on—
what was it, Anegada?—last year was one of my team's big-
gest collars, dollar-wise, for the year. I'll get back to you in
a few."

True to his word, Agent Rosenbaum was back to me in
less than thirty minutes. "You ready for this one, Constable?
Coral."

"Coral?"

"Yep. There is an active smuggling enterprise moving something called 'blue coral' out of somewhere in the area of the USVI, BVI, or BWI to China. From there it is processed into jewelry and sold around the world. Very high-end stuff, I'm told."

"But we have coral all over. And jewelry is made out of it right here in the Caribbean. There's no need to smuggle it."

"This stuff is different, Constable. The way I understand it, what you're talking about is what you see in the duty-free shops down there. It's branch coral, varying in color from white, to pink, to gold, to, in the rarest instances, black. The black coral is old and slow growing, usually less than a tenth of a millimeter per year. It sells for about a buck a gram. Pricey shit but nothing like diamonds, emeralds, or rubies.

"Blue coral has been around for years, too. It's rare, and expensive, but the color is mostly a washed-out, almost gray tone. But not the stuff that's being smuggled now. It's old, slow growing, and it comes from deeper waters. At least that's what the jewelry world speculates because no one has ever seen the source. And when it's been worked and polished, it's supposed to be eye-popping, with a lustrous deep lapis color. Combine that with rarity and you get something worth smuggling.

"My contact tells me that the going rate for unworked blue coral branches is ten dollars per millimeter. Last month, ICE seized some from a container ship out of Barbados that put in to San Juan because of engine trouble. There were fifteen branches on board, each between one and one point five meters long. You do the math and that comes to between $150,000 and $225,000 for the shipment."

Agent Rosenblum continued. "My guy at ICE tells me the stuff has been coming onto the market over the last couple of years in a very controlled way. To him that indicates a single source, with no competition. Now get this—based on the amount of product showing up in the world marketplace, he estimates the wholesale value of the coral coming from that single source is between $20 million and $30 million each year."

"Why doesn't ICE stop them?" I asked.

"That's the beauty of it for whoever is doing the smuggling. The unworked coral is going direct to China from somewhere in your neighborhood without entering US waters. ICE has no reason to intercept it. JITFS has no jurisdiction because it's not drugs or funds from drugs. The Chinese couldn't give a rat's ass, even though they are a signatory to the Convention on International Trade in Endangered Species. Probably the right palms are getting greased in the People's Liberation Army. It's the perfect smuggling crime, with the only law enforcement in the area being the local cops or customs wherever it's originating. You know how small the force is for the BVI and how stretched it is. Well, the same goes for Barbados, Anguilla, Sint Maarten, Saba, or wherever in the area the coral is coming from. Get it by the local boys and whoever is harvesting the stuff is home free."

"And ICE doesn't know where it is originating?"

"Nope. They've narrowed down the region to the Eastern Caribbean, but that's it. They've notified the local cops, including the BVI, but, no offense, Constable, the locals are too busy making sure there aren't pickpockets on the cruise ship docks to worry about a little coral they don't even know exists migrating out of their jurisdiction. Hell, we spent the last twenty years just trying to get some attention paid to narcotics smuggling in the EC and that was wrecking lives and getting people killed. How much attention do you think a hunk of rock taken out of the deep sea and turned into a piece of bling is gonna draw?"

"Maybe mine, when it starts getting people killed."

"You really think it got your victim killed?"

"It might have."

"Well, be careful, Constable. ICE thinks these folks are pretty sophisticated and if they've started using violence, that's a potent and dangerous combination."

Chapter Twenty-eight

I had no sooner rung off the call with Agent Rosenblum than the phone on the station desk rang again. After picking it up and listening to the voice on the other end, Bullfoot shoved the receiver in my direction, saying, "It Inspector Stoutt."

Rollie began with the sigh he usually reserves for incoming calls. "Constable Creque, the testing has come back on the knife in the Konnerth case. The blood on it is not the victim's blood."

"Is there any way to tell whose it is?"

"Not whose," Rollie said. "What's."

"What's?"

"Yes. Not whose blood, what's blood. It is fish blood, probably marlin or wahoo, although why the lab in San Juan went to the trouble of determining that after learning it wasn't human, I'll never understand. No wonder it takes days to get results from them."

The thoughts came fast. No physical evidence linking Robin Kingsmill to Michele Konnerth's death. Maybe the wrong man in jail. Henna Beckles moved up the list of suspects. The stunned silence from me prompted Rollie to ask, "So what else do you have to tie your suspects to the murder?"

The answer, the true and unvarnished answer, was nothing. Nothing but a bad attitude and a skewed moral compass on the part of Kingsmill. Nothing but an association with Kingsmill on the part of Johnny Harley. My only physical evidence was the shoe print, which did not match Kingsmill's shoe size, nor Harley's, but might match that of Henna Beckles. Then there was the witness who didn't communicate much, and when he did, it was with Lego blocks. And let's not forget that he was eight years old. Oh, and he was telling me the two men he saw were in a blue and yellow boat with a silhouette that didn't match that of the victim's boat, which was found adrift. So, nothing. I had nothing.

"I'm working on some leads." It was true but just barely. But it was apparently enough for Inspector Stoutt.

"Okay," he said. Just okay. Like "How's that sandwich?" "Okay." "Want to get a drink after work?" "Okay." "A woman is dead, fed to the sharks." "Okay." Almost as an afterthought, Rollie asked, "Do you need some help?"

Did I need some help? I had help. The amiable Bullfoot, all smiles and healthy appetite, connected to the Gordian community but not the fastest bonefish in the school. The mostly absent Sergeant Chalwell. I needed someone to talk with, to bounce ideas back and forth.

"Can you send Anthony Wedderburn back?"

After a second, Rollie said, "Consider it done."

The first words out of my mouth to Bullfoot after hanging up the phone were "How can I find where Michele Konnerth was doing her fieldwork?"

He pondered briefly and said, "I bet Mr. Gribanov know. He takes his dive groups out to Fallen Jerusalem sometimes. I bet he see her out dere."

As if on cue, Yuri Gribanov strolled in the station door, smiling his relaxed smile while chatting amiably with Sergeant Chalwell, who trailed him through the door. Unlike Mr. Gribanov, the sergeant scowled and seemed out of sorts.

"No reason to be out of humor, old chum," said the Russian in his acquired English accent. "What you think is a problem is not really, and can be made to go away in any event." His eyes fell on me. "Oh, Constable Creque, I see you are still a guest on Virgin Gorda. I hope you are enjoying your time with us."

"Yes, everyone has been most accommodating," I said, my mind flashing briefly on an image of Jeanne Trengrouse washing dishes in the cottage on Church Hill. Would I forever associate the scent of dish soap with the act of love? "Good morning, Sergeant Chalwell."

"Good morning. How goes your investigation?" the sergeant said, lightening his scowl by a couple of degrees.

"Not as well as I had hoped." I proceeded to summarize the lab findings on Robin Kingsmill's knife and the ripple-soled shoe print found on Michele Konnerth's boat, all in a low voice so that Kingsmill and Johnny Harley, by all appearances sleeping in their cells, did not overhear. I omitted Henna Beckles's ownership of ripple-soled clogs from my summary. Why, I don't know. It certainly seemed important, as it made her a suspect in my mind, but somehow I didn't feel comfortable with Sergeant Chalwell knowing that information.

"What is your plan for the investigation moving forward?" Chalwell said. "Because right now I think you need something more than what you have to make a case against . . ." And he nodded over his shoulder at the sleeping figure of Robin Kingsmill.

"I'd like to go out to Fallen Jerusalem to see where Ms. Konnerth was doing her fieldwork," I said.

Sergeant Chalwell's scowl returned, and he had just begun, "I don't see—" when Gribanov interjected. "I can take you. I used to see Ms. Konnerth at Fallen Jerusalem fairly often taking dive excursions out to the area. I can show you exactly where she was doing her research."

I thought I saw a flash of surprise, or consternation, in Sergeant Chalwell's eyes but it was gone as quickly as it appeared. He shrugged. "If that's the direction you want to take your investigation."

I thought about waiting the half day or so it would take for Rollie Stoutt to get the word to Anthony Wedderburn and for Anthony to make the trip to Virgin Gorda on the *Lily B*. Then I could use my own boat and work with the assistance of my trusted friend. But I wasn't in a temporizing mood and

Gribanov could put me in the right area from the outset.
"When can we leave?"

"I take it you need equipment?"

"Yes."

"I need to go to the shop, then, for gear, and we can leave
immediately after that."

Bullfoot drove us to Captain Tankhauler's Dive Shop to pick
up equipment and then to the dock. By early afternoon, we
were anchored over a mixed boulder-and-sand bottom in
ten feet of water on the leeward side of Fallen Jerusalem Island. The bottom sloped gently up to a minuscule sand
beach nearly hidden by a tumble of boulders angling out
from the shore.

"This is where I saw her boat anchored most of the time,"
Gribanov said.

I looked inshore beyond the narrow beach. Above the
sand was a chaotic mess of granite boulders ending in a pebbly flat dotted with the mixed vegetation known as Antil-
lean scrub thorn. We were close enough to land to see that
the place was not visited often; there were no footprints
on the shore, even far above the high-tide mark, and none
of the telltale sand paths in the vegetation that spring up
when even a few humans frequent an area.

I shrugged into the buoyancy compensator and tank; put
on fins, weight belt, and mask; and tested the regulator. With
water this shallow, it seemed almost silly to put on scuba
gear. On Anegada, I regularly free-dive for conch in twenty-
foot depths using only a mask and snorkel. Because Yuri

Gribanov had gone to the trouble of outfitting me, I felt almost obligated to use the gear.

I held on to my mask and hoses and took a long stride off the boat into the light green water. Once I was under, the water was air-clear, like most of the water in the BVI that wasn't in moving current or in a harbor with heavy boat traffic. Gribanov had done a nice job of gauging my buoyancy in setting up the weight belt, and I hovered just below the surface surveying the floor of the small bay. Sprats flashed to my left, their panicked course paralleled by the near-motionless silhouette of a great barracuda. One scissor kick of my fins set me gliding along inches above the sand bottom, with its usual detritus—broken coral, decaying seagrass, empty shells. Then, a few more yards to seaward, they began to appear on the seafloor, first one, then a handful, then dozens and hundreds, echelon upon echelon of lumpy black sea cucumbers resembling nothing else in the sea and nothing on land other than the donkey dung that gave them their common name. Here they lived their sedentary lives by the thousands, a city of unattractive creatures filtering unsuspecting bits of food into their mouths with hair-sized tentacles, having non-contact sex by spewing egg and sperm into the chance currents for fate, or Mother Nature, or God, to bring the two forms of gamete together to perpetuate their race, and generally uglying up the otherwise beautiful surroundings. And here Michele Konnerth had spent days, weeks, months of her young life, communing with the unlovely little beasts, watching every move of their nearly immobile existence, probably and understandably looking forward to nights of drunkenness and wanton sex after hours hovering over their turdesque ranks.

Unlike Michele Konnerth, I was not required by my occupation to linger with sea cucumbers and I did not. After a broad visual sweep to assure myself I was not missing something important, I paused to orient toward the shore. Gribanov's dive boat appeared suspended in midair at the end of its anchor line between me and the beach, its green hull providing the contrast to set it apart from the pure color of the cloudless sky above. I turned seaward, picked my line based on several of the more prominent boulders, and started deeper. Half an hour later I returned from the violet depths, having seen nothing I had not seen a thousand times before in the waters surrounding Anegada, and certainly having seen no forests of rare blue coral.

I surfaced briefly at the dive boat, where Yuri Gribanov waited with the practiced patience of a veteran dive master, neither asleep nor fully awake in the shade of the wheelhouse. I called for him from the stubby boarding ladder, and he took my gear aboard. Then I swam the twenty yards to the beach and put the day's, and maybe the week's, only footprints in the sand.

There was not much to see. The pristine sand below the tide line gave way to the cluttered garbage dump of the modern, unmanicured beach found now on all out-of-the-way islands. Wine bottles, fishing net, motor oil cans, and plastic bottles competed with the more traditional forms of flotsam and jetsam to fill the upper beach. After picking my way through carefully to avoid broken glass or the errant rusty nail, I came to a humpback-whale-sized shelf of granite, cooking-hot in the afternoon sun. Quick steps over the roasting stone brought me to the scrub thorn and, after a few uncomfortable minutes' walk being pricked and scratched, into the more open and arid middle of the island. The overgrowth gave way to a field of runty gray-green beach grass, able to survive on the salt-laden moisture blowing in from the waves crashing on the windward shore. Turning, I was high enough to see the cove where the dive boat waited and, turning again, realized the field where I stood had a commanding view of the sea to the windward side as well.

The sharp edges of the beach grass sawed against my ankles as I stepped toward the windward shore. The grass was undisturbed, until I came to a slight depression. There the grass had been pulled away from a circle about six feet in diameter and the sand that made up the soil was smoothed to provide a comfortable place for an animal or a man to rest. The rocks that had been moved out of the sandy circle had been placed along its windward side, forming a low wall. "Low" is perhaps an understatement; the barrier was no more than eight inches high, hardly enough to break the incessant wind blowing across the grass, or to keep anyone in or out.

The only way the wall would provide shelter was if you were prone. I lay down in the sand behind it. A flat stone in the middle of the wall was slightly lower than the rest, and by placing my chin on my hands, I could peer over the top of the stone. I realized then that the wall was not meant to shelter but to conceal. The low gap allowed me to look out to the open sea and yet be all but invisible behind the stones. The flat stone provided a perfect rest for a pair of binoculars or a spotting scope. Or, I supposed, a rifle. Had Michele Konnerth been using this perch to look out on a smuggling operation? Or was this a guard post for the smugglers, and had she been spotted from it as she passed by in her boat attempting to determine what the smugglers were doing?

Thirty seconds later I had my answer when I spied a folded scrap of paper jammed into the narrow space between two of the rocks forming the wall. Pulling it from its hiding place, I noted that it did not yet have the crisp-fragile texture that paper left in the elements on a beach acquires after a couple weeks.

I unfolded the paper. Three words—"UNDER THE FLOORBOARDS"—were written in a looping, precise hand I recognized. I had first seen it a few days ago.

The note had been written by Michele Konnerth.

Chapter Twenty-nine

    I held the note in my hand and studied it, trying to divine more from it than its written content, like a Pentecostal apprehending the Holy Spirit through a laying-on of hands. On close inspection, the meticulous script had a fragile quality to it. The scrap bearing the writing was from a wire-bound notebook, the paper coarse and cheap, ragged chads clinging where the sheet had been torn away. This all gave a sense that the note had been written in haste. Had the writer been found out, scribbling the message and jamming it between the rocks as someone approached?

    Crouching, I examined the rest of the area for other notes or evidence of any type. Nothing. Even the sand inside the semicircle of stones was devoid of prints, the action of the elements in the few days since Michele Konnerth had hidden in the shelter sufficient to reduce signs of her presence to rounded humps and shallow smooth indentations. The nondescript rise on Fallen Jerusalem was no more revealing of its secrets than a captive spy in a paperback Cold War melodrama.

The same could not be said for the words. Their message was clear—*something* was located under the floorboards. Their message impelled action—*look* under the floorboards. Michele Konnerth had placed something there important enough to spend precious seconds, seconds when an assailant approached, seconds that could have been used to flee, writing a note to make certain someone would look under the floorboards and find what was there, even after she was gone. I had now become that someone.

I stood and folded the note back into its original shape, then sealed it inside the two plastic sandwich bags I habitually carry in the pocket of my swim trunks. Ten minutes later, after a quick walk through the beach grass and scrub thorn and a cleansing swim to the dive boat, I was helped aboard by the strong hands of Yuri Gribanov.

"Anything?" he said, appropriately, but not overly, curious.

"Nothing but sand, rocks, and thorns." Why I revealed nothing to Gribanov I do not know. True, he was not a police officer and had no right to information about the investigation, but there would have been no harm in describing to him what I had found. He was not a suspect. He was not associated in any way with the events surrounding Michele Konnerth's death. He really deserved a tidbit; he had brought me all the way to this forsaken rock and waited while I poked around for hours. Something just kept me from telling him.

Maybe it was because he had once been a spy. Everyone knows from TV that you should never give a spy, active or retired, any information.

Freeing the anchor from the sandy bottom, Gribanov turned the boat in the direction of the Yacht Harbour. After a few minutes of chitchat about possible dive sites around Anegada, we both fell silent, the diesel drone of the dive boat inboard the only sound. I thought about where the floorboards mentioned in the note in my pocket might be. By the time we rounded the south break wall and entered the dredged channel of the Yacht Harbour, I had reached a firm conclusion.

Luther Quince looked up from his carving only when I had knocked forcefully on the porch post and he felt the vibration through the legs of his rocking chair.

"Good afternoon, Mr. Quince," I said. Luther didn't look me directly in the eye or respond to my greeting.

"Woman!" he thundered, loud enough to wake small children from their afternoon naps on Jost Van Dyke, miles away.

"Man, can you not just get your sorry backside out your rocking chair and come get me if you need me?" Dessie Quince screamed at the top of her lungs as she emerged from the elaborately carved front door, her sparse hair wrapped in a fuchsia bandana. "Oh, Constable Creque, how nice to see you again." She dropped her voice into full coquette mode. "Won't you come in?"

"Watch that woman, policeman. The devil became female

the day she was made," Luther said in, for him, a confidential tone of ninety decibels.

Assured that domestic balance, if not bliss, was being maintained in the Quince household, I stepped into the room Dessie called the parlor. Luther stayed on the porch, carving and muttering at an ear-splitting pitch about Satan's daughter. Dessie offered me a seat on an ancient horsehair sofa. The room smelled of potpourri, fried onions, and dust.

"I'm sorry to trouble you again, Mrs. Quince," I began.

"No trouble at all, Constable." She displayed a toothless smile and said sweetly, "Please call me Dessie." A bird-wing flutter of her eyelashes accompanied the invitation.

"The reason I stopped by, Mrs. Quince—"

"Dessie," she insisted.

"Dessie . . . is to take another look at Michele Konnerth's things in your guesthouse."

"You are always welcome here, Constable, but you have all of Michele's things already."

"I do?"

"Well, not you personally." Dessie placed a purring emphasis on the word "personally." " 'You' as in the police."

"What do you mean?"

"A policeman came round and packed up all of Michele's things—clothes, papers, everything—yesterday morning. You didn't know?"

"No. What was the policeman's name?"

Dessie was briefly lost in thought. "Oh, dear, I'm not sure he gave his name." Then, blaringly loud, directed to Luther on the porch: "Old man, what was the policeman's name who came and got Michele's things yesterday?"

"Mr. Policeman, woman," came the shouted response.

Dessie turned to me. "I guess we didn't get his name."

"What did he look like?"

"He was a white man. Medium height, medium build."

A description of every white belonger and 90 percent of the tourists in the BVI.

"What color was his hair? His eyes?"

"His hair was brown . . . maybe more black, I guess. I didn't notice his eye color."

"Did he have any distinguishing marks—scars, tattoos, or birthmarks?"

"No," she said. "He smelled nice."

"His vehicle?"

"I didn't look to see what he was driving."

Great. An exceptionally ordinary white police imperson-ator had carted away all of Michele Konnerth's worldly possessions. The only thing I knew for certain about the man is that he was *not* my main suspect, who remained locked in a holding cell in the police station.

"Dessie, I'd like to look out back around the bachelor cot-tage where Michele stayed again," I said.

"Do you think the old man can trust us out there alone?" she whispered.

The bachelor cottage on the Quinces' back lot had been neat and spartan when I had last seen it. Now it was just plain empty. Every stitch of clothing, every scrap of paper, every piece of equipment that Michele Konnerth had brought there was gone. The few sticks of furniture remaining gave the place the sad air of a home just before removal of the last load on moving day.

I walked slowly around the single room, listening to my steps for the hollow sound that might reveal Michele Konnerth's hiding place under the floorboards. When that tactic proved unsuccessful, I got down on hands and knees, crawling along each row of boards, looking for a telltale break in the decades of grime in the cracks to reveal the hiding place. I moved the bed and found a place where the space between the boards was microscopically wider. Fitting the blade of my penknife into the slot, I prized and twisted, and was rewarded by the board's lifting a fraction of an inch. More effort and the board popped loose, revealing a dark space extending down to the bare dirt below the floor of the house.

There are no poisonous snakes on Virgin Gorda but the brown recluse spider calls all islands of the BVI home, and the dark hole below the floor was a perfect habitat for it. With no small trepidation, I reached in up to my shoulder and felt round the dank space. In seconds I pulled up a plastic bag with a book-shaped object inside.

The book was Michele Konnerth's field notes for the period after January 18. I read, scanning the early pages rapidly when it became apparent that they were devoted to observations on the life of the donkey dung sea cucumber. Then, in an entry dated March 20, a new topic appeared—a strange boat with two men diving on the Atlantic side of Fallen Jerusalem Island. It was just a mention but that alone was unusual; until that point, Michele Konnerth had been the consummate scientist, confining herself strictly to her research subject. After this one notation, nothing was out of the ordinary for another couple weeks until this entry:

The two mysterious men were back again today, diving in the same place for the fifth time in the last two weeks. It would not be unusual to do this—after all, I dive in the same spot almost every day—but they seem so secretive. First, there is their approach. They always come directly to the spot from far out at sea, rather than coming along the coast where they might be easily observed. Second, they seem to be trying to camouflage their boat with this weird, hairy netting they hang along the hull and around the wheelhouse. It certainly works. I cannot even tell the color of the boat under the muddy brown/dark green netting. I don't think they have seen me. Fallen Jerusalem is between where I anchor and where they anchor. I wouldn't have seen them at all if I had not come ashore for a bathroom break and to stretch my legs.

Then the entry two days later:

They are back again today and I am sure they are up to no good. They seem to be pulling something out of the water and putting it in the boat. They are always careful to work from the seaward side, keeping the boat between them and the land so the view of whatever they are pulling from the water is blocked.

Five days later:

The water on the windward side has been calm for the last three days and the two mystery men have been at it each day, tossing something over the side of the boat from the water, over and over. Only one of them is diving, the black guy. The white guy stays in the boat, lifting whatever they bring up from the water over the side of the gunwale and storing it under some canvas on the work deck of the boat.

On April 13:

The mystery boat and the two men were back again today. Whatever they are doing has to be illegal. Maybe one of those narco-submarines sank with a load of drugs and they are salvaging it. I could go to the police but what would I tell them—two guys go diving every day? I need proof and I think I know how to get it.

On April 15:

I set up my observation post today before they arrived. Just laid out some rocks I arranged to look natural and waited for them to show. They were there like clockwork at nine a.m. I brought my binoculars this time, hoping to see what they were pulling from the water when they tossed it into the boat, but I couldn't quite make it out. My mind is made up, though—whatever they are doing can't be legal, with the way they try to conceal it when they bring it over the gunwale. Thank God the wind came up and they had to leave after three hours. I'm not sure how much longer I could have lain in that position. Tomorrow I'll bring my camera with the long lens, and get some pics of them in action. Maybe a still photo will show what they are pulling out of the water and I can turn it all over to the cops.

It was the last entry. Michele Konnerth's body, or what was left of it after the shark had done its work, was found on April 17.

Chapter Thirty

After extracting myself from an invitation from Dessie Quince for "tea and whatever may follow" and shouting, "Good-bye, sir!" to Luther, I turned my steps toward the police station. As I passed by First Bank near the center of Lee Road, Anthony Wedderburn fell in beside me.

"Hello, old man. Just arrived, answering the call. I see your Virgin Gorda brethren have not yet seen fit to place the keys to their Land Rover into your hands. Let's hope this case concludes before you need to replace the soles on your shoes," De White Rasta said, a puckish grin on his face and mischief in his eyes. "Speaking of concluding this case, Inspector Stoutt says the gent you almost plugged with your Webley may not be our man after all."

"It's beginning to seem that way, Anthony. I'm glad to have you back. I need your help," I said. I used the rest of the walk to the police station to fill De Rasta in on developments, including the white policeman who had visited the Quinces and taken all of Michele Konnerth's possessions.

"It seems as though the gentleman, whoever he was, failed to obtain what he was looking for and it found its way into your hands," De Rasta observed. "Dr. Konnerth may have stumbled upon some unsavory characters."

"The question is, Anthony, how do we find them?"

"You could do what she did, set up on Fallen Jerusalem and wait until they show, then call in the *St. Ursula* to catch them in the act."

"We could but my guess is they won't be doing any coral harvesting in the near future. The coral isn't going anywhere and they can afford to lie low until the heat is off."

"You sound just like one of those American private detective sorts on the telly," Anthony said.

"That's where I heard it."

"So what is the next step, old man?"

"I'm not sure." That didn't sound much like the lead investigator in a murder case, at least a competent one. I did not feel very competent at the moment.

I was saved from coming up with an answer to that question by our arrival at the police station. Constable George had just come in for the four-to-midnight shift a few minutes earlier. Alone in the station, he greeted us in warm Bullfoot fashion.

"Where are the prisoners?" I asked.

"De tourists in Her Majesty's prison all got released by de magistrate dis mornin', so dere was room for dem on

Tortola. *St. Ursula* pick dem up dis afternoon and take dem to Road Town."

"Looks like I get my old bunk back," said De Rasta. "With any luck, Mrs. Scatliff will do better tonight than fungi, saltfish, and callaloo."

"Don't count on it, Mistah Wedderburn. Sergeant Chalwell say de prisoner budget runnin' low," Bullfoot laughed.

That made my mind up. It was the end of a long day and I decided a return to the warm embrace of Jeanne Trengrouse was what I needed most. Since I had asked for Anthony to return to Virgin Gorda, I felt I couldn't leave him to stay by himself in the musty jail cell. "I could see if you can stay where I'll be tonight," I offered.

"Don't tell me you have a dozen cousins here and we could have been sleeping somewhere other than jail since day one," Anthony said.

"Actually, I have an invitation to stay at the Trengrouse cottage," I said. I detected an upturn at the corners of De Rasta's lips.

"Ms. Trengrouse is letting out rooms?" Anthony asked, breaking into a mischievous smile.

"Not exactly," I said. Bullfoot and Anthony exchanged a knowing guy-grin. "But I could ask if she would let you crash on her couch. It has to be better than the metal bunk here."

"Thank you, Teddy, but I'll bide here. I'm beginning to develop a taste for fungi." Anthony, the soul of discretion. "See you in the morning."

With no prisoners to watch, Bullfoot was more than

happy to give me a ride to Church Hill. On the way, I asked him to stop at the Supa Valu so I wouldn't arrive empty-handed. As with all island stores, the pickings were slim and basic—box milk, sweet potatoes, toilet paper, beer, mosquito coils. I despaired of finding anything suitable for an admirer to bring to his lady but then, in a corner, I spotted a dusty heart-shaped box. Candy, left from last Valentine's Day. It would have to do. I couldn't show up with a sack of dried pigeon peas. At the counter to pay, a display board held a gift for Jemmy as perfect as the candy for Jeanne was mediocre. A Swiss Army knife, with its array of gadgets, is the ultimate for an eight-year-old boy.

"How thoughtful," Jeanne said after greeting me with a long kiss at the front door. I had cleaned the dust off the cellophane wrapper of the candy box, but it looked even sadder in her hand than it had on the store shelf.

"It's the best I could come up with on short notice," I said, sheepishly thinking that I would probably have been better off arriving with nothing in my hand.

"It's lovely. Dark chocolate is my favorite. We can take it with us."

"Are we going somewhere?"

"I thought it would be fun to go on a picnic," Jeanne said.

"Is Jemmy coming with us?"

"No. Madda is coming to watch him in a minute. I want you all to myself for a couple of hours, with no little-boy ears or gabby birds nearby."

"Okay, but I have something for Jemmy," I said. "A Swiss

Army knife. Something a boy his age should have, one with lots of gadgets. My dada gave me one when I was eight and it was my prized possession."

"Is it safe for him to have that?" Jeanne asked. "I assume one of the gadgets is a blade. Couldn't he cut himself?"

"He could. I did, even after my father explained to me how to hold it and how to be careful. But it teaches responsibility and it will make him feel like he is growing up, to be trusted with something like a knife."

Jeanne knitted her beautiful brow in thought. "I remember cutting my finger with a knife when my mother was teaching me how to cook, chopping an onion for tortie. I was eight, the same age as Jemmy. I guess maybe I've been sheltering him, telling myself he can't do things most boys can because of the way he is. But I can't know and he can't know if he never gets a chance. All right, I think he can be trusted with it, provided you teach him how to handle it."

"Of course."

"Jemmy," Jeanne called softly. "Come see Constable Creque. He has brought you a gift."

Jemmy drifted quietly into the room, eyes cast downward. I explained that I had brought him a gift that I thought every boy should have when he was grown up enough to be responsible. He took the proffered pocketknife in his hand, turning it over and carefully inspecting it. I showed him how to fit his fingernail into the slot on the top of each blade to open them, and how each utensil on the knife functioned. I saved the straight blade for last, explaining that it was sharp and could injure if not used correctly.

Then I showed him how to hold the knife while cutting, and how to cut by pushing the blade away rather than pulling it toward you.

Jeanne watched silently as Jemmy took the tool and began opening and closing blades. The boy stopped and looked up to her, and she nodded to him. He moved off to his room, his new possession in hand.

"He will do well with it," I said.

"I know," Jeanne said. "He needs that. Needs a man around. I didn't think so, but seeing him just now . . ."

"Jemmy's a good kid. He'll be fine, whether there's a man around or not. He has a good, caring mother."

Jeanne stepped up to me, caressed the side of my face with her hand, and kissed me, gently, sweetly, and what seemed like almost sadly. Then, stirring herself as though she were awakening, she said, "I'd better get this picnic together. My mother will be here soon."

Jeanne busied herself with packing a basket while I watched her, back to me, move with sinuous grace from counter to pantry to stove. Watching her was a reliving of the domestic felicity I had thought I had at one time, and had learned so harshly that I did not. The drift to melancholy had just begun when a woman who could have been Jeanne's slightly older sister bustled in the door. She had the same striking blue eyes, grace, and directness as Jeanne, tempered by, I guessed, an additional score of years.

"You must be Teddy," she said, blue eyes appraising and, after a moment, approving.

"Yes, ma'am. Pleased to meet you."

Jeanne intervened with quick introductions and then we were on our way out the door, I still in uniform and Jeanne in a yellow print sundress that showed off the smooth skin of her neck and shoulders nicely. Her step was light as she led the way, and served to make mine so.

"Where are we having this picnic?" I asked.

"In a beautiful place where you can learn something about me and my ancestors."

The difficulties of the day fell away as we walked hand in hand along Church Hill Road, moving southeast, the land growing more rural and wild as we went, until there were no houses nor any sign of man. Larger trees lining the road gave way to scrub thorn but the loss of shade did not mean an increase in the heat, due to the powerful wind sweeping up from the sea. Soon our path opened out of the flora to a desolate rocky coast, barren of all vegetation, with a roaring sea below.

"This is where we will have our picnic," Jeanne said, spreading a blanket and placing the basket on top to prevent the wind from tearing it away. It was a dramatic place: the sea foaming against the rocks, the blustering wind, and views south to Fallen Jerusalem and north to the green mound of Gorda Peak. I noticed structures made of local stone a few hundred yards away, a tall tower and squat square buildings, all ruins.

"What are those?" I asked, pointing to the northeast.

"Those are the reason I am here, and the reason I brought you here today," she said. "But first, would you like something to drink?"

I agreed, and she produced a lime, a bottle of dark Cruzan rum, and two glasses. Dared I drink, after what I had done to myself in the last year? If not, was now the time to explain why? I decided the answer to both questions was no. "I'll pass on the rum today, Jeanne. Any water?"

I could tell she read something in my eyes. She must have decided there would be plenty of time for explanations. "Sorry, no ice," she said as she poured water for each of us. She toasted. "To us and happiness; they are one and the same."

We clicked glasses and drank, eyes locked together. The glasses were put down and we kissed, drawn-out kisses, until passion overcame us and we made love, Jeanne astride and covering me with the flowing skirt of her yellow sundress, the world and she all golden for fleeting moments, the past of pain, deceit, and failure forgotten. Then we lay back in each other's arms, the hard rock beneath a welcome bed we would not have traded for the luxury of a suite at the Ritz.

We drowsed in the late-day sun, until she sat up and said, "Another toast. *Yehes ha sowena whath dhewgh why ha 'gas henath.*" She made me raise a glass and drink.

"What does it mean, and in what language?" I asked.

" 'Health and prosperity always to you and your descendants.' It's a traditional Cornish toast, taught to me by my grandfather. That is why I brought you here. Well, that and to do what we just did, but mostly to show you this place and what it means. Come on."

Jeanne was up and had me by the hand, leading me to

the ruined chimney tower and buildings. The rocks we passed on the way had sparkling veins of white, green, and pinkish gold. Jeanne noticed me staring and said, "That's right, you've not seen anything like that on Anegada. Those veins are minerals in the granite rock. The white is quartz, the gold is feldspar, and the green is the reason I'm here. It's tin-copper."

"Why do you say it's the reason you're here?"

"It is. My great-great-grandfather came here from Cornwall in England to mine copper when the mines there were depleted. He fell in love with a local girl—my great-great-grandmother—and stayed when the mines shut down. I think he had to truly love her to stay in this desolate place. He and she used to live in the workers' quarters here before they became ruins. When I was a little girl I used to come and play in the mine shaft, until one day Madda found out and I was forbidden. I still like to come out now and then. It makes me feel connected to that part of my history. I even learned a few words of the old Cornish, including that toast I just gave. And Madda returned to her maiden name after Dada went and ran away, to keep the heritage, so I did, too. 'Trengrouse' is Cornish for 'the homestead by the cross.' Madda says the place the name comes from is no more, lost to time." Jeanne looked wistfully out over the surging ocean, as if she might see the country crossroad from which her ancestor came, though it was four thousand miles and eight score years distant.

"Come now," she said, seizing my hand and leading me into the abandoned mine shaft. Cut into the granite rock, it descended quickly. Jeanne produced a flashlight from the pocket of her sundress and led the way. Soon light and sound from the outside world faded behind us. Jeanne stopped at a low-ceilinged intersection of the shaft we were following with three other shafts.

"I wanted to show you this," she said, playing the light against the far wall. Flecks of mineral sparkled in the beam, now safe from miners' drills and picks. There, etched in the stone, appeared the following:

PEDER TRENGROUSE 1863

"My great-great-grandfather carved that, the year the mine closed. I like to think he came down here because he missed the old life and his old home. He gave it all up for the love of my great-great-grandma, stayed behind when the others went home." She ran her fingers tenderly over the etched name. Turning the light to illuminate her face, she asked, "Have you ever kissed a girl in a mine, Teddy Creque?"

"No."

Her eyes were blue fire in the indirect light. She pressed her body against mine. "Have you ever made love to a woman in a mine, Teddy Creque?"

Before I could answer, she switched the light off.

Chapter Thirty-one

The slightest hint of the rosy dawn shone around the edges of the plantation shutters when I heard the noise. Bare footsteps on the teak floor and the click of the wooden latch on the front door. I sat up, concerned, only to be pulled down into a tangle of bedclothes, frowzy hair, and the sweet perfume of Jeanne Trengrouse.

"It's just Jemmy, gone for one of his daybreak excursions," she said, snuggling into my chest. "But now that we're awake . . ." The slender fingers of her left hand played along my stomach and toward points south. We made languid morning love to the euphonic tones of the wind chimes outside the window. I was beginning to like this island.

After, we drifted off in each other's arms for half an hour, until suddenly Jeanne sat up, pecked me on the cheek, and bustled out of the room.

The clatter of pots and crockery in the tiny kitchen gave way in a few moments to the aroma of coffee, bacon, and eggs, enough to revive any man, even after an afternoon, and a night, and a morning, of lovemaking. I soon found myself wrapping my arms around Jeanne as she wielded a spatula over a sputtering frying pan, remembering the times I had done that with another woman, with Icilda, before it was all gone.

I was saved from further bleak thoughts by Jeanne's melodic humming and a flurry of morning activity. Sir Winston Churchill decided the day was far enough along for him to be released from his canvas cover and made his wishes known by bleating, "I needs out!" followed by a string of expletives sufficient to make a McNamara Road hooker cringe. Only the removal of the night cover halted the cursing, and just in the nick of time, as Jemmy returned a minute later. He immediately seized my hand and dragged me to his bedroom.

A three-quarters-complete skyscraper I did not recognize filled most of the floor space in the room but Jemmy steered me to the corner where the yellow and blue boat construction remained.

"Bad-men boat, bad-men boat," he insisted, drawing my hand down to touch the model.

"Yes, this is the bad men's boat," I said. My acknowledgment seemed to satisfy him. He released my hand and returned to the kitchen. I studied the odd blue and yellow checkerboard pattern of the boat's hull again. What was I missing? The dimensions and the configuration of the model matched scores of craft that plied the waters around Virgin Gorda. The paint job was the key.

A call from Jeanne that breakfast was served broke my

train of thought. The boat would wait for the bacon and eggs.

"Finding the boat is the solution," Anthony Wedderburn pronounced with the finality of a judge passing a particularly severe sentence. Anthony, Constable George, and I were seated on hard chairs around the single desk in the Virgin Gorda Police Station, hashing out possible leads in the death of Michele Konnerth. Sergeant Chalwell leaned against the chipping paint of the front door frame, sipping coffee. Outside, a benevolent sun, tempered by the southeast breeze, shone on another flawless Virgin Gorda day. Ground doves pecked in the middle of the macadam road, with no traffic to disturb their quest for seeds and insect tidbits.

"I still think you have your man with Kingsmill," Sergeant Chalwell said. "I already told you the Trengrouse boy is unreliable and this checkerboard-boat thing proves it. I've never seen a boat that color in these waters, not in all my forty-seven years. No, Kingsmill's your man. Maybe you should go question him again, in Road Town. He might have softened up now that he's had a few days in a real prison."

I doubted it but I didn't say as much. There was no reason to antagonize the sergeant. He had plainly reached his conclusions and would not allow them to be disturbed, a luxury a police officer might permit himself in a quiet place like Virgin Gorda. Or Anegada, as I had learned.

"I think a further interrogation of Kingsmill may be in order, Sergeant, but as long as Anthony is here with the *Lily*

B, it can't hurt to take a cruise along the shoreline to see if we spot any boat that might have something resembling a blue and yellow hull. Let's go, Anthony," I said. I tried to be polite and not challenge Sergeant Chalwell, but the fact remained that the investigation was mine to run as I saw fit.

"Suit yourself." Chalwell shrugged. "Just remember it's a long way around the island and marine fuel is $5.15 a gallon. Don't expect to be reimbursed out of the Virgin Gorda station budget."

"I think the Anegada station budget has sufficient funds for this search," I said. Chalwell responded with another, less emphatic shrug.

An hour later found De Rasta and me motoring out of the Yacht Harbour at no-wake speed, having first done a lazy circuit of the docks looking for a blue and yellow checked workboat. Turning northward, our course would take us past the ferry dock and Little Dix Bay, beyond Mahoe Bay and Nail Bay for a look around the broken rocky face of the Dogs and into the tourist paradise of the North Sound, at the far end of the island.

Anthony stood hard against the short center console of the *Lily B* as we motored, scanning port to starboard and back, a hand shading his eyes.

"What makes you think we'll find this boat that your young friend insists was involved in the murder?" he said. "There is a great deal of ocean out there, old man. I know that from just the last ten minutes of looking. Why wouldn't the murderers just hide it? Or even scuttle it?"

"First, Anthony, they may not even know they were seen.

While the area around The Baths is busy with people and boat traffic on even the slowest of days, even the early morning jogger who first saw the shark attacking said there was no boat in the area. That means there was a window of maybe ten minutes, between when there would be enough light to distinguish color and dawn, when the boat could be seen as a silhouette only. Even if you do sunrise yoga, or jog, or want to try some fishing before the crowds arrive, you don't come that early. The operators of the boat—Michele Konnerth's killers—don't need to hide the boat or scuttle it because they know the odds are microscopically small that anyone was there to see them in that ten-minute window. Besides, a boat in the Virgin Islands is like a horse in the Old American West; no one who has any experience living here would get rid of their boat without a pretty strong idea that they had been seen."

"So you think it's just a matter of looking in the right nooks and crannies?"

"Which we are going to spend the day doing," I said.

And which we did, wending our way in and out of small bays, checking every dock, anchorage, and hurricane hole big enough to hold even a single vessel larger than a canoe. We did a loop around Mosquito Island and Prickly Pear Island, exploring every swimming cove, snorkeling site, and protected area where a boat might spend a day or an hour.

And we found boats—ketches, schooners, racing yachts, motor cruisers, cigarette boats, fishing boats, catamarans, trimarans, single-hull sailers, tenders and dinghies, barges and trawlers. There was not one with its hull painted in a blue and yellow color scheme.

Noon found us at the Bitter End Yacht Club, after rounding Saba Rock offshore in the final lap of a fruitless morning. After a grouper sandwich at a table shunted off into a corner for the local trade, we headed back to the *Lily B* to gas up and continue the search. The boy pumping gas could only manage monosyllabic answers but even so we were able to clearly conclude that no vessel painted in blue and yellow checks, or swirls, or paisley, or plaid, had ever fueled up or driven by the dock at the Bitter End. There was nothing to do but work back on the Atlantic side of the island.

Pebbly, unpopular, and devoid of any boats, Joe Bay, and then Dog Bay, slid by. Ben's Bay held a motor vessel at anchor, its upper deck a mass of oiled and tanned bodies that erupted in a scramble of swimsuit-donning as we idled upwind, except for one brazen blonde who rose and stood at the rail, undoubtedly convinced that we would be as pleased at the show as she was to provide it.

"Royal Virgin Islands Sunscreen Police," De White Rasta shouted in the direction of the exhibitionist. "Just checking to make certain you've applied SPF 30 or above in the last half hour." Ignoring a suggestion from the flaxen-haired naturist that we board to check if she had missed any spots, we continued south at low speed.

Midafternoon found us overlooking the headlands at Copper Mine Bay, taking in a land view the opposite of the sea view Jeanne and I had experienced the prior afternoon. The time since the encounter with the bargeful of sunbathers

had been distinctly unexciting—we had seen no vessel in
two hours of slow cruising. I was sure that the area around
Copper Mine Point had no safe harbor for any vessel, so the
only prospect was for a turn around The Baths and a short
stretch north to complete our fruitless circumnavigation of
Virgin Gorda.

"How near are we to where the young lady had her hiding spot to watch the smugglers?" Anthony asked. He was
the first person I had heard refer to Michele Konnerth as a
lady since her death, myself included, and it struck me how
wrong it had been for all of us to describe her in any other
way. True, she had led a life, after working hours, that most
in these conservative islands would view with moral disap-
probation. But she had come to the Virgin Islands for a good
and noble cause, and if the reason she was killed was because
of what she had discovered, even this diversion had been
born out a concern for the sea and the earth. She was a good
person, despite all, and from then on I resolved to join
Anthony in referring to her as a lady.

"Very near, maybe a ten-minute ride, Anthony," I said.

"I would like very much to see the place." De Rasta
squinted into the southeast distance.

Without a word, I put the *Lily B* up on plane with a heading for Fallen Jerusalem Island.

Chapter Thirty-two

I wondered how Anthony was enjoying conditions topside. My guess was not very much. The current I drifted in was quartering the surface winds, which had risen from the southeast as they often do this time of year in our islands. The wind and the current collided on the surface to form a nasty chop, made more complicated by a long swell coming in from the northeast, generated by a storm somewhere off the west coast of Africa. Put it all together and it is what I have heard some charter captains call, as their passengers chummed from the rail, sloppy.

I was fine, twenty feet below the surface, riding the current with an occasional lazy kick of my fins, a passenger on a sightseeing flight, supported not by tenuous molecules of air, but the more substantial and reassuring lift of salt water. A hundred feet below, at the edge of the surface light and my vision, a monochrome jungle rolled past, its kaleidoscopic colors muted by the thick prism of water between it and the surface.

I supposed that Anthony could not complain, as the ride I was taking was his idea. After he had seen the hideout from which Michele Konnerth had watched the smugglers remove whatever they were removing from the water, he stood staring out to sea for a long minute.

"We should go see what's out there," he finally said.

"I'm not sure what that would do for us," I replied. "We can see there is no one out there now. I know of no one who dives the east side of Fallen Jerusalem. The currents are strong. There are no attractive sights, no wrecks or walls, just the rapid slope away from the island."

"Don't you want to know what's down there, old man?"

And, suddenly, I did. The reason Michele Konnerth was dead was possibly down there, and I had to know.

So, half an hour ago I had donned the thirdhand scuba gear that had been unused in the stern locker of the *Lily B* for over a year and rolled over the side, leaving De White Rasta to mind the boat and follow the bubbles as I flew along in the current. I was not really sure what I was looking for. I thought I was searching for blue coral, the rare commodity Agent Rosenblum had told me was being smuggled from the area, but maybe it was gold, or drugs, or artifacts, or one of the many other things that man takes from the sea to fuel his greed and dreams.

Whatever I was searching for, I wasn't finding it. What passed as I was carried along by the ocean's unseen hand was impressive, magnificent, striking, but also, well, ordinary for a dive in the BVI. Great barracuda hung between me and the myriad small reef fish on the bottom. A school of amberjacks flashed by, aggressive as pit bulls in pursuit of a terrified cloud of mullet. A juvenile white marlin scythed near the surface at the edge of my vision. Boulders crusted with every imaginable variety of live coral sat in a suspended landslide sloping seaward, their every nook and cranny holding a lobster, a damselfish, an octopus. But for the dive thus far, I had found nothing worth risking jail, nothing to be secretive about. Nothing to kill for.

In the rushing river of current, my half-hour drift had carried me almost the full length of Fallen Jerusalem. I was sure I was nearing the southern end of the field of vision for Michele Konnerth's hideout. Then I saw it, ahead and below, approaching rapidly, an open park, a cricket pitch in length at most, where nothing abided except a sparse copse of branch corals, black and dead, projecting from the flat of a plateau on the slope to the fathomless bottom, a sunken *deadvlei*. With the push of the current, I had only a heartbeat to decide, and dove on an inverse parabolic course to the bottom. I didn't have enough air for decompression stops on my ascent, so I could spend only a few minutes in the coral. The short time did not prove to be a problem, as the current increased as I neared the tangled coral forest. I fairly flew through the mass of branches, reaching out to snap off one specimen the size of my index finger before I was carried beyond the last of it. I pushed quickly to the surface. Anthony was only a hundred yards away when I broke through and he motored over with alacrity. Still, by the time he reached me, I was green around the gills from bobbing on the surface. Climbing aboard, I vomited over the gunwale as soon as I took the regulator from my lips.

"I've been doing that for the last twenty minutes in this infernal codswallop," Anthony said through clenched teeth. Then he managed a smirk. "It gets better when your stomach is emptied. It should take you about two more tosses."

It only took one, induced by De Rasta's remark. As soon as I was free from my fins, tank, and weight belt, we put the *Lily B* up on plane and rounded the south end of Fallen Jerusalem, headed for the still waters of the leeward side. Even there, if we cut the engine and drifted, the queasiness returned. We opted to creep slowly north, the forward motion ironing out the chop on the leeward side and the breeze in our faces providing some measure of relief. After a short time running in this manner, I felt sufficiently restored to show Anthony the coral specimen I had retrieved during the dive.

The fragment of coral branch was like nothing I had ever seen. Most coral is either bleached white by the sun or, if harvested before bleaching, is of a pink, red, or black hue. This piece, though it had appeared black in the depths, was a rich lapis color, with marvelous highlights of deep green and gold appearing and fading as it was turned in the sunlight. And this was without the benefit of a jeweler's effort to polish the gem. It seemed it actually *had* been polished.

"Maybe it has been polished by the current brushing bits of sand and the like against it for years and years," Anthony suggested.

"That could be, but who really knows," I said. "One thing

I do know—this piece of coral is dead, long dead. From what I saw down there, its companions are in the same condition, probably for the same period of time. Who knows what killed it, but one thing is fairly certain: the coral on that plateau is not a renewable resource." Of such things is rarity made, and the combination of rarity and beauty ensured a high price and a lucrative harvest for those who gathered the stark limbs from below.

But gathering and selling rare or endangered coral was also illegal under Virgin Islands law and under the Convention on International Trade in Endangered Species. I needed to know if this coral met those criteria. The best way to learn was to ship my specimen to Agent Rosenblum for a look by his friend at US ICE. Fortunately, Virgin Gorda actually has "overnight" package services, albeit at exorbitant rates and with "overnight" often actually meaning two days. Three hours later, I placed half of the two-inch specimen of blue coral into the capable hands of FedEx, with a telephone commitment from the irascible Rosenblum to have an answer for me within an hour of receiving the package. Now all I had to do was wait.

But waiting is not something I am particularly good at. I have the scars to prove it.

Chapter Thirty-three

After what had happened to me beside the lonely well at sunset on Anegada a year ago, I thought I had become a better police officer. At least I told myself that. I told myself that now I looked at an investigation from all directions, not discounting any possibilities, eliminating no suspects until the case was resolved with certainty, by confession, or irrefutable evidence, or both.

Every instinct told me the investigation of Michele Konnerth's death and probable murder would be resolved through some link to the illegal harvest and smuggling of blue coral that she had stumbled upon. But because I was a better policeman now, because I looked at all the angles, I could not yet eliminate all other motives for her murder. And the most likely other motive had to relate to Michele Konnerth's messy personal life. The one loose end related to that personal life was Michele's lover Henna Beckles. The things that made Henna Beckles a loose end were the ripple-soled clogs she wore and the single ripple-soled print found in Michele Konnerth's abandoned boat.

It was well beyond the cocktail hour by the time De White Rasta and I set off to the Mine Shaft Cafe. We did have the luxury of the Virgin Gorda station's police vehicle, surrendered by Sergeant Chalwell after a mild "I told you you were on a fool's errand" response to my description of our wasted circumnavigation. I suppose he could not justify withholding the Land Rover's use; shortly after we arrived at the station, he left, walking home for the night, with Bullfoot assigned to the desk for the evening.

The Mine Shaft was a shimmering oasis in the pitch-dark slope above Copper Mine Bay. The usual raucous crowd of tourists and belongers, fueled by painkillers and piña coladas during the two hours from sundown to the present, announced itself over the sound of the Land Rover engine as we entered the parking lot.

"Just another day in party-dise," Anthony said as we walked to the entrance. Inside, most of the crowd hooted around a sailboat race in a cake pan of water, the boats wine corks with toothpick-and-paper-napkin sails, the two captains' inebriated charter customers in tank tops and sunburns, each huffing mightily to push their phellem schooner across an imaginary finish line first. The race was presided over by one of the charter captains, his hand raised, about to declare a winner by smacking the inch of water in the pan and drenching the participants and spectators. At home in Pittsburgh or Peoria, the majority of the crowd would have called this dull and childish, but after a week in the sun, and a quart of Cruzan rum and fruit juice, it was high entertainment.

The wood and stone bar supported six patrons too far gone to take part in the miniature regatta. The bartender's white-shirt-clad back was all that appeared as she dug around in the dim recesses below the wood countertop for who knows what.

"Excuse us, barkeep," Anthony said as we approached. The bartender surfaced fully, revealing blond hair, rosy cheeks, and the palest of pale complexions.

"Damn, left Belfast, the rain, and the wick boyfriend behind but there's no getting out beyond the peelers," she said in a thick Irish brogue.

"We're looking for Henna Beckles," I said. The dainty barkeep eyed my uniform. "She's not in trouble," I added.

"It's her evening off," the girl said.

De Rasta resurrected the easy, somewhat-stoned smile of his ganja-smoking days and laid on the charm. "Here, lass, we're hoping she can help us. One of her friends was killed."

"Ya mean Michele, the girl ate by the shark? Henny's been away in the head over that. I think she loved the girl. Killed the fish already, ain't youse?"

"Yes, but Ms. Beckles may be able to help us with some details for Michele's family," I said, not quite a lie.

"Well, she's most likely home, since that's what she's been at since it happened, home and work, won't go out for a bit o' fun."

"Where is home, miss?" De Rasta said, voice warm and low.

"A wee shack off North Road, down the third path as you head back toward The Valley." The bartender tossed her blond locks in De Rasta's direction and smiled back. "The cops here are nicer than in Belfast, not that it would take much."

The pitch black of the Virgin Gorda night had been alleviated somewhat by a gibbous moon. Even so, finding the third path took two turns around and a knock on an old woman's door. It was nearing ten o'clock when we bumped the Land Rover to the end of the correct path.

The bartender was right to call Henna's place a shack. It was cramped by Caribbean standards and ramshackle by any standard, its construction reminding me of the Cow Wreck Beach Bar and Grill on Anegada—a jumble of plywood, driftwood, and tin, adhering together through no discernible means. The pallid glow of a Coleman lantern shone in the single window as we approached. A slightly sleepy and more than slightly drunk Henna Beckles answered after half a dozen sharp raps on the buckling driftwood door.

"What time is it?" she said by way of greeting.

"Ten," I said. "I hope we are not interrupting your evening." A mostly empty bottle of white La Cana rum and a half-full glass of the same sat on the battered table in the middle of the single room. A tower of dirty dishes waited in a dry sink. There was a pungent curry-and-fried-onions odor in the air. And on every inch of wall not otherwise taken up by the single bed and the battered armchair rounding

out the shack's furnishings were paintings—marvelous paintings of scenes from the islands: Virgin Gorda, St. Lucia,
Barbados; a riot of colors, sea blues, verdant greens, hibiscus
pinks, velvet blacks; paintings of houses, birds, boats, people,
trees, flowers. The life of the islands depicted on the walls
of this drunken woman's shack.

Following my eyes, Henna Beckles said, "You didn't
come here at ten o'clock at night to admire my paintings."

"No, we didn't, but they are most impressive."

"Can't sell them. No gallery wants them. I couldn't even
sell them on the sidewalk to tourists back home in Speight-
stown. Same with my photographs. They are all in that trunk
under the bed. Good thing I know how to pour drinks, so I
can make a living. Speaking of drinks, either of you officers
want one?" She reached for her glass and took a healthy swig.

"Oh, remember I am not a police officer, Ms. Beckles,"
De White Rasta said, extending a hand. "We have met.
Anthony Wedderburn. I'm a civilian assisting Constable
Creque."

"Pleasure. You want a drink? No? Takes the edge off."
She tipped the glass to her lips again.

"Ms. Beckles," I said. "The last time we spoke I did not
have as much information as I do now. I have learned that a
boat may be involved in Michele's death. It has an unusual
hull color, blue and yellow checked. Did you ever see such a
boat?" I wanted to ask to see her ripple-soled clogs, but not
yet. I snuck a glance at her feet—bare.

"Never saw a yellow and blue checked boat. What kind?
Sailboat?" She slurred the "S" in "sailboat."

"No, more of a workboat." My eye fell on a painting across the room. "Like that."

I pointed. The boat in Henna Beckles's painting was a spot-on copy of the Lego model put together by Jemmy Trengrouse, except the hull of the boat was all green.

"That painting was done at the Virgin Gorda Yacht Harbour," Henna Beckles said. "The boat is a dive boat."

Of course. I had been on it. Mr. Gribanov's dive boat. No wonder the shape of Jemmy's model had been familiar to me.

"Yes, I know the boat," I said. "But the one I'm looking for has blue and yellow hull paint."

"Never seen nuthin like that. That all you wanted?"

"No. I also want to see a pair of shoes you own." May as well be direct. "Ripple-soled clogs. You wear them for work, I believe."

"Why?"

"We found a print on Michele Konnerth's rental boat. The *only* print on the boat. Of a ripple-soled shoe."

"Not mine."

"I saw you have ripple-soled clogs the last time I spoke with you at the Mine Shaft."

"I only wear them for work. I never wore them on her boat, or any boat. The salt water would ruin them."

No sense arguing. "Can I see the shoes?"

Henna sighed, dropped to her knees beside the bed, and pulled out the same clogs I had seen her wearing at the Mine Shaft. She wobbled to her feet and handed me the shoes. And started to cry, drunk crying, loud racking sobs, wiping her nose with the back of her hand.

I examined the clogs closely, looking for blood drops or stains on the soles and on the wild pattern of the uppers.

"I loved her. She was everything to me," Henna Beckles bellowed. Anthony took her in his arms, and she curled into his shoulder, snuffling noisily.

Nothing was apparent from my examination of the shoes. I needed to take them to Rollie Stoutt to see if he could find blood using chemical tests and to see if the sole matched the print found in Michele Konnerth's boat.

"I'll need to take your shoes, Ms. Beckles," I said.

Henna nodded dully and slumped from De Rasta's arms into the straight chair at the table. "They are my only ones," she mumbled.

"What?"

"They are my only shoes."

"I'm sorry but I need them for my investigation."

Henna Beckles looked away into the dark corner of her little shack, and waved De Rasta and me away with the back of her hand. As we went out the door, the clink of the rum bottle against the jar she used as a drinking glass punctuated the end of our interview.

As we stepped into the night, Henna Beckles wept. "She's gone. And now they even took my shoes."

Chapter Thirty-four

The next day dawned cloudless, windless, and hot. Dogs slept in the black shade of parked cars. Humidity, on most days pushed away by the trade winds, made the air an almost physical presence, heavy and sodden. In the police station, the cell walls perspired like a defendant in the witness box.

Anthony Wedderburn and I had spent the night in the cells. It had been too late to barge in on Jeanne Trengrouse by the time we left Henna Beckles's shack, so we had crashed at the police station. Bullfoot was dozing on desk duty when we came in. Sergeant Chalwell arrived at eight, accompanied by Mrs. Scatliff and enough johnnycake and coffee to feed and caffeinate an army.

After breakfast, Bullfoot walked off for his home, Sergeant Chalwell went out on road patrol, and I called Inspector Stoutt at Scenes of Crime in Road Town. With uncharacteristic helpfulness and, even more baffling, enthusiasm, Rollie volunteered to come to Virgin Gorda to examine and test Henna Beckles's shoes. "Been in the office too much lately," said the one man who never seemed to get enough of his office. An hour later, the *St. Ursula,* its bow carving the only irregularity in a sea as flat as a tabletop, coasted into the Yacht Harbour. Inspector Stoutt stood in the cockpit next to the helmsman, for once unaffected by a trip on the water.

"We can apply some Luminol to the shoes right here in the cabin," Rollie said, closing the curtains to the ports and rendering the cabin blacker than a cloudy, moonless night. Rollie produced a spray bottle, barely visible in the pitch black, and sprayed the shoes. "If there is blood, you'll see a blue luminescence, starting slowly at first and gradually increasing in intensity, unless the shoes have been cleaned with bleach, in which case the blue will kind of flash across the shoes rather than giving a blue glow."

Four minutes passed with no blue, or any other, glow. Rollie flipped on a light and opened the porthole curtains. "Nothing there. Let's check against the print." He pulled a photocopy of the shoe print from Michele Konnerth's rental boat from a folder and placed one of Henna Beckles's shoes alongside. "This shoe is smaller than the print, and see how the ripple pattern is tighter in the shoe than the photocopy? These have just transformed from being evidence to being just a pair of shoes."

Rollie handed the clogs back to me. In minutes, the *St. Ursula* cast off, pushed up on plane, and turned toward

Road Harbour. Inspector Stoutt had spent only fifteen minutes on Virgin Gorda, though that was more than enough time to clear Henna Beckles of responsibility for her lover's death.

"I must confess, I am not disappointed that Henna Beckles is not the killer," Anthony said as we walked along the Yacht Harbour's main dock.

"Nor am I, although it really does leave us at loose ends for a suspect," I said. My eyes fell on Yuri Gribanov's dive boat, tied up at a finger of the adjoining dock. "If only we could locate that blue and yellow boat. It's got to be almost identical to Gribanov's *Tankhauler,* just blue and yellow instead of green."

De Rasta halted and put his hand on my arm to stop me. "Or not," he said. Then, smiling: "Oh, Dean Fritzsimmons, forgive me, but first-form art was so long ago."

"What, Anthony?"

"Dean Fritzsimmons, my housemaster at primary school, taught art to all us tykes. We just wanted to color, or dabble in paints, but he drilled the color wheel into all us first formers. You know, blue and red combine to make violet, red and yellow make orange, and . . . blue and yellow make green. Maybe instead of looking for a boat that is blue and yellow, we should have been looking for a boat that is green."

"But if Jemmy saw a green boat, why wouldn't he build his model with green blocks, instead of mixing blue and yellow? Unless . . ." I never finished the sentence. Finishing the sentence was a waste of breath, breath I needed as I sprinted along the dock, through the Yacht Harbour grounds, and out onto Lee Road. De White Rasta running hard at my heels, we burst from the entrance at the same time a rickety red Toyota pickup truck turned from Millionaire Road onto Lee. I stepped in front of the truck, surprising the grizzled old-timer steering the vehicle's load of broken Sheetrock gingerly around the corner.

"Hey, policeman, you near got yourself killed, steppin' in front of me like that," he yelled as I opened the passenger door and jammed inside with Anthony close behind.

"Take us to Church Hill. Now," I said. The old fellow's eyes went wide for a beat, but he put the gas pedal to the floor, which moved the pickup to its top speed of thirty-five, and gripped the wheel like we were leading the car chase in *Bullitt*. Ten minutes later, he deposited us in front of Jeanne Trengrouse's cottage, received my thanks on behalf of the RVIPF, and sped off without another word.

A loud knock, a call of "It Babylon!" from an alarmed Sir Winston Churchill, and Jeanne appeared at the door.

"Teddy, I missed you last night," she said. Then, over my shoulder, "Oh, hello, Mr. Wedderburn. Is this official business?"

"It is. Is Jemmy here?"

"In his room."

I moved by her to Jemmy's room, announcing myself with a light knock on the door frame. Jemmy was in his usual position on the floor, placing the finishing touches on Rome's Colosseum, in its current state. The model of the ruin was done in a precise repeating sequence of blue, red, black, yellow, and white blocks, the same as all of Jemmy's past works other than the blue and yellow "bad-men boat." No green blocks. Never any green blocks.

Jeanne and Anthony crowded in the doorway behind me. "He never uses any green blocks," I said, more to myself than to either of them.

"That's right, Teddy," Jeanne said in response to my statement in the air. "Jemmy's first set of blocks had only the five original Lego colors. Those colors are the only ones he'll use. He just puts any new colors off to the side. He had so many that I finally gave away all the colors he wouldn't use to the O'Neill twins down the hill. Their blocks are all orange, gray, brown, purple, and, yes, green. Did you come all the way up here to talk about Legos?"

"As a matter of fact, yes." Then to Jemmy, "The bad-men boat, Jemmy."

The jagged wall of a Colosseum arch was being constructed at a blinding pace but I thought I detected the slightest tilt of Jemmy's head in my direction.

"The model of the bad-men boat, Jemmy, you made it blue and yellow. Blue and yellow make green, don't they, Jemmy?"

The small hands adding blocks to the Roman amphitheater stopped, but Jemmy did nothing to indicate agreement with my statement.

"The bad-men boat is green, isn't it, Jemmy, not blue and yellow?"

For the first time since I had known him, the child turned his eyes, the same intense blue as those of his mother, to mine. And nodded, in a movement I might have missed had

Jemmy not focused all my attention on him through the use of those eyes.

"I think we have found the bad-men boat, Jemmy, but only you can say for sure. Will you come with me to look at the boat we've found and tell me if it's the one you saw when the bad men put the lady overboard?"

The blue eyes remained fixated on mine with no hint of the thought process I was certain was taking place behind them. Then, just as I had concluded that Jemmy had left our conversation and returned to that place in his mind where he spent most of his time, he stepped toward me.

And took me by the hand.

Chapter Thirty-five

I thought about knocking on some of Jeanne Trengrouse's neighbors' doors until I found one with a telephone and calling to try to reach Sergeant Chalwell to give us a ride to the Yacht Harbour. I hesitated because he was probably on patrol far away at the North Sound and wouldn't appreciate the long trip back. Especially if I was asking him to abandon showing the flag to all the tourists and resort owners there to transport a child he considered an unreliable witness and his troublemaking mother to follow up on a clue based on Lego blocks and an interpretation, however accurate, of the elementary aspects of the color wheel. I somehow didn't feel I would be successful in explaining it all in a way that would bring Chalwell hurrying back from whatever shaded bar or sun-kissed beach he was policing at the moment.

Reading my mood, Jeanne Trengrouse solved our transportation problem by disappearing behind the cottage, to return with her rusty bike, followed by another even rustier, and another that was nothing short of a total wreck. The largest, assigned by her to me, had a back fender that would accommodate Jemmy. Seeing the bicycles, Sir Winston kicked up such a squawking fuss that Jeanne brought him out to ride along.

It had been years since I was on a bicycle but the old adage about riding a bike proved true. It did not hurt that most of the trip was downhill, with the trade wind, now stirring slightly, at our backs. The five of us coasted away from the house down Church Hill, a bizarre combination of police caravan, family outing, and low-budget traveling circus. It was a pleasant midday ride, with a visibly nervous White Rasta wobbling in advance and gaily laughing Jeanne on my left, the fire-engine-red Sir Winston, feathers fluffed, calling, "Make way!" loudly and regularly, poised on her shoulder as we cycled through The Valley to the Yacht Harbour.

The Yacht Harbour bar hummed with happy conversation from the noonday drinkers as we pedaled past, but the docks and harbor basin itself were quiet.

"Is the bad-men boat here, Jemmy?" I asked, kneeling beside him. He took my hand and marched slowly along the first arm of the docks, stopping at the dock finger where Gribanov's *Tankhauler* tugged lightly at its lines.

"Bad-men boat," Jemmy said, standing to the right and slightly behind me to shield himself from whatever evil might lurk within the green hull.

As it turned out, no evil lurked there. I called, "Permission to come aboard," as is customary. There was no response, so I stepped over the coaming onto the deck. A quick two steps down into the cabin showed everything stowed and shipshape. There was no one on the boat.

Without any warrant to search, I did not want to taint any evidence that might be on *Tankhauler,* so I stepped back onto the dock.

"Anthony, would you please escort Ms. Trengrouse and Jemmy home?" I said. "I am going to the station to see if we can get transport to bring in Mr. Gribanov for questioning. Switch bicycles with me so you can carry Jemmy."

With little enthusiasm, De Rasta said, "I think I can manage it, now that I have my sea legs back."

"I'll get your bike back to you later," I told Jeanne.

"Later is fine," she said. "I'll keep a light on." Her eyes said she meant it.

I watched humans and avians turn and begin the long trek uphill before heading for the station.

The police station was open but empty when I pulled on the front door, with the eerie quiet that an almost-always-occupied place takes on when it is vacant. I was not two feet inside the door when the station's sole telephone began to ring.

"Virgin Gorda Police Station, Constable Creque," I answered, leaning against the desk.

"What a friggin' waste of law enforcement talent, havin' you answer the phone," Agent Rosenblum said at the other end of the line.

"We do what we have to do. It is a small operation here in the BVI, as you know, Agent Rosenblum."

"Small operation or not, the way you turn things up, you should be out in the field. If I had you on my team, you would not be answering the damn phone." Astounding. A compliment from Agent Rosenblum. A sure sign the apocalypse was upon us.

He continued. "I got the sample you FedExed just as my buddy from ICE was wrapping up a meeting here. I showed it to him and he nearly wet his drawers. That stick you sent is a piece of the blue coral half the customs outfits in the Western Hemisphere are trying to find the source of. ICE wants to know, now, where you got it. I'm guessing off a boat because it stunk like the bottom of a bilge when I opened the package."

"I didn't get it from a boat. I got it off the bottom of the ocean. I found a forest of the stuff down here off a small island, Fallen Jerusalem. I think it may be the source of the coral being smuggled to China."

"That's great. That's friggin' amazing. I'll let the ICE weenies know and I'll bet they get in touch with your government to set up a joint operation to shut down the smuggling."

For a beat or two, I was elated. For a beat or two, it seemed like the right resolution. US ICE, with me and others from Her Majesty's Customs, would stake out the coral forest and catch Mr. Gribanov and his accomplices in the act. It might take a while but it would all work out.

Then I thought about Tom and Judy Konnerth, mourning their only daughter. And I thought about Yuri Gribanov, slick enough to bargain his way out of the KGB. It was easy to envision a scenario where a captured Gribanov would negotiate a deal to make some or all of the smuggling charges against him go away in return for divulging the names of others on higher rungs of the smuggling ladder. Maybe in the process he bargains himself to lesser charges, or no charges, for the death of Michele Konnerth. I thought about the sound of Tom Konnerth's voice, in far-off Blue Earth, Minnesota, breaking as he talked about the death of his little girl. And I knew I could not wait for ICE, and the bureaucracy of a joint operation, and the shrewd negotiations of Yuri Gribanov that were sure to follow.

That was not what I told Agent Rosenblum. I told him, "Great. I can use the help. I'll keep things on hold down here for a few days to give the ICE folks time to put things together." It was the last thing I intended to do. I would move forward as fast as I could to button up the case against Yuri Gribanov for the murder of Michele Konnerth. I determined to deliver what little peace of mind I could to those two suffering old people who would be passing their last years alone.

"You know, Constable," Agent Rosenblum said, "we could use someone like you at JITFS. The British Virgin Islands are not represented on my strike team. I could put in a word with your boss, make some calls."

"Thank you, Agent Rosenblum, but I am satisfied where I am."

"Think about it, Teddy. And good luck with the blue coral." The line went dead.

I had plenty of time to think because RVIPF regulations required secure transportation to be available for the arrest of any suspects, and also required two officers, with at least one armed, to take part. I had to wait for both, which meant waiting for Sergeant Chalwell to return from his road patrol. It meant spending the latter part of the morning cooling my heels when my heels and the rest of me wanted nothing more than to collar the Russian and bring him in.

Chapter Thirty-six

The station door finally opened a few minutes before noon. My expectation of help was dashed when the figure entering backlit against the midday sun was that of Mrs. Scatliff, a tiffin of food, from which savory fragrances emanated, in each hand.

"This the sergeant's lunch he want delivered but it's enough for the both of you if you not piggish 'bout it. Conch stew an' peas an' rice. The stew's made with Scotch bonnet peppers, the way the sergeant likes." Mrs. Scatliff plopped the tiffins on the desk and exited as Anthony Wedderburn entered. He appeared to have spent the time since we parted in a steam bath, his face scarlet and his blond locks plastered against his forehead.

"I'm surprised to see you here, Teddy. I thought you and the local gendarmerie would be out chasing down Mr. Gribanov," he said. I explained the need to wait for transport and backup and filled him in on my conversation with Agent Rosenblum.

"So your old friend Agent Rosenblum comes through for you." A smirk played across De Rasta's lips. He knew my history with Agent Rosenblum and relished the turn it had taken. "It will probably take the Yanks a couple of days to ready their operation. Will we be returning to Anegada in the meantime? I'm becoming homesick for Belle Lloyd's conch fritters and sparkling conversation, not to mention the sophisticated ambience of the Cow Wreck Beach Bar and Grill."

"You'll have to wait a few days, Anthony. We're not going anywhere except to bring in Yuri Gribanov for the murder of Michele Konnerth. And then we are going to spend whatever time is necessary interrogating him until we learn the identity of his accomplice."

"Interrogate the former spy for the Evil Empire, eh? I'm sure the techniques you honed during your many years extracting confessions from the criminal hordes on Anegada will come in handy for that. Are you not going to wait for US ICE?"

Anthony's jest stung more than a little but only strengthened my resolve. "I intend to accomplish everything we need to accomplish with Mr. Gribanov before they ever arrive."

Anthony's response had only reached the stage of the arching of a skeptical eyebrow when Sergeant Chalwell bustled in the door. His crisp shirt and cool countenance were in sharp contrast to Anthony's appearance, attesting to a morning of "patrol" cruising the byways of Virgin Gorda without ever stepping from the air-conditioned comfort of the RVIPF Land Rover.

"I see the old girl's been in and brought lunch." He rubbed his hands and smacked his lips in exaggerated anticipation of Mrs. Scatliff's conch stew. "Appears to be more than enough for the three of us to share."

"Sergeant Chalwell, I need to speak to you about my investigation—" I began.

"Well, is it an emergency?" Chalwell interrupted.

A moment's hesitation and a truthful "no" on my part followed.

"Then we can talk over lunch. No sense letting this get cold." He clattered open the tiffin of stew and inhaled deeply the rich scent of meaty conch, lime, thyme, bay leaf, and searing Scotch bonnet pepper wafting from the pot. Five minutes later, we three were seated around the station house desk, a paper plate of steaming pigeon peas and rice covered with conch stew before each of us, the painful-pleasurable fire of the first mouthful tracing the food's progress from our tongues to the pit of our bellies, our foreheads beaded with pops of perspiration giving just enough relief to encourage further consumption.

"So, Constable, what did you need to talk to me about? Did you find that blue and yellow boat?" Sergeant Chalwell's questions came with just enough sarcasm in his voice to convey that he thought we would never find it, primarily because such a boat didn't exist. It was like when my dada used to ask about the success of my treasure-hunting forays when I was a child.

"In a manner of speaking, yes," I said. I explained about seeing the boat in Henna Beckles's painting, and Jemmy Trengrouse's subsequent identification of the *Tankhauler* as the "bad-men boat."

"I want to bring in Mr. Gribanov for questioning." When I said this, the sergeant's face soured. "After lunch," I added, hoping that it was only the prospect of an interrupted meal that had darkened Sergeant Chalwell's countenance.

"On the word of that half-witted kid and his trouble-making bitch mother? Not on my watch." Obviously, word of my relationship with Jeanne Trengrouse had not found its way to Sergeant Chalwell. I hoped.

"I can't ignore the lead without any questioning," I said.

"What makes you think it is truly a lead?" Sergeant Chalwell put down his fork and placed his hands on each side of his plate. I could have sworn he was going to push himself up from the desk and leap across it at me. Instead, he seemed to take a mental step back, and his body relaxed. "What makes you think that when Jemmy Trengrouse says the *Tankhauler* is the 'bad man's boat' he is not talking about the prior accusation?"

"The prior accusation?" I was lost for a second.

"Yes, the prior accusation that Jemmy Trengrouse made. I told you about it. He accused a prominent Virgin Gorda citizen of indecent assault. I investigated and determined the accusation was unfounded. His mother pushed the matter over my head, all the way to crown counsel. A charge was preferred and a trial occurred, with an acquittal as its result. The prominent citizen, whose name I avoided mentioning to keep from stigmatizing him based on the false charges, was Yuri Gribanov. Mr. Gribanov has been a model citizen of Virgin Gorda, both before and after the charges, and I will not have him dragged through the mud again just because that . . . child . . . says 'bad man' whenever he sees anything associated with Yuri."

I was taken aback. Was Jemmy just reasserting that Yuri Gribanov was a bad man because of what may have occurred in the past but was not proven? Doubt crept in, doubt about my instincts, doubt about my abilities as a police officer, the same doubts I had experienced in the past, in the horrific case that had won the Queen's Police Medal for me and had extracted a cost from me that could never be squared by ten, a hundred, a thousand, QPMs. I reasoned that I had somehow developed the necessary instincts from the experience of that, my one and only case to date. Well, I told myself that. So I persisted.

"I only want to interview the man," I said. "It doesn't need to be custodial. It doesn't even need to be here at the station. I'll just ask him some questions at his home, or business."

Sergeant Chalwell looked down at a paper napkin on the table between us, picked it up, wiped his hands, and tossed the crumpled napkin in the wastebasket beside the desk. "I didn't think it would be necessary to tell you this but Yuri Gribanov has an alibi to account for his time on the night of Michele Konnerth's death."

"Who?"

"Me." Chalwell stared at his half-eaten plate of stew.

"What?"

"I'm not proud of this but it is nothing illegal or immoral. You know Yuri is my friend. Sometimes we go out in the evening, drink some rum, chat up some belonger sistren or tourist pum-pum in a bar, have some laughs, do some limin'. The right kind of girls like the badge, or if they don't, they think whispering in the ear of an ex-spy makes them a James Bond girl. It's all harmless fun.

"The night Michele Konnerth died we were out, spent the evening in the North Sound, at Mouse Milk's place, Hog Heaven. The crowd was sparse, and no unattached ladies, so we leaned pretty heavily toward the drinking side of things. We closed the bar down at three a.m. When we left, we were both pretty soused, though not completely legless drunk. I had the Land Rover and drove us to Yuri's house up at Olde Yard. He passed out in the passenger seat on the way. When we got to his place, I carried him in and tossed him on his bed. I decided to crash on his couch rather than drive the rest of the way home. While no one's on the road on Virgin Gorda at three thirty a.m., there was no sense taking any more chances than I already had.

"I was still there the next morning when Elsie Scatliff got word to me that Bullfoot was looking for me, that there had been a shark attack at The Baths. When I left at seven o'clock, Yuri was still in his bed, his clothes on, in the same position I'd put him in when I'd brought him in. He didn't go anywhere after three thirty in the morning. He was in no shape to."

Sergeant Chalwell looked me in the eyes, his own weighted

not with shame but with mild defiance, a misbehaving child caught in the act, knowing his behavior was bad but not worthy of severe punishment. Or, in this case, any punishment at all. True, if DC Lane got wind of this, there would be a suspension for driving an RVIPF vehicle while admittedly intoxicated. Chalwell counted on me to not turn him in, to be one of the boys and not rat out a fellow officer. And he was right; I knew when I wrote up the investigative notes, the story he had told me would be sufficiently sanitized to avoid his conduct being called into question. I would do it because that was the code, what policemen did for their comrades. I had not learned that on Anegada, where I was the only officer, but I had seen enough American television to absorb the lesson.

"All right, Sergeant Chalwell. I guess Mr. Gribanov has an alibi," I said. The sergeant nodded, rose from his seat, and walked out without another word.

Anthony Wedderburn cleared his throat and said, "I guess that takes care of the green-boat theory. Where do we go from here, old man?"

Where indeed.

Chapter Thirty-seven

    De White Rasta picked at a pigeon pea, the last on the stained plate before him. A fly circled in through the open station door and headed straight for the remains of lunch, ready to contest De Rasta's sovereignty over the last crumb. Tasty as it had been at the start, the lunch I finished in silence after Sergeant Chalwell's departure rested on my stomach with the unease of a lone mouse at a cat convention.

    The investigation of the death of Michele Konnerth was at an impasse. Two suspects were in custody, the swinish Robin Kingsmill and his unfortunate sidekick Johnny Harley, but the physical evidence I thought I had against them had fizzled. I had to admit to myself that there would be no basis to consider them suspects, and certainly not to hold them, were it not for Kingsmill's arrogant attitude and foolish attempt to escape arrest. Henna Beckles was off the list, eliminated because her shoe didn't match the print on the victim's abandoned boat and, more important, because she was utterly destroyed by Michele's death. Anyone who loved and mourned as deeply could not carry off a murder as calculated as that which had befallen the young doctor. And there was no longer Yuri Gribanov, who might have been a lot of things but probably was not a smuggler of rare coral and certainly not a murderer, given his airtight alibi from the highest police official on Virgin Gorda. I could surely corroborate the alibi with the bartender, and probably with a handful of patrons at Hog Heaven, if I cared to make the effort.

If I cared to make the effort. And why was it an effort? Because ever since I had come to Virgin Gorda, Isaac Chalwell had been putting roadblocks in front of me. And discouraging contact with and denigrating the testimony of the one real witness to the crime. Even making movement around the island difficult by limiting—no, withholding—access to the police vehicle.

A poor policeman, the kind of policeman I had once been, would not have made the effort. Why bother to confirm an alibi provided by a non-suspect police officer, someone who was by definition a reputable witness? A poor police officer might have said maybe this just needed to go in the books as unsolved. Or maybe now the time was right to wait for US ICE to come in and see what they turned up. That would have been a poor policeman's instinct.

I was done with that, had left it behind as I crawled bleeding on the sand on a desolate beach on Anegada a year ago. My instinct now said something was not right. My instinct now said a good cop would follow up.

"Come on, Anthony. We are going to pay a visit to Hog Heaven," I said.

"Sounds charming," De Rasta said. "I hope we are not walking."

"Then get your thumb ready and be prepared to show a discreet but enticing amount of leg."

It was not leg but a smile that De Rasta used to secure our transportation. Ten minutes' walk from the police station, he flashed his toothy grin and flagged a mud-brown Datsun to the side of Handsome Bay Road. This was after four previous vehicles had not even decelerated in the face of my authoritative efforts as an RVIPF constable in full uniform.

"Cheer up, Teddy. It took years of practice for me to get it right," Anthony teased as we squeezed into the rear seat of the aging car. The driver and her companion, two belongers on their way to their jobs as housekeepers at Leverick Bay, giggled at De Rasta's bad jokes and puns all the way to the dusty turnout for Hog Heaven.

I had expected Hog Heaven to be the typical tourist bar, with its obligatory collection of island kitsch decorations and walls painted gaudy primary colors. A place that roasted a pig on Saturday night to lend credence to the name. But one look as we approached told me that Hog Heaven was not about roasting pigs but an homage to Harley-Davidson motorcycles. It was a biker bar, a thing I had seen on TV. I didn't know such things existed in the BVI. A full-sized Harley

Sportster was parked inside, just to the left of the bar. Hubcaps, club vests, black T-shirts, German army helmets, American flags, Harley posters, neon beer signs, and assorted items of cast-off leather clothing decorated the dark walls, giving a claustrophobic feel to the place. The smattering of early-afternoon customers didn't fit the look. Belongers all, they wore the usual Virgin Gorda uniform of board shorts and colorful tattered T-shirts.

There was no one behind the bar, so I asked a dread-locked geezer seated at the far end where the proprietor was.

"Mouse Milk? Him out back moppin' de pig," the man said, then shouted, "Hey, Mouse Milk, police here for you an' it ain't Chalwell."

I seated myself at the bar and dropped into patois. "Why dey call he Mouse Milk?"

The old man laughed. "Him raised on mouse milk. You see. But he cook a good pig, you stay round fa dinner."

The back door banged open and closed, seemingly on its own, and the scent of roasting pork wafted in. Then a dwarf, clad head to toe in biker leathers, popped up behind the bar. I saw he stood on a purpose-built step-box that brought him up high enough to reach the bar but still failed to put him on eye level with his customers.

"Are you Mr. . . . Mouse Milk?"

"I him. Dis my place. What I do fa you?"

"I'm Constable Teddy Creque and I'm here as part of an investigation about the lady who was killed by a shark at The Baths."

"I hear you got de criminal, mon. Him a bull shark, yes?"

"Yes, right. But there are some follow-up issues. The night before the shark attack, six nights ago, was a man named Yuri Gribanov in here?"

"Yuri, yeah, him come in two, three night a week. Yeah, he here. Him wit Sergeant Isaac Chalwell of de Royal Virgin Islands Po-lice Force, like usual. You could ask de sergeant dat, you don't need to find dat out from I." Mouse Milk furrowed his brow.

"I know. We're just trying to fill in some details that Sergeant Chalwell could not remember," I lied. Mouse Milk's quizzical expression said he didn't quite believe me. I continued on. "Did Mr. Gribanov have a great deal to drink that night?"

"No, not dat much. He here wit Isaac for de usual two, three hours, and he mebbe have two rum in de time."

"When did he leave?"

"Him an' Isaac leave together, what, 'bout nine, Mobie?" Mouse Milk directed his question to my geezer friend.

Mobie shook his dreads in agreement. "Yeah, dat 'bout right. Yuri an' Isaac, dey never stay late less dere some pum-pum in here dey think dey got a chance at. Dat night dey gone long 'fore I got home at ten. I 'member 'cause de old lady ax me what I doin' home so early, interrup' her TV watchin'."

"You sure?" My question was general, open to both Mobie and Mouse Milk. They both looked at each other and gave an affirmative nod.

"Dey not in trouble, Yuri an' Isaac?" Mouse Milk said. "Dey both uphill mans, sight?"

"No, no, just cleaning up some details, loose ends before my final report. Thank you, gentlemen."

"Hey, Constable, you stay 'while, pig be ready. Best pig in de Virgin Islands." Mouse Milk smiled. " 'Sides, we got a po-lice discount fo' you and you friend."

"Smells great, but we have to be moving on, get back to the station. Thank you again, Mr. . . . Mouse Milk."

"Do you believe what they said?" I asked De Rasta as we trudged west on the road that followed the spine of Fanny Hill. The prospect of a ride back to The Valley seemed remote; even the stunning views of Mosquito Island, Prickly Pear Island, and Saba Rock, emerald jewels in the azure pool of the North Sound, couldn't brighten the mood.

"I do, old man. They had no reason to mislead us," Anthony said.

"So Chalwell lied to us."

"I think those chaps would recognize legless drunk if they saw it. And, despite the fact that I saw neither a clock in the entire establishment nor a watch on any arm there, including that of Mr. Mouse Milk, I think they are able to ascertain the difference between nine p.m. and three a.m. So, yes, I think Sergeant Chalwell lied to us."

"That means, at best, Chalwell is covering for his friend Gribanov and, at worst, they are working together harvesting and smuggling blue coral. And maybe they are both responsible for Michele Konnerth's death."

"Jemmy Trengrouse did say he saw a white man and a

black man on the boat Michele was thrown from," Anthony said.

"Jemmy and Jeanne are in danger," I said. "We have to get them off the island and bring in extra officers to arrest Gribanov and Chalwell." I started to jog and De Rasta fell in beside me.

We had covered a quarter of a mile and just broken a sweat when a bright blue four-by-four with rental-car plates and four sunburned occupants approached, bound for the North Sound. "I'll handle this one, Anthony," I said as I stepped into the middle of the dirt road and raised my hand to halt them.

Chapter Thirty-eight

The twenty-year-old Suzuki Samurai that skidded to a stop before me was barely large enough to hold the four tourists aboard, let alone De White Rasta and me. An outraged burst of staccato French, punctuated by mysterious hand gestures the meaning of which I was probably better off not knowing, greeted me when I pulled open the driver's door.

"Do you speak French, Anthony?" I asked, hoping to quell the uproar through communication in the group's native tongue.

"I had a classical education. Latin and Greek."

So much for diplomacy. I grabbed the driver by the arm and pulled him as gently as I could from behind the wheel, all the while making what I hoped were reassuring noises to the other occupants. I jumped into the driver's seat, De Rasta wedged himself onto the rear bench between two plump matrons, and we were off, leaving the driver stamping and shouting in the middle of the lonely road, far from, well, anything.

Twenty-five minutes later we slued to a stop in front of the cottage on Church Hill. My French passengers, by now convinced they were about to die in a Caribbean backwater at the hands of a crazed native policeman, displayed momentary relief when Anthony and I exited and then set up a roar of Gallic epithets as they turned the car and sped out of sight. In seconds, only the tinkle and ding of wind chimes disturbed the drowsy afternoon silence.

I rushed the door, banged loudly on the frame, and when there was no answer, save a squawk from Sir Winston, pushed inside, Anthony at my heels.

"Jeanne! Jemmy!" I called. The main room was empty, as were the bedrooms. The chimes now took on an ominous quality, their previously happy tintinnabulations transformed to the mournful bong of funeral church bells. A stockpot of callaloo bubbled on the small stove, its brilliant green color an indication that it had not been cooking long. A ripe mango stood on a cutting board on the counter, a knife placed beside it, as if it had been put down to answer the door.

De Rasta and I moved outside, calling, the only answer the whisper of the trade wind and the ting of the chimes. After circling the cottage in opposite directions, Anthony and I reconvened inside. There was no sign of anything out of the ordinary, certainly none of struggle or abduction and no clue as to where Jeanne and Jemmy had gone.

"When I left them, I told them to remain here, as we

might need Jemmy for identification of Gribanov when you brought him in," Anthony said. "I thought they would be safe here."

"So did I. And they may be all right, Anthony. Maybe they just stepped out for a short walk," I said, without conviction. Sir Winston Churchill leaned and swayed on his perch, squawking and frilling his crest like an aging fan dancer in a small-time burlesque show.

"If only the bird could speak intelligently," De Rasta said. On cue, the flawless British diction of Yuri Gribanov rumbled from deep inside the throat of the gaudy macaw. At first, the bird spoke so rapidly that the words being said were unintelligible, running and tumbling over each other in a mess that could be discerned as British-accented speech but little else. Then the bird's shining black pupil seemed to display comprehension, and the words slowed to the pace of normal conversation. The result was as if Gribanov stood with us in the room.

"Take care, madam, and make no quick moves. I have used this gun before and will not hesitate to do so with you if necessary. You and the boy put on your shoes. You are coming with me for a little boat ride."

"Well, I'll be judged a monkey's uncle," Anthony said, the closest I have ever heard him come to an expression of shock or surprise.

I wanted to say to the bird, Repeat that, just to make sure I had heard correctly, but Anthony was already out the door, banging down the front step and around to the rear for one of the bicycles that were there. I followed him, hesitating for

a moment on the porch, hoping to hear a car we could com-
mandeer on the road. The only sounds were the whisper of
the wind and the incessant chimes. I bounded around the
back. Thirty seconds later found us racing our bikes like two
schoolboys on a lark. But we both knew it was no lark; the
lives of Jeanne and Jemmy hung in the balance.

The trip was downhill and went quickly along Crabbe
Hill Road until I drew to a halt at its intersection with
Millionaire Road. A choice had to be made. I assumed Sir
Winston's words about the boat ride meant that Gribanov
intended to dispose of Jeanne and Jemmy at sea, possibly
in the same way as Michele Konnerth. His boat had been
at the Yacht Harbour, and while we might not catch him
before he cleared the harbor, there was a decent chance of
at least seeing the boat's course if we went there immediately.

Or I could go to the police station and call for assistance.
I could also send Anthony there while continuing to the
Yacht Harbour myself. The problem with either Anthony's
or my going to the station was Sergeant Chalwell. If the sergeant was fully in league with Gribanov, we might encounter an armed Chalwell, and we were not armed. My old
Webley .38/200 was in the console locker of the *Lily B* and it
would just take too much time to retrieve.

I decided to go after Gribanov and I couldn't send De
Rasta to the station alone. After ten seconds of hesitation,
I said, "Come on," to Anthony, and pushed off toward the
Yacht Harbour.

"Get the barman to let you in the office and call headquarters," I said to Anthony as we pulled in the gate. "Tell them we have a hostage situation on a boat, the *Tankhauler*, which has just left the Yacht Harbour and we need the *St. Ursula* and armed officers as soon as possible. Tell them that I am in pursuit in the *Lily B*."

From the corner of my eye, I caught the image of De Rasta throwing his bike down and running into the bar as I sped down the dock to the *Lily B*. At the end of the next dock finger over, Garfield, the boy I had spoken to a couple days earlier, sat hand-lining in a blue-striped grunt.

"Garfield," I called. "Have you seen any boats go out in the last hour?"

"Yep, Constiple Teddy," the boy said, tossing the wiggling fish into his dirty Styrofoam cooler. "Seen two. Two drunk mens from de bar took out a Moorin's sailboat 'bout half hour ago. Almost hit de seawall on de way out." Garfield pointed to the northwest. "You can see 'em out dere now. Dey de one wit' de luffin' sail."

I was readying the *Lily B* while Garfield spoke, checking the gas tank connected to the outboard to see if it had enough fuel. Almost empty.

"What about the other boat?" I said.

"De dive boat," Garfield said, concentrating on cutting a chunk of bait and threading it onto his hook. "De Russian dude owns de dive shop was on it, wit' a lady and a little boy, littler den me."

I checked the spare gas tank. Empty. "Which way did they go?"

"Dey went dat way." The boy pointed south, in the

direction of The Baths and Fallen Jerusalem. " 'Bout fifteen minutes ago."

The breeze was freshening as I cast off my lines and idled
the one hundred feet to the Yacht Harbour's rusting one-
pump gas dock. No one attended the pump, not surprising
in a sailor's harbor on a sailor's island. I fueled, left a twenty-
dollar bill and a note on the pump, and was pulling away
when a shout and a thump heralded the arrival of De White
Rasta aboard. He had completed the call to headquarters
and sprinted along the dock, jumping the last four feet when
I failed to hear his calls over the sound of the *Lily B*'s outboard.

Picking himself up from the deck, Anthony said, "You
could have pulled away a tad faster, old man, to make it more
of a challenge."

"Sorry, Anthony. I didn't expect you to come. This might
be—no, this will be—difficult and dangerous. I can still drop
you at a dock finger before we clear the harbor."

"Nonsense, old man. I would not miss it for the world.
'Dangerous' and 'difficult' are my middle names." De Rasta
beamed. "Well, actually Percival is my middle name, after
my dear mother's favorite uncle, the Viscount Inchcape, and
Bronwyn is my third name, after my papa's bird-shooting
chum Baron Monteagle of Brandon. Ah, there it is, too much
information. Suffice it to say that I understand the perils
and join you in harm's way with full awareness."

"Suit yourself," I said. There was no time to quibble.
"Hang on."

I pushed the throttle forward and had the *Lily B* up on

plane before we cleared the harbor break wall. Turning
south along the coast, I swept the horizon, hoping my skill
at spotting bonefish on sun-dazzled flats would translate to
picking out the profile of Gribanov's dive boat in open water.
It proved remarkably difficult. My eyes, trained by long experience to penetrate the surface of placid water seeking
movement and shadow, were seldom used, like those of a
blue-water sailor, to discern objects at the distant edge of
the earth's curvature.

As we ran full out, Anthony rummaged in the console
locker to come up with my battered binoculars. An ancient
set, they had no image stabilization nor any other modern
bells and whistles, and they had been dropped dozens of
times, including once in the water. One lens was slightly
fogged but Anthony, once he found them, braced against the
console and in two minutes was pointing to a microscopic
dot on the horizon.

"I think that's them, though it's difficult to be sure," Anthony shouted above the thundering outboard. "The boat is
the correct size and I think the hull color is right. I cannot
make out how many people are on board."

The boat followed a course tighter to shore than ours.
I corrected our heading and pushed the speed as high as
I dared in the moderate chop. The *Lily B* became fully air-
borne over the troughs, thumping down with teeth-jarring
smacks on the crests before roaring into the air again. De
Rasta abandoned all pretense of looking through the binoculars, grimly clinging to the stanchion post at the side of the
console, trying to absorb the shocks with his knees flexed.

The *Tankhauler* was larger than the *Lily B* and by definition slower. This would be especially true because Gribanov would not know he was being pursued yet, and wouldn't push as hard so as to have a more comfortable ride. But the head start he had would put him at the southern end of Virgin Gorda well before we could reach him. From there he could, if he discerned he was being chased, run north and duck from sight in one of the many small coves on Virgin Gorda, or head south using Fallen Jerusalem, Broken Jerusalem, Round Rock, and Ginger Island to mask his location.

I backed the engine on the *Lily B* to idle. I hoped it was the right strategy. I hoped I wouldn't regret it.

More than that, I hoped I wasn't chasing a boat with a cargo of corpses.

Chapter Thirty-nine

"What are you doing?" Anthony said. "We were gaining on them!"

"We won't catch them before they reach the end of the island and I don't want to tip them off to us yet. It would be too easy for them to hide from us if they sped up now."

De White Rasta watched with the binoculars as the *Tankhauler* swung to starboard at the south end of Virgin Gorda, below Penn Hill. "They seem to have turned left, but I can't be certain," he said after a couple minutes. "They have disappeared."

I shoved the throttle forward. The *Lily B* responded like a Thoroughbred to the whip. In moments we were on plane again, our speed at the maximum the hull would tolerate in the deepwater swell.

I set a course on a straight line to Gribanov's last position, turning to starboard around the southern point of the island after ten minutes of running hard. I backed off the throttle as we took an easterly heading to provide a smoother platform while Anthony scanned with the binoculars.

"Nothing," De Rasta said after two 180-degree sweeps. He dropped the field glasses from his eyes to look to me, hoping for direction. I had none to give. We drifted and slopped up and down in the higher swell coming in from the open ocean for five excruciating minutes, scouring the empty sea for any sign of Gribanov and his boat.

"We may just have to pick a direction and go with it," Anthony finally said. The prospect was not appealing. I knew if Gribanov had headed straight east, out to sea, after clearing the headland at the south end of the island, we probably would have picked him out searching with the binoculars. That meant he had opted to run either north along Virgin Gorda or south to Fallen Jerusalem and the uninhabited islands beyond. North or south offered a myriad of bays and coves to serve as hiding places. Or quiet spots to carry out an execution.

I was just about to turn to port toward Fallen Jerusalem when I caught a flash of reflected sunlight out of the corner of my eye, to the left along the rugged shore of Virgin Gorda near the abandoned copper mine.

"There, Anthony." I pointed.

"I don't see anything, Teddy," De Rasta said after a breathless three minutes.

A decision had to be made, a decision the consequences of which could mean life or death to Jeanne and Jemmy. Maybe the flash had been an automobile windscreen reflecting on a drive along the headlands, or, more likely, the sun glancing off the port of a boat hauling fish traps along the shore.

I gunned the engine and spun the wheel to take a course toward the cliffs of Copper Mine Point. We bounced hard in the sea swell. Anthony kept a death grip on the console stanchion to avoid being flung overboard; I did the same with the steering wheel.

Copper Mine Point rapidly transformed from a blurry promontory at the edge of the sky to a towering citadel of rock above a frothing sea. I lowered our speed, and Anthony searched the water between us and the ragged brink where the crags met the water. The pitching of the *Lily B*, the crash of the waves against the cliffs, and their rebound and reflection of the midday sun produced a confusion of motion that would have confounded the sharpest eye. It was impossible to focus on any location or object, impossible to pick something from all the movement and dazzle. It reminded me of searching for bonefish on a windy day with the sun moving in and out of the clouds. The trick in that situation was not to focus or to search, but to relax the mind and the eye, and allow the image of the fish to come to them.

I drew a breath, relaxed the focus of my eyes, and took a mental step back, allowing my eyes and mind to open and accept, as I had so often on the bonefish flats.

Movement, not on the water but on the rocky hillside above, attracted my attention. A speck against the gray-tan of the hill face. Now I could focus and parse the single speck into three, moving almost imperceptibly against the back-drop of stone and scrub.

"I need the field glasses, Anthony," I said, and when I brought the image into focus, there was the barrel-shaped figure of Yuri Gribanov, pushing Jeanne Trengrouse and Jemmy ahead of him. They were on a narrow track that could not be discerned with the naked eye, a path that led upward to the ruins of the copper mine where Jeanne and I had picnicked just days, and what now seemed an eternity, ago. Just then, Jeanne stumbled and fell to her knees, and I saw Gribanov roughly jerk her to her feet and shove her on-ward.

"That's them," I said, opening the throttle wide on a di-rect line to the intersection of cliff and sea below where they walked. It would only be a matter of minutes before Grib-anov would hear the engine noise and see us. And he would know we had seen him, his position on the barren hillside as exposed as ours on the open sea.

The unfamiliar coast did not present any ready landing places for the *Lily B*. Quite the opposite; everywhere I looked as we approached seemed to be green swell foaming against a sheer cliff face. But there had to be a place to land. Gribanov had put ashore somewhere.

The rocks and hill of Copper Mine Point now filled our entire view, and still no available place to put ashore. Grib-anov stopped and turned directly toward the *Lily B*. The sound of her outboard had finally overridden the smash and roar of the waves, and now the Russian knew he was being chased. He paused for a minute, appearing to take our measure, and then prodded his captives onward. I could see there was a gun in his right hand.

The footpath the trio took was now more easily separated from the surrounding country. The portion they had already traversed curved down and around an outcrop. I turned the *Lily B* to run parallel to the cliff, toward where I assumed the path would meet the water's edge, hoping that a boat landing would show itself at the cliff's base. It wasn't very promising. Every yard we traveled revealed only massive swells, unimpeded in their journey across the Atlantic, slamming against jagged rocks with a force that would dash the *Lily B* to a collection of toothpicks before De Rasta and I would have a chance to fling ourselves ashore.

Suddenly, we rounded an outcrop that opened into a cove. No, not really a cove. The space was far too small to merit that name. It was more of a J-shaped hook at the cliff base that provided enough shelter for a single boat. In that hook, tied fore to a rusty ring pounded into the rock and anchored aft in the riot of staghorn coral that grew to within four feet of the surface, was the *Tankhauler*. A flat rock slightly longer than a man's foot provided a step from the starboard side of the boat to the path that snaked up and over the outcrop.

The *Tankhauler* had been hastily tied and anchored. When each rushing swell raised the water level in the protected area, the boat raked against the flat rock. There was no place to tie or anchor the *Lily B*. I did the only thing I could do, rafting my skiff to the *Tankhauler* with lines from the bow and stern cleats. The two boats banged against each other with every surge of seawater into the confined space. At least the *Lily B* was not smashing directly against the rocks, but, rafted against the larger *Tankhauler,* she would go down with the dive boat if it was holed.

No time to worry about that. I unlocked the console and pocketed my Webley .38, hoping I would not need to use it but understanding I probably would. A nagging voice inside my head wondered how I would fare against a trained KGB agent in a gun battle, especially considering that I had missed Robin Kingsmill at a distance of four feet the last time I had fired the gun. I tried not to think about that. It didn't work.

"Stay with the boat, Anthony," I said as I crossed over the gunwale to the *Tankhauler* and then to the rocky shore. I was fifty feet along the crumbly path, already out of sight of the boats, when I heard heavy breathing behind me.

"Once more unto the breach, old boy," De Rasta said. The man thought Shakespeare fit all occasions. Maybe he was right. There was no time to argue, so after greeting him with a "Keep your head low," I turned and scrambled along the path.

Two minutes had us transitioned from half-climbing to a full sprint along the stony hill. Two more minutes had us in sight of the slower-moving three ahead, with Gribanov pushing and cajoling. They were nearing the ruins of the copper mine at the crest of the hill when Gribanov turned, spotted us, and snapped off a shot. The angry hum of a bullet ended in an explosion of shards from a rock an arm's length to our left. We dove for cover.

"No wonder the Yanks won the Cold War. The Russkis couldn't shoot and they knew it," Anthony laughed. A high, nervous laugh.

I raised my head for a quick glance, dropped down, and when there was no shot, took a longer look, just in time to see Gribanov push Jeanne and Jemmy into the mine entrance and follow them in.

"This time, Anthony, stay here," I said as I rose.

"I'm going with you, old man." De Rasta fell in beside me. "Even Quixote had his Panza."

"In case you didn't notice, Anthony, we are not tilting at windmills." I ran toward the black mouth of the mine.

Chapter Forty

As De White Rasta and I stood to the side of the mine's opening, ready to enter, I realized what folly it was. A stab of my head around the entrance corner revealed that we would be walking into a pit as dark as the thoughts of a condemned man on the day of his execution. The only source of light came from the entrance, so we would be lighted from behind, easy targets for the Russian to work on honing his marksmanship.

"If we go in, we'll be backlit," I said.

Anthony's usually-merry blue eyes turned steely cold. "Leave it to me. I'll get us in," he said.

I was as concerned as he—no, more so—about the fate of Jeanne and Jemmy, but some reason had to prevail. "Even when we get in, we'll have no light source, so how will we find them without walking up on Gribanov and getting shot for our trouble?"

De Rasta reached into the pocket of his ragged shorts and pulled out a tarnished Zippo lighter. The emblem on it, nearly worn away from years of use, was a lion and crown above a globe and anchor. A banner below the emblem carried the phrase *Per Mare Per Terram*.

Royal Marines. I glanced from the lighter to Anthony's eyes, my question evident.

"Misspent youth," he said. "This will light the way. We will go in blacked out and I'll light it up on your signal." Then he plunged into the entrance, rolling low to the far wall when he was thirty feet in. A bullet sung out of the mouth of the mine just before he stopped rolling.

There was nothing to do but follow. I duplicated De Rasta's dash and roll and drew a duplicate shot, this one alarmingly close to my left ear. I hoped that Gribanov's shooting was not improving with practice.

My roll slammed me prone against Anthony, his elbow catching me on the cheekbone just below my right eye. For a moment, the mine's darkness was supplanted by a thousand stars, until pain swept them away.

"This was your plan to get us in?" I hissed.

"We are in, are we not?"

"Only because Gribanov can't hit a barge with a cast net. But he's getting better. We do it my way from here on."

I began to crawl forward. Remembering the floor of the mine shaft was not level but undulated up and down like the swell of an easy sea, I knew we would move alternately from hidden to exposed. After a hundred feet of tearing knee and elbow on grating rock, I heard the shuffle of feet in the silence, far ahead. Gribanov was pushing deeper into the mine with his hostages, moving rapidly away from us.

I stood and De Rasta, close on my heels, followed suit, both of us pressing tight against the shaft wall.

I have been on the ocean, far from land north of the Anegada Trench, in a sea fog on a moonless night, and there was still *some* ability to see in those circumstances. No such luck here. Several hundred feet and around a slight curve from the entrance, all light seemed to have been sucked from the atmosphere. I pushed my hand out until it collided with Anthony's shoulder, then pulled myself close and whispered somewhere near to his ear, or face, "Put your hand on my shoulder. We're going to walk along the wall."

We edged forward that way, for what seemed an eternity, trying to be stealthy but occasionally kicking a rock or scraping loose gravel with a sound that seemed louder than a rock concert inside a submarine. Similar sounds could be heard, now and then, from ahead as Gribanov and his prisoners moved downward in the gloom.

I had to assume Yuri Gribanov knew the old mine, and knew it well. His entry into the mine made no sense otherwise; his escape could be easily blocked by simply waiting outside the entrance. He was counting on our following and must have believed that the darkness and his knowledge moved the odds in his favor. And he was right, for those two reasons and another—I could not risk firing a gun at him as long as he was near Jeanne and Jemmy. I would not risk it.

I paused to listen and De Rasta halted behind me. Ahead, there was a scuffing noise of feet against gravel, then the sound of flesh striking flesh, like a butcher pounding his fist into a quarter of beef. Jeanne's voice pierced the silence with an animal cry, born of pain but also angry and defiant.

Gribanov must have decided that Jeanne's outcry took away any advantage there had been to silence. In a calm, almost matter-of-fact voice, he called, "So, Constable Creque, we meet under very different circumstances. Your Ms. Trengrouse and her son are with me, as you know. Unharmed, for the present. They can remain that way if you simply go back the way you came."

"You know I cannot do that, Mr. Gribanov," I said. A salty bead of sweat trickled into the corner of my mouth.

"'Cannot' is a word often used in situations where it has no application. Like the instant one. Let me explain to you why you can, and should, go back, both you and your compatriot—Lord Wedderburn, is it?"

"Yes, sir," Anthony said. His even voice could just as well have been addressing his headmaster at Eton or his commanding ensign in the Royal Marines.

Gribanov continued. "You have a gun. I have a gun. If what Isaac Chalwell told me is accurate, you carry an ancient Webley thirty-eight revolver, six shots and then reload. I am carrying something much more modern, with a clip which holds . . . ah, let us just say it holds more than six shots. I suspect your Lord Wedderburn is unarmed, as he is not a police officer. Am I correct thus far, Constable?"

I said nothing.

"Your silence speaks volumes, Constable Creque. Consider as well our respective concerns should bullets begin to fly. I will assume you would be concerned about striking Ms. Trengrouse or her son. I can assure you I will keep them close to me in the event of any gunplay. I, on the other hand, have no such concerns about who is in the line of fire if the firing begins."

"You have an alternative. Surrender," I said. "You cannot get away. Surrender and no one, including you, gets hurt."

"There is that 'cannot' again, Constable. I cannot get away? But I can. If I come out of here alive—and I will come out alive—the police forces on this island will not touch me, at least for a period long enough for me to find my way to friendlier shores, as a different man with a different name. And if you think I 'cannot,' remember the money and effort expended by the *rodina* training me to do just that. Take a moment, Constable, to think about the logic of what I have said. You will understand that your best course is to walk away, and I will do the same."

"No," I said. The single flat word had the sound of a sentence pronounced in a show trial courtroom. I wondered if it sounded that way to Gribanov, out there in the darkness.

"Do you think you have the upper hand?" Gribanov said. "That you can wait me out, and the cavalry will arrive, like some American John Wayne movie? There is no cavalry, Constable. I'll wager no one knows that you and Lord Wedderburn are here, and if they discover you missing, with your boat gone, the search will be at sea, not on land. No, I think the cavalry is not coming. And since you persist in being unreasonable, I am going, with Ms. Trengrouse and the boy. Do not follow."

Muffled sounds of movement welled up from the empty blackness of the shaft, the shuffling of feet, the rustle of clothing. Then, "Teddy!" in Jeanne's voice, followed by a slap and more shuffling.

I moved forward, too rapidly, stumbling against a rock and nearly going down. The gloom of the mine instantly flared burning bright, an explosion of sound erupting on its heels, and a shot pinged off the rock wall, waist high. Then, as quickly, darkness and silence again, with the formless crimson image of the muzzle flash still lingering on my retinas and the sound echoing in my ears.

I stopped moving until these sensations cleared. Anthony whispered in my ear, "We need to get closer. When we do, I'll flick on the lighter and you take the shot. Otherwise, he will get each of us eventually, just by shooting at the sound we make. I'll squeeze your shoulder just before I touch off the lighter and step away to draw fire."

I had no better plan, so I pulled De Rasta's hand against my forehead and nodded. Ahead, there was more sound but it was becoming distant. I started moving again, my pace faster, Anthony behind with his left hand on my shoulder and, I assumed, his lighter at the ready in his right. The smell of sweat, not the sweat of clean, hard work, but the sweat of fear, rank and pungent, permeated the close air. The Webley felt heavy and foreign in my hand, a tool to save my life and the lives of those I loved, but alien and unreliable.

The tension and the absence of light did not impede us

much, and after a few minutes of sliding my hand along the mine shaft's rough wall as a guide, we seemed to be gaining on the trio ahead. De Rasta moved in absolute silence, never stumbling or scraping a foot. I managed almost as well, and the time or two my shoes kicked some gravel did not draw any fire from Gribanov. Maybe he was saving ammunition.

While Anthony and I were silent, the same could not be said for the three we pursued. As I heard the stumbling and murmurs ahead, I imagined I could pick out who was making the sound—a reassuring susurration from Jeanne to Jemmy, the quickly muffled protest of the boy when pushed, the ripple of clothing as Gribanov shoved mother and son forward.

There was no way to accurately judge, but I felt like we would soon be arriving at the room Jeanne and I had visited short days ago. The branching shafts leading out from that room would only compound the problem of following Gribanov. I decided catching him in the larger room, before he could enter one of the branches, would be the best chance to bring him down without injury to Jeanne and Jemmy. With luck, they could dive out of the way or flee down one of the shafts when the gunfire began.

I redoubled our pace and with that redoubled the noise we made. Our feet were no longer stealthy. De Rasta grunted, brief and sharp, as some part of him smashed into something in the darkness that I had unknowingly managed to avoid.

A scuff of stone fragments and a muffled curse and slap could be heard ahead. The sounds echoed louder than in the confined space of the shaft; Gribanov, Jeanne, and Jemmy had entered the large room. It would be only moments before they moved into one of the branches that spread out from there. We had to act now.

I sprinted forward into the darkness.

Chapter Forty-one

Running in total darkness, even for the hundred feet or so that I ran, is an unsettling experience. I felt the rush of air against my face and limbs, and the push and departure of the ground beneath my feet, but with no sight there was no way to gauge speed or progress. There was no way to know if the next step was onto solid land or into the abyss. De Rasta, no doubt surprised by my sudden acceleration, was left behind. I could neither hear nor see anyone ahead. It was as if I ran alone in the black void of space, a million miles from Earth, my life, and hope.

Except in space there is no sound, and I was making plenty of sound, so much that it drew the answering sound of another shot from Gribanov, and the attendant flash of light. There was light enough to briefly illuminate my path to a sprawling stop at the entrance to the room as a searing pain chopped my right leg from beneath me.

The pitch black returned as quickly as it had been erased by the flashbulb incandescence of the shot. Gribanov snapped another shot, which snarled its way impotently down the main shaft and provided another instant of dazzling light. He stopped after the second shot and all fell silent as we waited and listened—listened for what seemed an eternity but was only a minute or two. I lay where I had fallen and gingerly moved my hand to my injured leg, the pain flowing up and through me as I pushed my fingers into the warm blood. What I felt was not a bullet wound but a jagged gash from knee to ankle. I was not shot; my collision with the unknown object that had gashed my leg may very well have saved me from being shot.

I still held the Webley, having clung to it through my tumble, intuiting that whatever forlorn hope Jeanne, Jemmy, Anthony, and I had rested with my keeping my grip. The hand that held the gun had paid the price, three knuckles, I would later learn, sliced wide open and broken as they took the brunt of my fall.

In the midst of my self-triage I was startled by a touch against my shoulder. De Rasta, soundless as a ghost, had joined me. He moved his hand down my arm until reaching the Webley, and, assured I was still armed, whispered, "Now."

Before I could move, before I could react, even before I was certain what he meant, Anthony stood and flicked the flint on his Zippo lighter. The room was instantly bathed in light, not the harsh, sharp light of a gunshot, but a mellow golden flame, soft and allowing for easy adjustment of my light-starved eyes.

My eyes were not the only ones that adjusted quickly. After a moment's hesitation, Yuri Gribanov pointed his chin at De Rasta and began to raise his gun. I saw now that he carried a nine-millimeter Glock 17. It had a seventeen-round capacity, I remembered from my recent constable training. He had fired six, which meant there were eleven rounds left. Don't ask me how I managed to think all this through as Gribanov raised his gun; I just know I did.

While I was thinking, others were acting. Jeanne Trengrouse, held by Gribanov's left hand as he raised the Glock in his right, jerked mightily on that arm just as Gribanov fired two rounds—tap, tap, the mark of a skilled combat shooter. Both shots went just wide of Anthony, one slug sparking against a mineral deposit in the rock wall where it struck.

Anthony immediately doused his lighter. Gribanov had nine rounds left. Jeanne had managed to separate herself from Gribanov but Jemmy had still been next to the Russian when the room went dark.

I thought about taking a shot in the dark. I thought about how I would feel if my shot struck Jemmy in that black room. And I froze. I froze and everyone and everything in that pitch-black hole in the ground seemed to freeze with me, no sound, no movement, no light for a long count of maybe ten seconds. It was the longest ten seconds of my life. I thought it might be the last ten seconds of my life. It would almost certainly be the last ten seconds of the life of someone in that room.

You could almost hear the last beat of that ten-count, the

referee getting ready to slap the canvas beside the downed fighter, when the room was lit again, this time by the concentrated light of a torch. The torch light caught Yuri Gribanov dead center in its beam. Jeanne was holding the light. She must have pried it away from Gribanov when she broke his hold on her. She placed the light on the Russian and held it there, unwavering, like it was a weapon and she could kill him with it, dispatch him by merely exposing him to the light.

Gribanov turned a half turn toward the light as I pushed up on an elbow to fire the Webley. His shot and mine filled the chamber with sound and light at the same instant. I followed with four more. Gribanov staggered the slightest bit and dropped the Glock.

The beam of the torch canted to a drunken angle as its metal casing hit the floor.

"I'm shot," Gribanov said, and died.

De White Rasta's Zippo flicked to life, bathing the room in weak, wavering light. Anthony rushed to Gribanov, kicked the Glock far from where he lay, and, seizing an arm, knelt in the middle of the Russian's back. He needn't have troubled; after feeling Gribanov's neck, he said, "Dead."

I rose, the pain from my leg a roaring throb. As I did so, Jemmy Trengrouse emerged from the shadows and rushed to the torch, picking it from the floor and turning its bright beam on the prone figure of his mother.

"Madda," he cried, and fell upon her, hugging and weeping.

For a brief time, my thoughts flashed back to a dark

green copse in the wilderness of Anegada and another prone figure of a woman barely visible in the twilight. The year of emotion since that night on Anegada, a year lost to self-pity and self-loathing, to anger and regret, to might-have-been and should-have-done, came back in a flood and I stood, paralyzed, as the child wept over his mother. Then training took hold and I quickly limped the few steps to Jemmy and Jeanne. Jeanne was facedown, blood pooling beneath her, and Jemmy, in hugging her, had covered himself in blood as well. I knelt on my good leg beside Jeanne, gently pulling Jemmy away so that I might examine her wounds.

"Hold the torch on your madda, Jemmy, so we can see how she is hurt," I said, and the boy silently complied. As I finished speaking, Jeanne coughed and groaned, rolled to her side, and opened her eyes.

"She's alive," said Anthony, now standing over us with the flickering Zippo held aloft like some kind of odd subterranean Statue of Liberty.

"Of course I'm alive . . . ow," Jeanne said as I ran my hand along her bleeding arm and hit the neat round wound in the process.

"Is this the only place you are hurt, Jeanne?" I said.

"Yes. I . . . I guess I hit my head, too, when I went down. I passed out for a minute."

"Shine the light on your madda's head, Jemmy," I said as I propped Jeanne up to better see. "Yes, you have a nasty bruise, maybe a concussion." I gazed into her striking blue eyes, fearing to find a blown pupil, but the pupils were both equal, and as I looked I saw the panic and fear depart, replaced by calm and trust. I knew then that Jeanne would recover, that we were safe, and that the demons of the past year had been banished. Forever.

The wound in Jeanne's arm was a classic flesh wound, the bullet entering her bicep and exiting the other side, missing bone, vein, and artery in the process. She winced as I bound the wound with strips cut from my shirt, and cried and smiled at the same time when it was over.

"You are safe," I said, and we hugged, an awkward half embrace to protect her injured arm. "Do you think you can stand?"

"Help me. Let's get out of here."

She leaned into me and I lifted her to her feet and turned toward the mine entrance.

There was a light coming toward us.

Chapter Forty-two

The light was mere yards away in the main entrance shaft. Whoever it was would be on us in seconds. It was possible it was the cavalry come to the rescue, an RVIPF contingent mobilized on Anthony Wedderburn's hasty phone call from the Yacht Harbour before our pursuit of Gribanov began. But the message to headquarters had been of a chase at sea, not a hostage situation in an abandoned mine, so the chances of its being the cavalry were remote. It was much more likely that Yuri Gribanov's partner in crime was coming to assist him in disposing of Jeanne and Jemmy. And now that partner would have heard the shooting as he moved along the shaft toward us.

"Douse the light," I hissed. Immediately, the torch and the flame from the Zippo went out. "Get down and stay down, no matter what. Move away from me."

I stood in the center of the rock chamber as the light moved closer, scissoring through the inky blackness, its beam given definition as it reflected off dust particles in the heavy air of the mine. I had one shell remaining in the cylinder of the Webley. I thought about trying to find Gribanov's Glock, but Anthony had kicked it away into an obscure corner of the room and there was no way I could hope to find it in the dark.

"Hello, are you all right?" a voice behind the torch said, a voice that I had expected, a voice I had come to know well since arriving on Virgin Gorda. Isaac Chalwell. The torch flashed into the room, and my face, but I still saw he was armed, his service automatic in his right hand.

"What's going on? I heard shots," Chalwell said. Still playing the charade. Did he think he could talk his way around this?

I had my answer an instant later. Low and to my left, Jemmy Trengrouse shouted, "Bad man," as the light of the torch he held washed the room. The noise and the light behind me were sudden enough to draw my involuntary attention and I glanced for a fraction of a second to see Jemmy, standing resolutely, with his torch pointing away from Sergeant Chalwell, down one of the shafts branching from the room. I knew the danger was before me, not behind, and turned to again face Chalwell.

What happened next was so rapid that it is only now, after some reflection, that I can piece together what occurred. On turning toward Sergeant Chalwell, I was horrified to see he was in a shooting stance, raising his Glock in my direction. I began to move and raise my gun but I knew I would be too late and Chalwell would shoot first.

"Teddy!" Anthony shouted. Isaac Chalwell fired just as

De White Rasta hit me with a glancing body blow. Another shot, a fraction of a second after Chalwell's, exploded behind me. The blow struck by Anthony sent me flying, my Webley slamming against the rock wall, and I landed on hands and knees.

I looked up, expecting Isaac Chalwell to be readying for another shot at me. Instead, his torch and attention were focused on the entrance to one of the side tunnels leading from the room. I followed his gaze to see Bullfoot's crumpled body there on the floor, a gun, the gun that had fired the second shot, still curled in his dead fingers. He was in his RVIPF uniform, and when Sergeant Chalwell panned the torch along his body, I saw his shoes. A pair of black police boots, with ripple soles.

Chalwell rushed to where Bullfoot lay and took the gun from his hand. It was only then that I noticed there was a second figure prone on the dusty mine floor.

Anthony Wedderburn rested on the hard ground, facing upward. His gaze found me as I knelt beside him. There was no care or pain in his eyes, and not a lock of his short blond hair was out of place. He tried to speak but no words came, and then his eyelids fluttered and fell closed. A spot of dark blood betrayed the small bullet hole in his shirt, two inches to the right of his heart.

RVIPF deputy commissioner Howard T. Lane maintained a mask of professional distance as the two stretchers, holding the bodies of Constable Tybee George and Yuri Gribanov, emerged into the dazzling sun from the mouth of the old copper mine. An hour earlier, Virgin Gorda's sole ambulance had transported Anthony Wedderburn and Jeanne Trengrouse from the mine entrance to Taddy Bay Airport, where they were taken on a special VI Birds charter to Tortola. Word relayed from Peebles Hospital to the deputy commissioner had already confirmed what the Virgin Gorda EMTs had said before they transported Jeanne—her gunshot wound was as minor as a gunshot wound could be, threatening neither life nor limb, and her mild concussion would have no lasting effect. She would spend the night at Peebles so that she could be observed for any complications, and then return to Virgin Gorda the next day.

The prognosis was not so encouraging for Anthony. He had survived the airplane ride and made it to the hospital, but whether he would see the dawn of another day was uncertain.

After the ambulance transporting George and Gribanov's remains drove away, I sat down on the bare stony slope. My leg, while not broken, was gashed badly enough that it would not support me for longer than the few minutes when DC Lane, Sergeant Chalwell, and I had stood as the bodies were carried past us to the ambulance. I held my head in my hands as I sat and no one uttered a word, verbal statements already having been given to the DC by the sergeant and me earlier.

To Isaac Chalwell's credit, he had told the DC what I believed to be the unvarnished truth in his statement. "I didn't think that Yuri was involved and I didn't want to see his name dragged through the mud again. So I lied to

Constable Creque. I covered for Yuri. He was my best friend. Hell, he was my only friend. I just couldn't believe that he'd had anything to do with that woman's death."

DC Lane had warned Chalwell then. "Before you go on, Sergeant, based on what you have just said you will likely be charged with furnishing false information and perverting the course of justice. And you will lose your position as an officer of the RVIPF."

"I know, I know," Chalwell sighed. "But I failed in my duties as a police officer. Maybe if I had been more diligent, more aware, some of the people who died or were injured would not have been. If I had been a better policeman maybe none of this would have happened."

Been there, Isaac. Done that. And you can't get rid of it by confessing, or praying, or drinking, or rationalizing. Maybe you can't get rid of it, all of it, ever. I'm still waiting to find out.

"How did you know to come to the mine?" I asked.

"I didn't. It was sheer luck that I was close to the mine entrance when the shooting started, and I heard the shots."

"But how did you come to be close to the mine entrance?"

"Bullfoot and I were at the station when the Road Town marine base called and said the *St. Ursula* was on its way. The dispatcher there always calls when the *St. Ursula* heads to the area of Virgin Gorda, so that we can meet the boat and provide land transport and other assistance, if needed. I asked the dispatcher why the *St. Ursula* was coming and she said you and Mr. Wedderburn were involved in a hostage situation at sea. She didn't know much more, except that the boat involved might be traveling southward. I told Bullfoot to stay at the station while I took the vehicle out to see if I could assist from shore. I drove south along the leeward side, stopping to scan the water with binoculars a couple times along the way. The last time I stopped, I was just able to see the *Lily B* turn due east off Penn Hill. I drove back and over Copper Mine Road, figuring the best vantage point on the windward side was Copper Mine Point. You can get a clear view north up the windward coast, and also see south to Fallen Jerusalem, Broken Jerusalem, and all the way to Ginger Island from there. I had just stepped from the vehicle when I heard the shots and came to investigate."

"What about Constable George, how did he know to come to the mine?" the DC asked.

"I don't know." Chalwell pondered for a second. "He heard the same information from the dispatcher that I did, so he would have known the area where the boats were headed, but how he got into the mine is a mystery to me."

"I can answer part of that," said a voice behind me. I turned to see Rollie Stoutt emerge from the mine entrance with two uniformed officers. The officers were clean; Rollie looked like he had been mining coal in the Black Country of the West Midlands. Sooty gray dust powdered his face and neck, giving his normally sleepy eyes a startled expression. "I sent one of the officers here back along the branch shaft that Constable George had come from. He said the shaft narrowed but ultimately ran about a half mile to an opening large enough to allow a man to enter, just below Salt Spring. There was a Toyota pickup truck parked there, with the keys still in the ignition. My guess is that Constable George drove there in that truck."

"I'll bet we find it registered to one of his cousins or uncles," I said.

Rollie continued. "He must have known the mine pretty well. The officer reported that the entrance at Salt Spring was hidden by brush and scrub thorn, so that you couldn't see the opening until you almost fell in it."

"And I'll bet when we check Constable George's bank account, we'll find it holds amounts far in excess of a modest policeman's salary," the DC said. "Either that or there'll be money buried in his backyard. One way or the other, we'll find it."

Rollie rubbed his sleeve across his brow, streaking the dust and sweat in a long smudge across his forehead. "Oh, yeah, the officer found something else pretty interesting, so much so I went there for a look myself." He reached in one of his aluminum evidence cases and extracted a baggie. "There were branches of this, stacked waist-high along the wall of the shaft for about a hundred yards. Do you know what it is?"

In his grimy hand was a six-inch stem of coral, reflecting a deep lapis blue-black in the late-day sun.

Epilogue

At ten on the Saturday morning before Easter Sunday, I lifted the heavy black receiver of the landline in the Anegada Police Station and placed a call to Blue Earth, Minnesota. Tom Konnerth answered on the second ring and made me wait to convey the news I had until his wife could get on the extension. They listened in silence as I described the events of the last few days, and at the end Tom spoke a simple "Thank you, Constable." I was about to ring off when Judy Konnerth, silent throughout the call save for an occasional sniffle, spoke.

"Michele was all we had, Constable. We loved her very much. We're all alone now, just two old people, all alone."

I thought of Henna Beckles, broken and alone too, in her grief over the death of the woman she loved. "There is something you should know . . ." I began. At the end of my explanation, there was a long silence.

Finally, Tom Konnerth spoke, a gruff growl of emotion softening his voice to the point where it became barely audible. "We're simple people, Judy and me, and we don't claim to understand some things about today's world. But, truth be told, we suspected Michele . . . well, we knew, but Michele left things unsaid, probably thinking she was sparing us, and we did the same. You say they were in love, Michele and this girl Henna Beckles?"

"Yes."

"It must be hard for her, to lose someone she loved."

"She was having a difficult time."

"Constable . . . do you think if we came down there, to Virgin Gorda, she would meet with us?"

"My guess is she would."

"Then we will be down," Judy Konnerth said. "No one should grieve alone."

At eleven o'clock that same day, Jeanne Trengrouse knocked on the door frame of my office. "Ready?" she asked. She was wearing shorts and a long-sleeved T-shirt, winter wear for Anegada. The shirt covered the bandages on her arm. I had convinced her to come to Anegada to convalesce, and for a safe haven from prying eyes and wagging tongues. She and Jemmy had accepted my invitation because, she said, someone needed to watch over me while I convalesced. So we presided over each other's recovery, watched our children play together, and wondered how much time our mutual recuperation would require. We both concluded that we did not mind if it took years.

"I guess so," I said. I winced in pain as I rose from the desk chair, tried quickly to compose my face before Jeanne saw it, and failed.

"Are you sure you should be doing this?" she asked.

"Yes. Very sure. He was there when I needed him. He needs me now," I said. "Are you certain you don't need Madda and Dada to help you with the kids?"

"I've got it," she said, and I knew that she did. "Besides, if I need help, there's always Sir Winston."

We drove in my RVIPF Land Rover along the single paved street of The Settlement, past Dotsey's Bakery to the sandy lane that ended at the fishermen's landing. The *Lily B* was there, tied bow and stern to the dock, a gentle swell rocking her against the bumpers. One of the constables from the RVIPF marine base had brought her over from Virgin Gorda after she was recovered, drifting, off Copper Mine Point. Other than a scratch or two, she seemed none the worse for wear.

The same could not be said for her master. My leg still ached, the bandages applied by the Virgin Gorda paramedics still in place. But this was a voyage I had to make.

Jeanne waved from the dock as I throttled up the *Lily B* to run on plane. I usually stand at the helm but that day I sat on the ripped and faded cushion of the console seat.

There was only the slightest wisp of wind. The few clouds in the sky were off to the southeast, the portent of a late-day shower. For now, though, the journey along the inside edge of the Horseshoe Reef was a racing ride on the face of an aquarium, sunlight perforating the silken surface to reveal the recondite world of towering coral heads, flashing schools of bar jacks and sprats, the thick blue shadow of a barracuda lying in wait. It would have been a perfect Anegada day if my destination had been a happier one.

After the drive along the Sir Francis Drake Channel, the *Lily B* and I picked our way through the Road Harbour traffic of bareboats, coasters, and a hulking cruise ship to the marine base. One of the officers there gave me a lift to Peebles Hospital, and I rode the elevator to the fourth-floor ICU.

The ICU had been renovated since my sojourn there, but one institutional fixture from the old unit remained. Nurse Hattie Rowell scowled up from her charting at the new wood-paneled nurses' station as the elevator bell dinged, and then smiled when she saw its passenger.

"Constable Teddy Creque, as I live and breathe," she said, folding her chart closed. "To what do we owe this honor?" Then the smile departed. "Oh, yes, Mr. Wedderburn. Your Deputy Commissioner Lane and Inspector Stoutt just left. They told me about what happened on Virgin Gorda. It sounds like if Mr. Wedderburn hadn't put himself in the way of that bullet, I'd have had you back in here again."

"If I had been that lucky," I said. "More likely, I wouldn't have come out alive. Anthony is a hero. I hope you are treating him that way."

"Here in the ICU we specialize in heroes. Nothing but the best for him." If Nurse Rowell said it, I knew it was true.

"How is he?" I asked.

"Touch and go. He lost a great deal of blood before we got him here. He needed twelve units that first night. He's intubated and really hasn't regained consciousness since he was brought in." Hattie Rowell was not one to sugarcoat but she saw I needed something. "He's strong, though. You know what it's like. You've been here. We can do a lot but it's your own inner fortitude that gets you through when things are really bad. That man has a lot of inner fortitude."

"Can I see him?"

"For a short time," she said, slipping into the watchdog role she filled so well. "Three minutes. Bay two."

I remembered the time I had spent in bay two as I strode the ten steps to the room. I would not wish what I experienced there on my worst enemy. And now Anthony Wedderburn, De White Rasta, my best friend, my brother, was in that room of tubes, and machines, and death waiting on the threshold, all because he had saved me.

"Hello, Anthony," I said, false cheer in my voice. There was no acknowledgment, no movement from the ashen figure in the bed. I took his hand and found it cool, and dry, and as singularly lifeless as any living flesh, of man or beast, I had ever touched. He was situated to face a window that fronted on Road Harbour. I stood there, holding his hand, remembering when I had lain in that selfsame bed, the memories triggered by the smells of antiseptic and alcohol, and the drone of the machinery that forced the patient to live. I wondered if Anthony would ever again look out at the harbor, hear the dry rattle of palm leaves in the trade wind, savor the light sweet scent of frangipani, or wade in the warm surf of Cow Wreck Bay. I would have done anything, anything, if he could but have been given another chance, another opportunity to enjoy those simple pleasures. As it was, there were only two things I could do for De Rasta, and so I did them.

First, I prayed, prayed to the God I was still not sure existed, a formless, forlorn appeal that came to nothing more than "Please, God, please, just please."

And then I reached into my uniform shirt pocket for the item I had placed there earlier in the morning. The tears came as I pinned the Queen's Police Medal to the pillow beside Anthony Wedderburn's unmoving brow.

Acknowledgments

Thanks to friend and fellow writer Ed Duncan for taking on the task of being first reader for this book. Your encouragement and critical eye are much appreciated.

My gratitude to Minotaur Books and the fine team they have assembled on my behalf, including the amiable Joe Brosnan and the tireless Shailyn Tavella.

Humble thanks to super-editor Elizabeth Lacks for persuading me to make a critical change to this story, for editing with a light but insightful touch, and for tolerating too many emails from me.

To copy editor Aja Pollock, thank you for deftly applying the grammar hammer and punctuation pliers to fine-tune this work.

To my sensational agent, Danielle Burby, thanks for believing in me and taking me on. As Bogart said, I think this is the beginning of a beautiful friendship.

Finally, and of course, thanks to my beloved Irene—wife, friend, partner, and now, muse of my writing world.